HOT
WIRE

HOT
WIRE

JAMES
BROWN

ARBOR HOUSE
New York

Book design by Richard Oriolo

Manufactured in the United States of America

10 9 8 7 6 5 4 3 2 1

This book is printed on acid free paper. The paper in this book
meets the guidelines for permanence and durability of the
committee on Prodution Guidelines for Book Longevity of the
Council on Library Resources.

Library of Congress Cataloging in Publication Data

Brown, James, 1957-
Hot wire.

I. Title.
PS3552.R68563H6   1985   813'54   84-21732
ISBN 0-87795-630-8 (alk. paper)

This is a work of fiction. Any similarity to persons living or
dead is purely coincidental and exists solely in the reader's
mind.

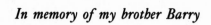

In memory of my brother Barry

For his friendship, his encouragement and trust, I thank Orlando Ramirez. For believing in this novel, and seeing it through to the finish, I also thank Stephanie Mann, Leslie Morgan, Susie Breitner, and Eleanor Johnson.

1

Lonnie Baer arrived at Los Angeles International as a ward of the court. Five-three. Wiry like a cat. He wore a tight black pocket T that showed the bumps up his spine, baggy Big Ben's, and a pair of Puerto Rican fence climbers one size too large. This time they got him in Barstow when he stopped for gas. An attendant looked in the Volkswagen and spotted the ignition lock broken and a pair of vise-grips on the backseat. A few minutes later Lonnie came strutting out of the bathroom nursing a Coke and found the sheriff waiting for him. Six months before that he caught a ride that left him just outside Bakersfield where there was nothing around but a pocked two-lane highway and miles and miles of cotton field. The road wasn't used much and he didn't think he could thumb another ride. Most of the drivers were old men and women. Afraid. The rest were trucks. Huge rigs with eighteen wheels, blowing smoke and scaring the hell out of Lonnie as they passed. They hardly saw him, much less stopped. Yet he felt good and full in the chest when he looked out over all that raw white cotton. The way the sun shone across the field as it wavered in the wind reminded him of whitecaps on the ocean, hissing, foaming bright and then

fading. He figured he'd be safe if he hid in the fields but
come dawn the CHP picked him up and sent him home
again.

The plainclothesman and Lonnie stood just beyond the
PSA gate. Passengers greeted family. Businessmen and students and others blended into the crowd and disappeared.
Soon the pretty stewardesses departed with their flight
bags and there was no one left except Lonnie and the cop.
He kept his head down and his hands deep in his pockets.
They stayed ten more minutes and then the plainclothesman nudged him and they went down the escalator and
through a long white tile hall and finally outside to where
the taxis and porters waited. He was back in L.A. and
didn't like it. His family would want to know why he left
and he didn't know what to tell them. Especially Sonny.
For two days now he'd been thinking of different explana-
tions, sometimes the same one over and over until he
memorized it. But everything that sounded any good was
a lie and Sonny always saw through his lies. There was
nothing he could say that wouldn't hurt Sonny.

"She probably couldn't find a parking space," the cop
said.

Lonnie nodded.

"But she'll be here."

They settled on a bench and watched the traffic. A plane
thundered overhead. Exhaust smudged the evening sky.
The cop kept one hand in his pocket and jingled his keys
like he had during the flight. It annoyed Lonnie but he
wasn't about to give the sonofabitch the satisfaction of
knowing he was annoyed.

"What does she drive?"

Lonnie shrugged.

Cars pulled in and out and changed lanes and double-
parked. His heart rose each time someone honked or a
woman built similar to his mother appeared in the passing
crowds on the sidewalk.

"Ah, she'll be here."

Lonnie said nothing. The cop reached over and put a hand on his shoulder.

"Don't worry."

"Jus' keep your fuckin' hands offa me, huh?"

A valet in a Chevy sped up the street, parked at the curb, and left the engine idling while he dashed inside to the Hertz booth. Blinking twice, Lonnie smiled to himself. It was new and shiny and nice. A Camaro. Probably a V8, possibly a 6. Four-speed. He shifted slightly on the bench and casually looked over his shoulder, through the big window, to the valet talking with a girl at the Hertz booth.

"We'll give her a while longer. Okay, sport?"

Sport. Come off it. Coaches and cops were the only ones who used that kind of shit.

The cop carefully rested his arm across the top of the bench. "Were you born here?"

"Huh?"

"Were you born here?"

"San Jose."

"I have a cousin there."

So what? Lonnie thought. Did the cop really think he cared?

"Does your mother work for a living?"

"What's with the questions?"

The cop frowned, removing his arm from across the bench. Lonnie hoped that was the last of the bullshit. They were all like that—nice—after they just finished screwing you. Maybe they felt guilty or something. If they did, good. Fuck 'em. "What's your phone number?" the cop asked. A few seconds passed. "You either know it or you don't. Which is it?" Lonnie shot him a cold stare. "Do you want to see if we can get ahold of her or do you want to spend the night downtown?"

Asshole, Lonnie thought. But he gave him the number anyway. The cop smiled and went to the phone booth a couple of yards from the bench. A 747 rose into the sky above the airport, leaving behind a long trail of almost invisible exhaust. Lonnie watched another plane make an approach and when it disappeared behind a building he found himself staring at the Camaro. Twenty, say thirty yards away, he estimated.

The sliding glass door to the airport hummed open and a fat man with strings of flowers piled high around his neck waddled out, followed by a crowd of tanned people. They all looked healthy but tired, and they were probably glad to be home. Some wore puka shell necklaces to accent their new tans, some wore Bermuda shorts and loose shirts with bright flower patterns. They moved slow and talked a lot. Lonnie's heart pounded. He looked at the Camaro again— the valet—the Camaro.

He needed a smoke.

Waiting until the thickest part of the crowd separated him from the plainclothesman, Lonnie paced himself and fell into step, following the people up the sidewalk toward the baggage claim. He didn't think he'd make it, could almost hear the cop shouting, the crowd whirling around, him running, and then some hero's big firm hand latching on to him from behind. But it was too late to turn back now. Whatever happened, happened. All he could do was stay hidden within the crowd and hope. He muttered to himself, *Don't believe it till you're there, don't believe it till you're there. Jus' keep walkin'* . . . A drop of sweat slid from his forehead, down his cheek. When he was parallel with the Camaro he did a quick double take, slipped between two young women, and came up beside the car. For a moment he stood listening to the motor purr softly and rhythmically, one hand on the door handle, in a daze. It didn't seem real, that he was here, that he was actually doing it. Then as if he just realized he hadn't forgotten anything, he flung open the door and jumped in and ground the gears to find reverse, hit the gas, pulled the wheel sharp to the right, slammed it into first, and cut off a shuttle bus as he shot across traffic to the left lane. By the time the crowd dispersed, by the time the cop had hung up and noticed the empty bench, Lonnie was gone.

He glanced in the rearview mirror and, seeing no black-and-white trailing him, pressed in the car lighter and reached down into his sock for two flattened, wrinkled Camels. Taking a deep long drag, he scooted the seat forward and exhaled slowly. There was only nine-oh-four on the odometer and the cab smelled of fresh plastic and vinyl. His hands trembled; he tightened his grip on the wheel. A couple of miles up the boulevard he turned onto the freeway. The Camaro was the newest car he'd ever driven and he wanted to push it to its limit—make the other cars stand still—but he held it at fifty-five, used his blinkers faithfully, and didn't tailgate. He got off at Western, planning on taking the back streets. Safer. Less traffic. Although he felt drawn toward home, although he was headed in that direction, he knew he wasn't going there. Maybe he could just sort of drive by and look once. For the hell of it. Before he took off again he at least had to let Sonny know he was okay. But it might be smarter to call instead. His throat swelled. He should get rid of the car. Ditch it in the Pep Boys parking lot on Sunset. Maybe then he could think clearly.

A few streets after he pulled off the freeway, while he was stopped at a red light, a black-and-white rolled up beside him. Stay loose, he thought, stay loose. They don't know shit. He tapped the accelerator lightly to make sure the engine wasn't dead and it hummed quietly, smoothly, powerfully. If he stepped down it would take off fast. Lonnie lit another smoke and tried to act nonchalant, tried to look older than his fifteen years, tried pretending he hadn't even noticed the cops.

Inside he was going crazy with fear.

The light changed.

Lonnie eased the Camaro into gear and started off. He held it two miles an hour over the limit to keep up with the flow of traffic and not attract attention to himself. Soon the black-and-white fell in behind him. Panic. Stay loose. He wanted to glance in the rearview mirror to see if they were checking his plates or if they had just changed lanes to make a turn. But they might see him looking and that would only make them suspicious. He drove for three blocks and then put on his blinker. Too soon. Couldn't turn for another block yet. Goddamn it, he thought. You idiot. He had to wait for a gap in the oncoming traffic and it seemed like an incredibly long wait and he worried that the cops were growing impatient and that he was holding up traffic. Then when he made his turn he misjudged the distance, forcing an oncoming car to brake. And he'd crept out too far and had to cut the wheel sharp so as not to hit the curb.

The black-and-white followed.

He cruised for a while, then hung a left.

The black-and-white hung a left.

"Shit."

Suddenly the red lights came on. He turned around in his seat and gave them an incredulous look. *Me?* You mean *me?* One of the cops nodded but Lonnie kept going. The siren went on. He ignored that, too. Finally the cop on the passenger's side rolled down his window and aimed the loudspeaker—*Pull over immediately . . . Pull over immediately.* They swerved into the next lane and sped up. Just as they were coming up alongside the Camaro, Lonnie stepped down hard on the gas. They faded back. He turned off Western and headed up into the Hollywood Hills. It was his best chance, probably his only chance to lose them. He knew the roads there, the bends, the curves, and what they'd handle. Since he was eleven Sonny had been taking him up to the hills and letting him race. He felt the road through his fingertips, through the vibrations of the steering wheel, and could pull out of a twenty-five-mile-an-hour bend at fifty without hitting the turtleback reflectors or rocking the car too much. And he knew how to fix cars, too. Had a feeling about them. A rhythm. A kind of sense that made a motor seem simple and logical. Maybe he didn't know the names of all the parts, but he could tear down an engine and put it back together in a couple of nights.

The road was winding and dark, the city below a valley of white dots. As Lonnie glided into a bend he glanced in the rearview mirror and saw the black-and-white far behind, its headlights snaking across the mountainside and then disappearing and reappearing. He knew he could ditch the car and hide if he got to the top of the hill and dropped down into Griffith Park where the roads were a maze and the brush was thick. The speedometer read fifty . . . sixty . . . pushing sixty-five. When he shot down a straightaway and into the last bend, he felt the Camaro dip to its left, tilting, too much weight, too fast on one side. The car pulled toward the edge of the mountainside, wheels screeching. His headlights shone on the fork in the road ahead. Almost to the summit. One way led deeper into the hills and dead-ended, the other way wound down into Griffith Park. He glanced in the mirror one last time before he dropped it to forty-five. The black-and-white was still far behind. He had maybe two good minutes on them, maybe more if they took the wrong fork. They were slower than he figured. But when he hit the summit, when he knew he had them, he spotted another patrol car racing up the road that led down into the park. Slamming into reverse, he backed the Camaro into someone's driveway, then got out and ran. A couple of minutes later he heard the first black-and-white skid to a stop at the crossroad. Soon the other one pulled up. Sirens wailed. Lonnie slid down a hill on his ass and tumbled through the brush, tearing his shirt and cutting and scraping his arms, stumbling and falling until he came to a street lined with homes. He ran across the front lawn of a house and hopped a fence into a backyard, hopped another fence, and wound up in another backyard. A big one. There was a pond full of lilies and goldfish, a small ornate bridge, a miniature stone tiki house, an Olympic swimming pool. A Weber barbecue stood on the porch under a plastic tarp, and in the far corner was a

forest of tall bamboo where Lonnie hid, behind the miniature stone tiki house, sweating heavily. He heard a black-
and-white cruising the street above him. The squawk of
P.B.s sounded through the neighborhood. Cops were probably going door to door now, asking questions, shining
their flashlights into bushes. People were probably standing in their front yards, wondering what was going on.
The safest thing to do, he thought, was to stay where he
was and pray they didn't search the yard.

Dry leaves crackled beneath him as he leaned back to rest
his head against one of the bamboo trees. He held his breath
a moment. Listened. They had turned their sirens off. A
warm sensation tingled in his throat, nice and pleasant at
first, like cold wine on a hot afternoon. But as it traveled
down it grew warmer and warmer until it burned, boiled,
a dull gnawing pain in the pit of his stomach. It racked his
lungs and ribs and made him feel thick and sluggish inside
like a poisoned animal. He slouched between his legs and
gagged. Nothing came up but a pasty green acid, bitter and
rancid. His stomach convulsed and contracted like a machine with no cutoff and he retched and spit until he
thought his guts would burst. Then, slowly, the pain subsided. Soon only a small ball of warmth remained locked in
his stomach, a soothing warmth again, one that made him
weak and light-headed like he was drunk. Sitting up, he
wrapped his arms around his belly and closed his eyes.

A few hours passed before he thought the neighborhood
had been quiet long enough to risk leaving. Most people
would either be asleep or watching TV. Lonnie rose to his
feet, stiff and slow like an old man. His jaws were sore from
grinding his teeth and his stomach still hurt like there was
a fist inside grabbing him. He peered out from behind the
trees. No lights shone in the back windows of the house.
Brushing himself off, he went to the swimming pool,
dunked his head, threw his greasy hair back. Then he unlatched the backyard gate, crept quietly along the side of
the house, and started the long walk down the mountain.

In the distance he could see the Capitol Records building on Vine Street. Behind him, if it wasn't night, he'd know exactly where to look to see the big HOLLYWOOD sign sitting cockeyed and ragged in the hills. Lonnie kept his head down, walked fast, and avoided streets with street lamps. Once a dog barked as he passed a house and he broke into a run for a full block. By the time he got to the city his left heel was blistered and his legs ached. He limped down the street, looking for someplace to stop and rest. Soot was thick in the cracks of the sidewalk. A young man stood beside the iron gates that protected the plate-glass windows of the Supply Sergeant. Hollywood Boulevard. A street he knew well. He'd hitched from Highland to Western a thousand times. Why all the tourists came here he didn't know. Did they really believe this was glamorous? An old woman standing outside a Thai restaurant regarded him suspiciously as he passed. He smiled weakly. She ignored him.

He wanted to call Sonny while he still had a chance but he didn't know what to say. Everything seemed so damn tangled with other problems. They weren't like math problems with the answers in the back of the book or like an engine he could strip down, fix, and put together again. He was afraid. Sonny would be angry. There was no excuse. His lips quivered. He had to find a phone booth. Stopping, he muttered to himself, *Men don't cry . . . Men don't cry,* until the tightness at the bottom of his throat relaxed. His eyes burned and watered. He told himself it was from the smog. Had to be. He wasn't crying, damn it. Not now. Not here on the streets like a heartbroken bum.

2

Mrs. Tania Baer liked running the water just hot enough to bear and soaking until her fingertips wrinkled. Close her eyes. Let her body go limp. But today she hopped in and hopped out and didn't do a good job drying herself. Shaking her head like a dog, she sprayed the walls with water. Then she wrapped her hair in a towel and wiggled into a blue satin jumpsuit. She posed in front of the dresser mirror, sucking in her stomach, trying for the wide-eyed innocent look that had worked ten years before.

She was short and chubby, with wide hips and chunky thighs rippled with cellulite. But with cork platforms she was four inches taller and liked to think she looked thinner. As she turned in front of the mirror she noticed a bra strap was showing and reached over her shoulder to push it underneath the cloth. Her hand cramped. She winced and tugged down the top half of the suit, twisted the bra around to her stomach, unlatched it and threw it on the bed. Her breasts were large and milky white with dark purple nipples, and they drooped without the bra. Dan liked her braless anyway, liked her to wear lots of perfume, too. They were all going out to dinner tonight after she picked up Lonnie. He'd promised to meet them at the airport restaurant.

Her purse was heavy with coins. She scooped them out and spread them evenly across the bed, counting silently as she separated dimes from quarters, nickels from pennies. She worked at Denny's and sometimes, on a good day, she might bring home twenty dollars in tips, maybe more. Today she had only made two dollars in cash, six in coin. A party of eight had stiffed her. For no reason—cheap is all. She always gave better service to bigger parties because the bill was higher and they were supposed to leave twenty percent. That would be the day.

She sighed and put the bills and quarters back in her purse, found her brush, and turned sideways in the mirror with a hand on her groin. Sucked in her stomach again. She wasn't fat. Not really. Her face looked drawn, her hair thin and brittle. A sharp pain shot across the bridge of her nose. Suddenly she wanted to cry, though she didn't know why. All day she had felt moody, wavering constantly between the desire to cuddle Lonnie and to grab him hard and shake some sense into that crazy head. It was a familiar anger, a quiet, mixed anger that confused her and made her feel helpless. But she should try to be happy now. Lonnie was coming home. They were all going out to a nice restaurant. He would meet Dan. Hopefully they'd like each other.

Only two buttons worked on the car radio and all she could get were loud, obnoxious disc jockeys and commercials. Clicking it off, Tania hummed the last bars of a song running through her head. She couldn't remember all of it, though, and after a while she grew exasperated and turned the radio back on. Now it was the news. Better than nothing. At least it filled the car with sound and made the ride seem shorter. Then she remembered something—not all of it—just a glimpse. Something she read in a child psychology class, a night class in adult education a long time ago. Tania had liked the course, earned an A, and she was mad at herself for forgetting what she thought she almost certainly should've remembered. Why did she do that? It was always the important things, too. Of course, maybe they just seemed important. She wondered how a person could know for sure if you couldn't remember.

Temperatures expected to be in the nineties tomorrow and through the weekend . . .

A string of red lights flashed on two by two. Tania panicked and locked the brakes. They squealed until her car stopped a few feet short of a big Ford ahead. Her face turned red with embarrassment. She stared at the Ford's license plate for a good minute without moving. When she figured the driver wasn't looking at her in his mirror anymore, she rolled down the window and leaned out. She moaned. Thousands of idling cars and the airport was still miles away. She glanced at her watch and saw that she had plenty of time left if they got the wreck, wherever it was, cleaned up soon, and if everybody didn't slow down to gawk like a bunch of vultures. Tucked above the sun visor was a pack of Virginia Slims and she reached for it, lit one, then rested her arm on the window frame, warm from the sun. Neither of the two older boys, she thought, had ever been as much trouble as Lonnie. Sonny was a good boy, watching out for the others, acting like a man although he'd become too smart-ass lately. Alex reminded her the most of her late husband. Impulsive. He never meant any harm, though. It was his damn friends who got him into trouble. But Lonnie . . .

Some sonofabitch edged his way into her lane without even signaling. Tania jerked her hands off the steering wheel, laughing at how ridiculous it was. What good was it going to do him? Her lane wasn't moving, either. Fumes from the idling cars were making her nauseated, and the heat, from remaining still in the sun, grew more intense. By the time she got there, she thought, she'd be so sweaty she'd need another bath. She rolled up her window, put out her cigarette, and looked down at her watch again. Five after four. Fifty-five minutes left. Ahead the traffic started to move, but within a few seconds it had stopped. Far in the distance she could now see two big yellow arrows flashing on and off. Goddamn Caltrans had closed two lanes. It took all the time she had before she even passed the bottleneck, and when she did she saw five men in orange uniforms standing around looking at the ground like they had lost something. She gritted her teeth, vowing to write the head of the department a nasty letter.

She parked in the first lot she came to. Locked the car. Ran. As she dashed across the street to the airport, her purse bouncing on her hip, what she'd been trying to remember came to her. It *was* in one of her psychology books, and it had to do with not reminding a person, or scolding or lecturing him or making a big scene, but just forgetting the problem for a while and talking about it later. It was good advice, she thought. She would act like nothing had ever happened. When the time came it would come naturally and she'd bring it up and they would talk and then . . . Well, she'd just have to take it a step at a time.

Another PSA plane landed. Tania looked through the crowd of passengers as they came down the ramp, her chest heaving. She couldn't remember ever running so much in her life. In a few minutes everyone was off the plane. A man shut the gates. She checked the board over the ticket desk. Her mouth dropped open. These people weren't from Barstow at all but Oakland, goddamn Oakland. Whirling around, she looked up and down the rows of seats in the lobby. A group of senior citizens sat waiting for the plane to Reno.

She had him paged.

Lonnie Baer, please come to the information desk.

Five minutes later she asked the clerk to try again.

Lonnie Baer, please come to the information desk.

She scanned the halls, turning her head left to right. Five more minutes passed. No Lonnie.

"Try again," she said.

"What's the flight number?" the clerk asked.

"Three-sixteen, I think. PSA." She dug through her purse for the slip of paper that she had written the flight number on. "It's from Barstow. Can't you tell from that?"

"There's no airport in Barstow."

"*San Diego.* You know what I'm talkin' about."

"It could've been delayed."

"What?"

The clerk pointed down the hall with a pen. "Check with the main desk."

Tania clenched her fists and rushed off. Nobody knew what was going on. Why didn't they hire decent help? At the main desk she was told Flight 316 had arrived on schedule forty-five minutes before and she started crying. Everything was falling apart. A porter came over to help her to her car. "I'm all right," she said, pulling away.

"You sure?"

"Go do your damn job."

The porter shrugged.

She met Dan at the restaurant and he tried to calm her. They had a drink, and just when it looked like she was getting hold of herself, she broke down again. Her eyes stung and objects around her seemed clipped and blurry. Dan suggested she call the police but she couldn't stop crying long enough to say anything that made any sense. So Dan called while she sat in the dark, sniffling, twirling the ice cubes in her glass with one finger. A candle flickered and illuminated the deep lines in her forehead, brightening the strands of hair that had come loose and fallen across her cheeks, shadowing the curl of her lips. The couple in the booth behind her talked in hushed voices. She knew it had to be about her although she couldn't actually make out their words. Ordinarily she would've gotten up and told them where to go, but tonight she didn't care what anyone said. All she wanted was Lonnie.

Dan returned to the table.

"He came in all right."

She bit her lip.

"But they lost him. He stole a car."

Her face contorted, like she was going to cry again. Dan hurried her to the bathroom, an arm around her waist. Then he stepped back into the phone booth and called her apartment.

"Lonnie?"

"This is Sonny." He'd just gotten home from an interview and was almost out the door again, on his way to drama class, when the phone rang. "Who's this?"

"A friend of your mother's. She's upset."

"What's going on?"

"I'll let her explain."

"Good."

"Oh . . . Sonny? Be nice, okay?"

"Sure, sure."

Tania came out of the bathroom red-eyed but collected. In control again, forcing a smile. She was about to ask Dan how she looked when he handed her the receiver. Her smile faltered. She wrinkled her eyebrows, puzzled. Dan nodded. As soon as she heard Sonny's voice she started crying again.

"What's the matter, Mom?"

She mumbled.

"Speak up."

The clinking of glasses and silverware traveled from the kitchen down the hall. Dan stood outside the booth next to the cigarette machine, arms crossed, as if he were guarding the area. His face was pink and smooth, and his eyes, because of a thyroid condition, protruded like big glossy marbles. He always carried a pocketful of coffee candies wherever he went and he was sucking on one now, rolling it under his tongue.

"Are you drunk or what?" said Sonny.

"*Drunk? I am not drunk.*"

"Where are you now?"

"None of your goddamn business."

"C'mon, Mom."

"I'm sorry I called."

"You didn't. Some guy did."

"I have better sense not to," she said in her most uppity voice, looking at Dan. The poor guy. He shouldn't have to deal with all this crap. It was good of him to be nice but really it wasn't any of his concern. He had two fine kids of his own. This was her problem and she was just sorry Lonnie had ruined another perfectly good night for them both. She knew he thought her kids were punks.

"Lemme talk to Lonnie."

"He's not here."

"Where is he?"

"I don't know."

"Whatta you mean you don't know?" Sonny said. "I thought you were picking him up."

"I was."

"Did he come in?"

"Uh huh."

"And you don't know where he is?"

"He stole another car."

"Jesus Christ."

Tania bawled harder.

"Calm down, just calm down."

She hung up. Dan led her back to the table and they had another drink. He insisted she have something to eat even though she said she wasn't hungry. All she wanted was to get drunk. According to what the police told Dan, he said, there was nothing anyone could do until they found Lonnie. No sense worrying.

After they finished their meal she followed him to his house in Encino. His kids had spent the night at their aunt's apartment so they had the place to themselves for a change. They made love but it was late and they were tired and Tania was worried and their stomachs were upset and full. When Dan came she held on for a while, her head on his chest, listening to his heartbeat. As much as she would've liked to fall asleep in his arms, he was too warm and she couldn't breathe comfortably. Dan kissed her lightly on her forehead, the tip of her nose, and they said good-night and rolled to opposite sides of the bed. He snored and sputtered in his sleep. Though she liked his body beside her, his fat hairy ass against hers, and the heat of it, it had been so long since she'd had someone in bed with her that she couldn't sleep.

Propping herself up with a pillow, she watched Dan's chest swell and fall. He was a nice man, a gentle man. Fat, but a good man. She pinched his ass and he moaned and threw an arm across her which she lifted off and gently rested beside her thigh. A car passed outside. She watched the headlights shine through the drapes and make patterns on the walls.

It was a strange time of night, she thought. So many people slept through it without ever knowing the difference. In a way she felt special to be awake now. She wanted to turn on the bed lamp, roll over on her belly, and read a magazine for a while, but she was afraid of waking Dan. Besides, it would ruin the special feeling. It was better just to relax, drift toward that edge where she could control her dreams. Make them good if they were going bad.

About three A.M. she climbed out of bed, kissed Dan on the forehead, and got dressed. Although she had planned on having good sex in the morning to make up for last night, she decided she'd better get home. Too bad. They never had much time together. He owned an upholstery shop in Sherman Oaks and had to work ten-hour days and weekends just to keep it out of the red. Next time, she thought. For sure. Next time she'd cook him a good breakfast, too. French toast and bacon, his favorite. But tonight she had to get home. The police might have already called. Tania shivered at the thought. Where was he? Was he okay? The way he ran off you'd think she beat him. People always blamed the parent, and that sure wasn't the case here. Lonnie wasn't giving her a chance. She put a hand to her head, feeling a little dizzy, a little hung over. It was hell to start the day worried and tired. Tired all the goddamn time.

In the kitchen she found a pad of paper and a pen, made herself a cup of instant coffee, and began to write:

> Dan, baby,
>   Sorry I had to go but . . .

She took out the *baby*. Too corny. The note had to be to the point and not mushy. But it had to make him feel good when he woke up, tired, only another long day of work to look forward to. She knew how it was. Damn right she did.

> Dan,
>   Sorry I had to go but I'd better stay near the phone. You looked so tired I didn't want to wake you. When you get up give me a call. I love you.
>
> > Love,
> > Tania

3

The stench was strong, the toilet was cracked, and the urinal was plugged with cigarette butts. On one wall hung a prophylactic machine that sucked up quarters but delivered nothing. Alex Baer zipped up and stepped in front of a mirror over the porcelain washbasin streaked with rust. Looking good, looking good, he thought. His shirt was half unbuttoned and he played with the black hairs on his chest as he flexed his shoulders so that the muscles bulged forward. *Fine.* His waist was small, his chest big and meaty, his arms long and muscular. There was a layer of fat around his chest and biceps, even his face, but he wasn't fat or flabby. The excess fit him well and gave the illusion of more strength than there really was. Powerful. Tight. Like a jock, he thought. He lit a joint and let it hang from the side of his mouth while he drew a comb across his head, patting each area, each hair down, until it was all just right. "Alex." He did a drum roll on the washbasin. "Alex Baer." He said it loud, said it twice and grinned. His hands slid down the back of his thighs and squeezed the muscles. Nice. Solid. The toilet drained; the air conditioner in the window whirred and vibrated. Fuckin' thing. Still ninety degrees and can't cool shit off. Just makes noise. He smacked the vent, flicked the roach into the urinal, and, swinging the bathroom door open with a bang, strutted up to the counter and bought another beer.

The floor at Pearl's was sprinkled with sawdust, the walls lined with eight-by-ten glossies. Vince Edwards. Spencer Tracy. And a lot of actors who starred in TV shows that had gone off the air years ago. Most of the photos were black-and-white studio shots, signed and dedicated to Pearl. During the Golden Age, Pearl's was supposedly where famous actors went to have a good chili dog and get away from the bland food of the studio commissaries. Then the gossip columnists wrote about it and Pearl's became popular. In. Tour buses made it a regular stop. It was great for business, but soon after Pearl died the chili dogs went downhill and now the place simply lived off its fading reputation. Tourists and rock groupies packed the tiny booths and sat for hours, heads turning in unison whenever some flashy local swaggered in, or a Rolls Royce or Mercedes rolled by outside.

Alex finished his beer and ordered another. An old buddy, Pete, was supposed to have met him here an hour ago. The plan was to head to San Diego—National City, wherever the hell that was—and conduct business. Pete was average height, slight in build, and had always appeared harmless to Alex. They had first met at Silverlake Lanes where they worked as apprentice bowling machine mechanics. During lunch they'd stroll out behind the big trash bins in the parking lot and smoke a joint or share a six-pack if one of them wanted to put up the money and walk to the 7-11 on the corner. Unless Alex felt generous he'd shrug and pat his pockets or say he only had a twenty and couldn't break it. So Pete usually bought. Behind his back he dubbed Alex the Scrooge. Said he nickel-and-dimed you to death.

They could've fooled around talking all afternoon and then suddenly they'd get a rash of calls over the loudspeaker. A ball jammed in the feeder. A fanatical bowler wanted a pin reset by hand. Some drunk broke the foul light again on lane fourteen and it wouldn't quit buzzing. And then there was the crashing, the constant crashing of balls on wood pounding Alex's ears, exploding into the backboards, the clattering and clinking and the smell of hot machines going nonstop for too many hours. Then a pin might stick in the turret and the machine would spit pins all over the floor. Three sets of ten. Everywhere. Seeing the mess when he was stoned made Alex want to rip off his work shirt, throw his hands into the air, and tell the boss to ram the job up his ass. It wasn't worth the hassle for minimum wage.

Aside from Silverlake Lanes he didn't see much of Pete although he thought he should've made the effort. The guy seemed nice enough and he always had excellent dope. Then one day Pete didn't show up for work. Alex quit soon after. Months passed. A couple of weeks ago Pete had happened to walk into Pearl's. They went outside and smoked like old times.

"Colombian."

"Where'd you get it?" Pete asked.

"Not bad, huh?"

"Nope."

"Got a friend," Alex said.

Pete agreed it was good but said he thought Alex had paid too much for it. He could get just as good Mexican for a whole lot cheaper. Yeah? Alex said. They smoked one of Pete's and he had to agree. If he had the money, Pete said, he'd let him in on a deal. He could get kilos for next to nothing compared to what Alex paid for Colombian. Coke, too. That did it for him.

He was in a stoned daze when Pete finally arrived at Pearl's.

They piled into Alex's Riviera, ate two black beauties to keep wide-eyed, bought a case of beer, and headed for San Diego. "I got a friend where we're going," Pete said, after they merged onto the freeway. "She's having a party to-

night." Alex nodded. He drove fast and chain-smoked.
Cigarettes tasted great when he was speeding.

Two hours later they were in San Diego.

An hour later they had tasted and bought the dope.

By eleven that night the Riviera was parked outside a
two-story house in National City with four kilos of Mexican locked in the trunk. A thin gray layer of cigarette
smoke filled the living room. Country music played on the
stereo. Some people stood around a buffet table of cold cuts
while others huddled beside a small bar in the den.

Alex was upstairs in the bedroom with a half-ounce of
cocaine, high and a little drunk, kissing his way down the
belly of the hostess. Her head was thrown back, lips shaped
in an O, eyes shut. A drop of fluid stained Alex's jockey
shorts. His gums, his mouth, were numb from the coke and
he barely felt the skin he kissed. She lifted her ass and
shimmied her panties down her thighs. Alex was rock hard.
He'd heard about older women. Experienced. Hot. She
pushed on his shoulders, moaning. Her breasts lay flat on
her chest. "Scoot up a little," he said. When she moved he
shoved a pillow under her ass, kissed the soft inside of a
thigh. The faint twang of a steel guitar sounded on the
stereo downstairs. Alex centered his kiss. A car started up
outside. He raised his head, froze, listened. The engine
coughed. "That's my car!" He hopped out of bed and
dashed to the window. His face turned pale. "That's my
fuckin' car!" Instantly he was sober, jumping into his
slacks, pulling on his boots, grabbing his shirt, running
downstairs.

Pete and another guy sat in the Riviera, boxed between
two cars. Alex circled his hand around for Pete to roll down
the window. He unrolled it halfway. Alex stuck his head
in, breathing hard, sweating, his face beet red.

"Where the hell ya goin'?"

"To pick up some ice," he said. "Relax." Alex stared him
square in the eyes. "You left your keys in your coat." Pete
laughed. "Like I thought you were busy."

"Move over."

"We'll be back in a minute," the other guy said.

"Who's he?"

"A friend."

"I don't like him."

Pete and the other guy exchanged looks and shrugged.

"Lemme in."

"You're getting excited over nothing."

"Stay outta this."

"Please, Alex. Get your head out of the window."

"Lemme in," he screamed.

"Roll up the window, Pete," the other guy said.

"Trust me, man."

"Don't pull no shit." Alex tried to keep the window from closing. "Owww." He kicked the fender. It sounded like an explosion. Pete unrolled the window enough for Alex to free his fingers. He rubbed and shook them for a second and then, with tears in his eyes, disappeared. Pete maneuvered the car away from the curb. A scream filled the air. He slammed on the brakes. Throwing the engine into park, he slowly opened the door to look around. Out of nowhere, out of the darkness, sprang Alex. They had a tug-of-war with the door that ended quickly with Alex sprawled on the street.

Pete revved the motor. "Did you hear that? I'll run you over. *I said I'll run your ass over, Alex . . . don't try me.*"

He drove slowly at first, then faster as they got farther down the street. Alex pounded the roof with his fists, screaming as loud as he could. Pete hit the brakes. Gas. Brakes. Gas. Brakes. Lights around the quiet neighborhood flashed on like blinking giants. They pulled over. The other guy unrolled the window a crack. "What are you trying to do? Get us busted?" Alex leaned over the edge, looking at them upside down, his hair hanging toward the ground. "We're just going to pick up some fucking ice."

"*Sure.*"

"Honest."

"Trust me, man," Pete said.

"Then lemme in."

"Okay, okay."

"Ya mean it?"

"Of course."

"Open the door and get out."

"Alex, my word is good. We're partners, right?"

"Get out and walk across the street."

"Trust me or I'll get on that fucking freeway."

Alex considered his choices. "Promise ya won't try nothin'?"

"Promise."

He jumped to the ground and brushed his hair out of his eyes with a sharp sweep of the hand. Then, as he reached for the door handle, Pete stepped on the gas and left him standing in the middle of the street. *"You sonofabitch."* He shook his fist. Suddenly he realized he had the coke. A grin spread across his face. Idiots, he thought. But they had his car. *"They got my goddamn car."* He ran to the corner and looked up and down the street, panting, listening for the clatter of his Riviera, hoping they were only circling the block to scare him. They were coming back, he thought. Sure, they were coming back. Don't worry. It was a joke. Some joke. He bent over and felt inside his boot for the baggie of cocaine. Even if they weren't funning, they'd be back. The coke was worth half as much as the Mexican. Patting his boot, smiling confidently, he sat down on the curb.

An hour passed.

Two hours passed.

This was a shitty joke.

Three hours later he was standing at the entrance to the freeway. Twenty cars had passed and he'd tried everything short of lying in the road. He tucked in his shirt, combed his hair so it looked shorter, and smiled when the headlights of a car shot toward him down the ramp. He did everything possible not to look like a wild mass murderer or rapist or hippie and still no one stopped. Soon he was flipping drivers off as they passed, their red tail lights fading into the long dark freeway. Stumbling to the side of the road, Alex leaned against a signpost and cursed. He was beyond exhaustion. What he needed was a good bath, a warm bed, a drink to calm his nerves, sleep. Sleep forever. *When I get those motherfuckers* . . . The driver of a beat-up truck carrying a load of scrap metal pulled to the curb and motioned him to hop in back.

4

Sonny Baer stared out the window of a plush waiting room overlooking Wilshire Boulevard. A middle-aged lady in a muumuu was trying to jaywalk the rush-hour traffic. Each time it looked clear she'd step out, then balk at the last second and scramble back to the curb like a nearsighted cow. Cars in the right lane swerved around her. Sonny found himself rooting for her, then grew bored and turned back to the script. A lump rose in his throat when he thought of all the times he'd auditioned and been rejected. Last time it was a hood for a TV cop show. Now he was up for a military guard who arrests two young environmentalists after they discover traces of radioactive waste in a schoolyard drinking fountain. Stupid. Silly. But he needed the part.

When he was thirteen, Sonny had done a Kellogg's Corn Flakes commercial with Jimmy Durante. It was the first part he'd ever tried out for and he was selected over a hundred other kids. He played a little punk in knickers and poor-boy cap, cocked to one side, who stomped on Durante's foot. Through trick photography Durante grows into a giant and hops around, holding his foot, moaning the Kellogg's pitch. A year later he did another for Kool-Aid which never aired. Work became harder to find as he got older. Eventually he changed agents and was advised not to do any more commercials. He had to be more selective. His career could be ruined before it began. Except for a small spot on a local soap opera, in which he played a dope-addicted high school kid, Sonny hadn't worked for three years.

Wrinkled copies of *Cosmopolitan* and *Los Angeles* lay on a redwood burl coffee table. A clock on the wall showed four-fifteen. Damn. He should be on his way to the airport to meet Lonnie but he knew the minute he left his name would be called. Two other actors lounged on the couch facing each other. They had sugar-coated voices, smiled constantly. One man had a habit of signaling quotation marks in the air with his fingers. They discussed meaningful relationships, identity crises, coping, and communicating on higher levels. Bullshit is what it was, Sonny thought. In the casting office down the hall he heard another actor shouting his lines. Overdoing it, phony as hell. The guy had it all wrong. This military guard, at least in this situation, would be relaxed. And if he shouted it would come from the diaphragm. Deep. Like a rookie cop trying to be tough even though he was scared and nervous. Sonny knew the feeling. But the guy had been in there a long time. Maybe they liked him? He lit a Camel and watched the smoke dissipate in the stream of air shooting from the air conditioner under the window. Somewhere in that smoggy sky his brother was approaching L.A. Shaking his head, he thought, Lonnie, you just can't take off every time things don't go the way you want.

A second later the secretary walked into the waiting room holding a clipboard to her chest. She had curly hair and wore tight designer jeans. The actors grew quiet, waiting to hear who she called next. Sonny dashed his smoke into the ashtray on the coffee table. Pouting as if she were truly sorry, glancing at her watch, she said, "It's been a long day. Why doesn't everyone go home and come back Monday for a raincheck?"

The two men sighed in chorus and bounced to their feet, smiling. Cheerful. Sonny gave them a dirty look.

"Have they decided?"

"They have a person in mind."

"Then what's with the raincheck?"

"It's not final yet."

"My ass it isn't," he muttered. They wasted his time for nothing when he could've met Lonnie at the airport. Dropping the script on the coffee table, Sonny pushed past the two men, out of the office. It was a shitty part in a shitty TV show anyway, he thought, entering the elevator, feeling for his car keys.

He drove his old 'Vette down Wilshire to Westlake, up a side street and to Pico and turned into the alley leading home. To his left were apartments and old houses. There were backyards and garages behind chain link fences and old wooden fences rotten at the posts, leaning as if they were about to fall. Sometimes in the afternoon or early evening a woman might be hanging laundry on her backyard clothesline, or Old Man Wheat might be out watering his rose garden. Occasionally a pack of kids on bikes weaved through the alley looking for a place to party. Dented trashcans and battered cars rested inside apartment carports, and, farther down, behind a tall fence, two stripped cars sat rusting in a field overgrown with foxtails and mustard weed. A NO TRESPASSING sign full of BB holes dangled by one wire on the fence. In the corner was a patch of earth where someone had tried to start a garden. On the right was a huge warehouse that ran the length of the alley. And across from a dynamo that hummed day and night was the Palms Apartments, where the Baers lived. The number on their garage was missing; the faded outline of a nine barely visible. It was an enclosed garage Lonnie used as a clubhouse until Sonny got his 'Vette a couple of years ago. Now car parts were strewn everywhere.

Sonny parked in the garage and went upstairs to the apartment. No one was home. The side tables in the living room were cluttered with McDonald's wrappers and paper cups and a half-eaten cheeseburger. Ashtrays overflowed with cigarette butts. A cushion was missing from the couch. He'd be damned if he was going to clean the place. It was Alex's turn. Besides, he didn't have time. Sonny stripped naked, took a shower, put on some jeans and a white T-shirt, and reached for his notebook on the dresser. On his way out he stopped in the kitchen and grabbed a chicken leg from a Colonel Sanders bucket in the refrigerator. That's when the phone rang. Mom. Drunk. He didn't know where she was calling from. And that guy, telling him to be *nice*—who was that asshole? After she hung up, he punched the wall so hard he bruised his hand. Goddamn Lonnie. What did he do now? The kid was ruining his life.

He hurried downstairs.

In the garage he found Stormin' Norman from apartment three sitting in his 'Vette. On weekends Norman stood on the corner of Sunset and La Brea and sold maps to stars' homes. He had small black surfer crosses and misspelled words all over his arms and hands like burn marks or tiny bruises. Whenever he got the urge to carve on himself he came to the garage with a bottle of India ink so he'd have Sonny or Alex or Lonnie for an audience. It grew old fast, though, and nobody cared or paid him much attention any more. Tonight he was with a friend.

The Mad Tattooist leaned over to his buddy and whispered something.

"Get out," Sonny yelled.

"Can ya give us a ride?"

"No."

"C'mon."

"I won't say it again."

He looked at the other kid and grimaced. There was something all over the front of his shirt, Sonny didn't know what, but it looked grotesque.

"Want me to tell your old man you cut school yesterday?"

Reluctantly the Mad Tattooist gave up his seat behind the wheel.

"And don't be fuckin' around in my car. How many times I gotta tell you?" He pointed to the seat. "Look at that. You got shit all over."

"Can I go with ya?"

"What are you? Deaf?" Sonny raised his hand but the Mad Tattooist danced away. He made a face and Sonny threw the chicken leg at him. It bounced off his shoulder.

"Cocksucker," the Mad Tattooist screamed.

The other kid bolted out of the garage and Norman, alone now, spit at Sonny and ran after his buddy. Sonny frowned. Little prick. When Lonnie was that age he was never that bad, never a brat. Lonnie was all right. Stormin' Norman was a punk. Lonnie held his own and didn't bother anyone. Never. Maybe that was the problem. The kid was too independent, held it all inside. Sonny revved the engine and sped down the alley and headed for MacArthur Park where the locals hung out.

An old man sat on a bench near the lake, brown bag in hand. The water was murky green. Five guys huddled around a battered picnic table, smoking dope. Shooting the shit. From behind, from a distance, one might have been Lonnie—small, wearing a red headband. Sonny parked and hurried down a windy path and through a tunnel that smelled like piss. But as he approached the group the small one turned around and he saw it wasn't Lonnie. His heart sank.

"Any of you know Lonnie?"

"Whatta ya want 'im for?"

"That's his brother, stupid," the small one said.

"Ya sure?"

"Yeah, I'm sure."

"Lonnie ain't been around lately."

"Didn't he get busted?"

"Again?"

"He looks jus' like 'im, huh?"

"That your 'Vette over there? *Nice.*"

"It'd look better lower."

"What's it? Sixty-seven?"

Sonny left. They didn't know shit.

He cruised around Belmont High, scanning the school-yard through a tall chain link fence. Prison, he thought. You couldn't blame Lonnie for hating the place. Sonny had hated it when he was here. The yard was empty except for a couple of men jogging the track. Unless it was Saturday, unless the basketball courts were empty, the chances of his brother being here were about zero. Maybe he should come back when it was dark. Kids stood behind the backstop and got high there at night. Lonnie might come around to meet a friend, though Sonny didn't know of anyone he was that close to. He cruised the side streets, looking into parked cars, slowing to a crawl when he came to a Transam loaded with guys. He cruised Sunset, then Hollywood Boulevard. Where the hell would he go if he hadn't left town already? Think. Sometimes he went to Pearl's with Alex to shoot pool. Not often, though, not by himself, anyway. Then there were the slot car races at Santa Monica Pier, but that place was gone. Destroyed. He and Lonnie used to fool around there a lot together before a storm washed it into the ocean. Even if it was still standing, he thought, it would be too far to drive. There just wasn't enough time.

Sonny had feelings inside that were right, powerful, that could move people. Spending his whole life working at Standard and living home and doing theater at night when he was really too tired for anything but sleep was okay for now. But Christ, not forever! The theater was obscure, the plays too arty. No one cared. If it wasn't for the actor's relatives, and the director giving away free tickets, there wouldn't even be an audience. Things had to change and grow and move toward something *big.*

A note was tacked on the theater door: REHEARSALS CAN-CELED. The same thing had happened twice last week. Not enough actors showed. He grabbed a bottle of sherry from the glove compartment, walked around back to the dressing room, found the spare key on the ledge overhead, and let himself in. The theater was dark inside, smelled musty like an old disorderly bookshop. He sat in the back row and put his feet up on the chair in front and took a long drink. The play was scheduled to open soon and the actors were still uncoordinated. Some didn't even know their lines yet. The whole play, he thought, was turning into a joke. They called themselves serious, but most of the actors were veterans using up their GI Bill or girls who didn't know what they wanted or women who had raised their families and now had spare time on their hands. To them it seemed a hobby—a place to socialize, to fill the gap. Which was fine, only they were blowing it for him. The play had to be good. A reviewer from the *Los Angeles Times* was supposed to come opening night. He figured if he got in the *Times* some people in the right places just might take notice and come see his performance.

All right, he thought. So he was late today. But it wasn't like he was screwing off at the beach. For a moment he wondered if he should try and catch his last class at LACC. No. He wasn't learning anything there. Just putting in hours like on any other job except it didn't pay. What he needed was a break. One goddamn break. A chance. A little recognition and a little money, and he could quit school and all the students and failed drama teachers and start making a career for himself. Degrees in drama from LACC to UCLA to the finest acting schools in New York didn't mean much here. College-trained actors were everywhere. What the industry needed and wanted was someone they could sell and they could sell him because he was handsome and had talent, too. He should be hunting for a better agent who wouldn't send him out for crappy parts in crappy television shows and make him wait hours in crappy waiting rooms and then not even get interviewed. He needed a *lead* role. But if he'd gotten the part today, if the casting directors knew their asses from their heads, he would have added a touch to that character to make it shine like no other actor could. Even a goddamn TV show was a start. Mom had told him college was a wise choice, that he needed a stable job to fall back on in case he didn't make it, but she was wrong. *Falling back* was for losers. It was a bum or a star, no compromises. Not with his dream. He knew all kinds of actors. Some were really good. But they always let themselves be detoured or get knocked down and were always too tired or frightened to keep getting back up. They lost before they'd begun. He had to push and keep pushing until he broke through into the clear.

Staring across the empty seats and aisles, the dark empty stage, Sonny had another drink and then carefully set the bottle on the floor. He reached for his wallet and pulled out a yellowed slip of paper, a review from *Variety* of a play he did a year ago on that same stage. Cautiously, slowly, so as not to tear the paper, he unfolded it along the same worn creases as he had many times before. His lips moved almost imperceptibly. "Sonny Baer, a dark, attractive young man of twenty, reveals an uncanny ability to give color to an otherwise colorless mixed-up youth. A sensitive portrayal . . . ."

Two A.M. The phone rang. Sonny's temples throbbed, and, twice, fumbling for his keys, he lost his balance and stumbled. He ran his hand along the wall for the lightswitch and, out of breath, picked up the phone on the fifth ring.

"How ya doin'?"

"Lonnie?"

"Who else gonna call ya?"

"You okay?"

"Naw. My leg's broken, my head's busted. I can't move my fingers."

"You shittin' me?"

"I'm in terrible shape."

Sonny raised his voice. "Don't be joking around. This isn't the time. You okay?"

"I'm okay. I'm sorry."

"That's all right."

"Sorry. Really."

"Forget it."

"Sonny . . ."

"Yeah?"

"I'm in trouble."

"Don't worry."

He heard Lonnie swallow hard. "You're the only guy I can trust, Sonny. I mean that." Pause. "You ain't mad?"

"I ain't mad."

"What about Mom and Alex?"

"Nobody's mad," Sonny said. "Where you calling from?"

"I jus' wanted to talk."

"I'll pick you up."

Lonnie hesitated. "I ain't sure I wanna come home."

"Then whatta you going to do?"

"I ain't sure."

"Then you better stay put."

Silence.

"Want to meet somewhere and talk?"

Silence.

"You still there?"

"Yeah."

Silence.

"Think straight, Lonnie."

"Okay, okay. Jus' talk?"

"Just talk."

"You know the El Taco?"

"On Western?"

"Yeah."

"Stay where you are. Don't go anyplace."

No answer.

"Just stay where you are, you hear?"

"I hear."

"Promise?"

"Promise."

"Be right down."

"Bye."

"Don't go anywhere."

"Bye."

Lonnie hung up.

Sonny walked downstairs to his car. Surely. Deliberately.

Across the street from the El Taco, stopped at the light, he saw a crowd and two patrol cars parked crookedly, only the front wheels touching the curb. Red lights flashed round and round against the walls of the buildings and into the sky. A clerk stood in the doorway of a porno bookstore. A few old men kept their distance as they watched, concealing thin green bottles under jackets. The people at the bus stop and the customers from the El Taco formed a semicircle around it all, like they were watching a street fight.

Sonny parked in a red zone and, leaving the door wide open, ran into the crowd. Three cops stood like stone walls, keeping everyone at a distance, hollering the way they do to get back, go away, get on with your business. Sonny squeezed through the crowd, parting people, saying, "Excuse me, excuse me," when suddenly he felt two hands on his chest pushing him backward. "That's my brother," he shouted. The cop continued to push. "That's my brother. *Listen.*" They didn't know what they were doing. Lonnie wasn't scum. Some fucking anecdote for the wife. Then it was over. He saw Lonnie being tugged, hands cuffed behind his back. The cop pushed his head down and shoved him into the backseat of a patrol car. The door was slammed shut and locked. For a second Sonny couldn't speak or move. His face burned. Two women behind him were whispering. They weren't worth his spit. He watched the patrol car fuse with the traffic up the street, the back of his brother's head growing fainter and fainter, until there was nothing left to see.

The officer in charge took him aside in the El Taco parking lot and asked for his driver's license, where he lived and worked, his relation to Lonnie and his mother's full name, if he was aware of what Lonnie had done. He replied briefly, emotionlessly, looking down at the ground. There was nothing he could do tonight, the cop said. They would contact his mother. Chuckling, he made a crack about Sonny's breath, something about how he'd like a shot, too, after a night like this. Go on home now. Sleep. Your brother will be all right. The casualness with which the cop spoke, the false concern, made Sonny want to put his fist down the bastard's throat. If he ever caught him off duty . . .

He got into his car and onto the freeway and drove in a straight line until it intersected and then he turned around and headed home. The apartment was still empty. Sonny poured himself a glass of Mom's vodka and stood beside the phone for what seemed like a long time. They should've called by now, he thought. They might have tried and nobody was here. They should keep trying.

He wanted to phone them himself but instead he turned on the TV and sprawled out on the floor. The last bars of the National Anthem accompanied a picture of an American flag waving in the wind. Coughing up a ball of phlegm, he turned the TV off, reached for his pack of Camels, shook one out, lit it. Took a few drags. Dashed it in the ashtray on the coffee table. The clock on the wall showed a quarter to four. On the way to his room he heard Mom's Toyota come clattering up the alley outside. He flipped on the light. Lonnie's bed was unmade. Sonny crawled on top and lay there, waiting, staring at the ceiling.

5

Tania's father spent his first fifteen years in America boxing as a middleweight. Her mother, Teresa Gianetti, was a second-generation immigrant from Italy. They lived in a tenement in Chicago with your usual amount of "hopheads," as her father called them, and casual low-lifes and hustlers. Transients. But mostly the tenement housed factory workers and carpenters, plumbers and ditchdiggers, laborers and craftsmen of all sorts.

Although Scott O'Malley was fast, he wasn't extraordinarily skilled, and he had a hot temper. In the biggest fight of his career, a preliminary match at Madison Square Garden, under a top-ranked heavyweight bout, he fought a Puerto Rican from New York—a then-undefeated up-and-coming star. The publicity posters featured a picture of curly-haired O'Malley glaring at his opponent at weigh-in, and the papers gave him three to one odds. He kept ahead on points until the eighth round when he was staggered by a flurry and became angry and wild and let go with one too low, hitting the boy below the waist. The fight was stopped. That was the first of seven disqualifications in his career. For a few years his temper worked to his advantage—he could fill a small auditorium with local fans who wanted to see a dirty fighter lose. But forty or so fights later, winning many more than he lost, he began having trouble making weight. His hands slowed down; his timing was off. He worked out as hard as he always had, only now everything he ate turned to fat. Two weeks before a match he starved himself and sat in a steam room for hours. Eventually he became too weak, too dehydrated to fight well.

So he went up a division even though he wasn't natural there. As a middleweight he at least fought men his own size and build, but as a light-heavy he boxed lean men comfortable as light-heavies, or young boys growing into heavyweights. After a couple of years his ears were cauliflowered and riddled with broken blood vessels, his nose had been broken five times, and a cut above his left eye had been opened so often that now it bled from the slightest blow. Every opponent knew about his eye and worked it until it swelled shut. Soon the fans were leaving early or not coming at all. They'd seen what they wanted too many times.

One night after a particularly brutal fight, his doctor told him to quit or he'd lose the sight in his left eye. There was a time he wouldn't have listened. O'Malleys didn't give up. But he'd been tired lately, frustrated, and his manager was spending less time with him than he was with the newer, younger boxers. The eye was a good excuse to get out of the business without losing what remained of his pride. He fought once more and then slowly, over a period of months, stopped training.

By this time O'Malley had two kids and needed steady employment, so he hired on as a security guard at a rubber factory on the edge of town and began coaching his son. Ernie was a big kid but he was still awkward, like a chubby, floppy puppy who hasn't grown into its paws yet. After a month of training O'Malley lied about Ernie's age and entered him in a YMCA match for boys twelve and older. Although sixteen-ounce gloves were used, Ernie had his jaw broken in the third and final round. For the next two

years, whenever O'Malley mentioned fighting, his wife
cursed him in Italian and pulled her son to her bosom.
Ernie was relieved. He didn't like boxing for the simple
reason that he didn't like being hurt or hurting someone.
And long after the jaw healed he complained it still pained
him and that it didn't set right when he bit down. The jaw
story only worked for a while, though.

Eventually, his big-boy awkwardness turned to grace.
When he was seventeen he captured All-City as a lean
light-heavy. Shortly thereafter O'Malley arranged his son's
first professional bout, which he won by knockout in the
sixth round. Half the money he gave to his father; the other
half he spent on an old beat-up Plymouth. The motor sputtered and coughed and the transmission turned out to be
packed with sawdust. It only ran for a week. Again Ernie
fought and this time he used half the money to buy a rebuilt
transmission from a junkyard. When his father wasn't
working him out, he went to the city library and read
Chilton manuals as if they were magazines, taking elaborate
notes, staying late until the librarian shooed him home.
Word circulated. Soon the neighbors who owned cars came
to him for advice and repair work. Slowly, Ernie began
faking injuries so he could skip training and build a business for himself.

Mrs. Teresa O'Malley was an old-world woman who
believed there was a yes or no answer to all questions. What
she said was final. No back talk. Tania often tired of plead-
ing with her mother and would run to Ernie's room, sit on
the edge of his bed, fold her hands in her lap, and talk with
him until her frustration subsided. He seemed to know
what he wanted and where he was going. It had nothing to
do with boxing. Listening to Ernie made her own dreams
seem possible. It was her mother's sense of propriety, a
sense of waiting and waiting, that made her fear she might
never enjoy life like she imagined other girls did.

When Tania reached the tenth grade Mrs. O'Malley
bought her a sewing machine and Tania dropped out of

school to work. Her mother said if you spoke English, if you could write your name, you'd had plenty of education and it was time to help the family. She made a sign which she displayed in the window of their ground-floor apartment: ALTERATIONS & CUSTOM TAILORING.

The landlord referred business to them, particularly Mr. Allswang, whom Tania considered incredibly obnoxious. He wore a toupee and carried a folded newspaper in his coat pocket that he fanned at people whenever they lit a cigarette or cigar or pipe. But he owned a popular restaurant on the good side of town and they did all his personal suits and his employees' alterations. In her broken English, Mrs. O'Malley often said if you worked for Mr. Allswang you were the best. No one could question the quality of your craftsmanship. Tania wasn't impressed. She thought her mother was belittling herself and the family by being overly respectful of Mr. Allswang and it angered her. He was a loser no matter how many restaurants he owned. She couldn't picture herself sewing for him or anyone else for the next ten years.

Ernie fought once more. This time he kept all the money and drove his old Plymouth to California.

It was snowing the day they received a package from Gilroy, California. Inside were apples, dried prunes, and oranges the size of softballs. There was a letter taped to an apple. Tania split the envelope cautiously. The package could only have come from Ernie. Her father held an orange in one hand and grimaced while his wife looked in wonder at the fruit. In the envelope was a snapshot and a twenty-dollar bill. Ernie stood ankle-deep in the Pacific. On the back it said: "It's always summer here." Mr. O'Malley muttered a curse and dumped the fruit in the garbage. After that, the days droned endlessly for Tania. Mr. Allswang came around more frequently and stayed too long. One time she caught him staring at her and refused to drop her eyes.

Tania wrote her brother, and in his reply he enclosed bus

fare. Later that night she packed two suitcases and slipped out of the apartment to hide them in the closet under the staircase in the hallway. The next morning she told her mother she was going to pick up donuts at Tommy's Bakery, like she did every Saturday, and instead boarded the Greyhound for California.

She lived with Ernie in a cottage in back of an onion farm, trying to save enough to attend secretarial school at night. First she worked at a fruit stand on Highway 101, then she waitressed at a diner in Salinas that had a huge neon onion out in front in garish shades of yellow and green. For a year she wrote her parents twice monthly, hoping they would forgive her, but they were bitter and never answered her letters. As far as they were concerned she was just like her brother now. No good. That spring, at the age of nineteen, Tania met and married Gus Baer, an ironworker for Local 358, and postponed her plans to attend secretarial school. They moved to San Jose where she lived for thirteen years and had three sons. Like her father and brother, Gus was wide across the shoulders although not as tall. He had high cheekbones like a Sioux and a dark, weathered complexion from working long hours in the sun. His forearms were thick, his hands large, and his fingers callused and rough as sandpaper.

Sometimes on the weekend he splurged on a case of Pabst, a hunk of sharp cheddar, and a loaf of sour french, and drove the boys to Gilroy for the afternoon. They'd run through the fields like a pack of wild dogs, pulling up the scallions, eating only the good part, throwing the tails over their shoulder. Ernie and Gus would sit in the kitchen drinking, talking, occasionally glancing out the window to make sure Lonnie wasn't being picked on too much. "The Republicans, the Democrats, they ain't doing a goddamn thing for us," Gus might say, sitting back in his chair. "Never did. And I don't expect 'em to, either. They're sonsabitches. They're *all* sonsabitches." His eyes would grow misty. He'd sweep an open hand across the table as if he were covering the entire country. "You know what's going to happen, Ernie? I'll tell you what's going to happen, goddamn it. It's getting so a man can't eat to live no more . . ." Then he'd lean forward, shaking a fist while he rambled on, Ernie nodding and agreeing.

Gus died building one of San Jose's first skyscrapers. A cable carrying a beam snapped and hit the railing, making him lose his balance. He grabbed for a solid beam but missed. As he fell his head hit the outside railing on the sixth floor and then again on the fourth floor. His body bounced off the ground like a basketball. His skull was as soft and wet as a sponge, his face no face at all, his bones mush.

The settlement was small. Tania went to work at Ford but she was laid off with six hundred others on the line nine months later. Bills came due. She borrowed from her brother until she found a job cocktailing at night in a local bar, leaving Sonny to watch over the boys. He was ten and Alex was eight. Lonnie was almost five. But she soon gave her boss notice, thinking there had to be something else, something better to do with her life. Needing time to herself, she turned her sons over to Ernie while she scouted the country for a new place to settle.

It was summer then, and Ernie had quit his job to open his own business. The overhead was high—rent on the garage, the cost of tools, advertising flyers which the boys stuck on windshields—and sometimes he wouldn't get home before ten or eleven at night. His third customer was a used car lot dealer who offered him good money to fix a car just long enough to sell, promising him more jobs in the future. But Ernie considered himself an honest man and refused the proposal. People who knew little about engines would, whether they liked it or not, often receive a short lecture regarding what was wrong with their car, and possibly why, when they came to pick it up. If they paid good money for repairs, for parts, he figured they deserved a good explanation. And when an engine was shot to hell, instead of patching it, he'd suggest the owner buy a rebuilt from a Mexican he knew in San Jose who did quality work. There were too many backyard mechanics around, he'd say. Sure, they'll slap you an engine together cheap. With worn-out parts! What do you have? The same problem in six months.

To keep the boys busy, to keep their minds off their mother and father, he made a list of chores for them to do while he was working. Sonny cooked and washed the dishes one week, Alex the next. Lonnie cleaned the bathroom, polished the faucets, vacuumed. On Sunday they carted the week's laundry to the laundromat. On Tuesday Sonny delivered TV flyers. Mornings Alex delivered newspapers. On Friday Lonnie bagged the returnable bottles and cashed them in at the market. And on Thursday Tania phoned them after nine P.M. when the rates went down. Once she called from Humboldt, once from Crescent City, once from Long Beach. She always told each son how much she missed him. Are you behaving? Not giving Ernie a hard time? Her brother, who usually spoke last, would tell her all was fine, they were all doing fine, which wasn't always true. Lonnie had recurring nightmares and convulsions, sometimes waking up at night frothing at the mouth as his eyes rolled back inside his head.

They were sitting on the couch watching the late show the first time it happened. A crash came from the bathroom. Ernie ran and found him on the floor with his head thrown back, his body vibrating. They wrapped him in a blanket and rushed him to emergency at the county hospital. Doctors tested for epilepsy, thought he was poisoned and pumped his stomach, but they couldn't find a thing wrong. A month later he developed blistering rashes on the meaty sides of his calves, and at night he lay in bed scratching until his skin felt moist and cool with blood. Ernie bought salves and antibacterial sprays, and finally he took him back to the county hospital. A cream was prescribed. Pills. Neither worked. The sheets were always spotted and crusty by the end of the week.

Then when summer ended his brothers started school and they couldn't watch over him. So Ernie brought him to the shop, cut the arms and legs off an old pair of coveralls, and gave him a white painter's cap to wear. He swept floors, fetched tools, cleaned parts. After an hour or so his uncle told him to take a break and he went out back to play in the junk. There were flywheels with missing teeth, crankshafts, valves, and open transmissions that looked like huge seashells inside. Lonnie watched the farmworkers in the field in the distance while sitting on top of a rusty engine block, timing chain in hand, absently pulling it taut, then letting it collapse. The workers were hunched over, many in straw cowboy hats, moving from side to side as they thinned weeds or topped onions. The air smelled sweet and acrid. At noon the bodies rose, the older men and women more slowly than the young, hands on the small of their back. Ernie called him inside about that time, told him to wash up, and they would walk to a nearby diner for lunch.

An old two-ton, flatbed Dodge appeared across the field at quitting time, raising dust in its wake, honking its horn as it bounced along the bumpy dirt road. Lonnie watched the Mexicans form a line and hand in their tools—knives if they were topping onions, hoes if they were clearing weeds. Then one by one they slowly climbed into the back of the truck and sat, cramped, shoulders touching shoulders. Gone. The field vacant and quiet, he knew his uncle would soon be closing shop for the day. Sometimes he'd hear his name, sometimes Ernie came out, sat on the rusty engine block, and talked with him while he drank a cold beer.

In the spring Tania came for the boys. Her face was tanned and she looked strong and healthy again. She had a PBX job lined up in Los Angeles and, although it wasn't exactly what she wanted, it would do for now. L.A. was a big city with lots of opportunities. Another, better job would come along for her once they were settled. That had been ten years ago.

They left Gilroy at night with their small car packed with all it could carry. The rear end nearly scraped the ground. Just before dawn they pulled into the Coronet Motel on Hollywood Boulevard. Alex was asleep in the backseat between two cardboard boxes, huddled in a faded gray blanket. Tania placed a finger to her lips and whispered to Sonny to keep Lonnie down while she went in and signed the register. The man might see them and make her pay extra. Then the dome light came on. Alex groaned. Then it was dark again. When Mom's footsteps had trailed off across the asphalt Sonny reached inside the glove compartment for her pint of vodka and stole a long swallow. Shivered. His head was below the window but he could still see the motel swimming pool, soft blue and bright, shimmering. He could see up, too, and he searched the sky for the tops of palm trees. All the postcard pictures of Hollywood had palm trees. He had another drink, capped the bottle, smiled. Hollywood. Suddenly he heard a whimper and looked down and saw his little brother crying. Taking him in his arms, he held him tight, chest to chest, trembling, there in the car in the parking lot.

A man inside a wire cage heaved a cloth sack full of towels into a laundry bin.

"The Dodgers lost."

"No kidding."

He patted his back pocket and grinned.

"You'll get your money," the cop said, walking away, leaving Lonnie. The man in the cage leaned out the service window. "When hell freezes over. Huh, Kiley?" he hollered. "When hell freezes over." Muttering to himself, he tugged his pants up around his belly and faced forward.

"Stay behind the red line and strip."

Lonnie pulled off his shirt, unlaced and took off his shoes and socks, unbuckled his pants and slipped them off. He

looked like a refugee in a CARE ad. Skinny. His ribs stuck
out. You could count them.

"Everything."

A couple of seconds passed.

"Including shorts."

Lonnie dropped his boxers. His cock drew up into itself
like an accordian, and he tried his best to hide by pivoting
one leg and standing sideways. Down the hall, as he stood
naked, he spotted a janitor pulling a squeaky bucket-on-
wheels behind him, never looking up while he mopped a
roped-off section of the corridor. On the rope hung a sign:
DANGER WET FLOOR. The man snapped a string from around
a fresh stack of towels with one quick jerk.

"Turn around, bend over, and spread your cheeks."

The concrete floor was cold. His feet, moist, stuck to the
painted red line when he shifted.

A bolt clinked into place behind him. There was a cot on
one side of the room and a small toilet in the corner. The
window opposite the door was covered with a heavy wire-
mesh screen. Resting his elbows on the ledge, he looked out
over the fences below. On the road outside a pair of headlights glared and then dimmed as the car passed the center.
Far in the distance, street lamps glowed. It was late. The
sun would be up soon. Most people were asleep. He imagined the neighborhood. Tracts. All the same except for the
trim or the design on the garage door. Nothing was worse
than an old tract. The only nice ones were owned by old
people who had the time to keep up the yard. Rose bushes
bloomed outside the front window. Beds of gladiolas and
violets mixed with other flowers Lonnie didn't know the
names of. Birds of Paradise came up to the white picket
fence and everything was perfect and calm as if waiting for
something. Lonnie remembered walking by these houses
and wanting to lie in the flower beds because they looked
so damp and dark. Soft. It was like ocean water. Sometimes
he wanted to swallow it in big gulps, but he knew it tasted

terrible, or to immerse himself in the gentle roll of the waves, but knew he'd freeze if he tried. These beds were the same. Then there were days when he walked past the beds and wanted to jump the picket fence and rip the flowers and rose bushes up by their roots and scatter them across the lawn. Something inside of him would have been released. Satisfied. But he knew he would never do it. For the first time since his arrest, since he was questioned, booked, photographed and brought here, he wanted to let his body go limp, his face relax and cry. He thought of Mom, he thought of Alex. He thought of Sonny and he wondered how long he had waited for him outside the El Taco.

Lying on the cot, he stared at a drawing scratched into the wall of a cartoon woman with huge breasts. It had to be recent. The other graffiti was painted over.

Two days later.
"The sign says no smoking."
"So what?"
Alex lit up.
"They been in there more'n an hour."
Sonny strolled over to the door. He wore a white shirt and gray slacks, and his hair was neatly combed. From inside the office he heard the probation officer asking Mom if she'd go to joint counseling with Lonnie. They had psychiatrists and counselors working for the city just for this reason. It wouldn't cost her a thing. Suddenly the door burst open and Sonny jumped back, startled. Tania barged out, clutching her purse in both hands, flying into one of her tirades.

"You know what he said?" She took a few steps and stopped, took a few steps and stopped. "Huh? You know what he said?" She blinked and looked at Sonny, then Alex. "He said Lonnie was nuts. *Nuts.* He said *I* was nuts." Spinning around, she hollered in the direction of the office. *"You're nuts, mister."*

"Shh."

She stared at Sonny.

"He'll hear you."

"He better."

"The sonofabitch," Alex said.

"The sonofabitch is right," Mom said.

"He didn't say you were nuts," Sonny said.

"The hell he didn't."

"The sonofabitch," Alex said again, pounding a fist into his palm.

"You're blowing it for Lonnie," Sonny said.

Mom pointed a finger at herself in amazement. He reached for her but she moved away.

"Watch it," Alex said.

"Shuddup, you jerk."

"Don't call me no jerk, asshole."

Sonny ignored him. "Are they going to let him go or what?"

"I don't know," Mom said. "I don't know, I don't know, I don't know."

"Let her alone," Alex said.

She plopped into a chair. Alex knelt in front of her and held her hands steady so she could light a cigarette. "I can raise Lonnie," she muttered, as if to herself. "I don't need a brain surgeon to tell me. You'd think my baby *murdered* somebody. *Hear that, mister? He ain't no murderer.*"

"Goddamn right." Alex nodded. "This family don't take shit from nobody. I mean *no* body."

"They can't steal my baby."

He patted her on the back. "Jus' let 'em try, Mom. Jus' let 'em try and see what goddamn happens."

Sonny clenched his teeth. His nostrils flared. "*What in the fuck is going on?*" Threw up his hands. "*Are you guys out of your minds?*"

They glared at him like they wanted to kill. Just then the door opened and Sonny and Alex and Tania all straightened up. The probation officer walked out with Lonnie, a hand on his shoulder, Lonnie smiling weakly, bowing his head. He spoke calmly. Lonnie could go home now. Of course there wouldn't be a trial, but a hearing. It would be held within thirty calendar days, they would be notified of the exact date, and at that time the judge would make the final decision as to whether Lonnie was granted probation or sent to a boys' ranch. If he kept out of trouble the judge might go easy on him. It depended. He would be lucky, though. This wasn't a first offense.

"Let's go."

"Wait a second," Sonny said.

"C'mere, Lonnie." She grabbed his arm and pulled him away from the PO. "C'mon Alex . . . Sonny."

Sonny took her wrist in his hand.

"Get your stinkin' claws offa her," Alex said, bracing himself.

"I ain't stayin' here anymore." She jerked free of Sonny and, dragging Lonnie down the hall, hollered behind her, "You'll be hearin' from our lawyer, *mister.*"

Alex gave the PO one last dirty look before he disappeared around the corner with Mom and Lonnie. Sonny started after them, then balked and spun around.

"Sorry about this," he said, shaking his head.

The PO shrugged like it was nothing.

"She isn't always like that."

"Don't worry about her. Watch out for your brother. If he screws up now, I tell you, the judge will come down hard." He smacked his lips. "Do what you can." Smiled. "All right?"

Sonny nodded and then hurried down the hall. It would be simpler if it were just he and Lonnie. Alone. So they could talk.

Alex had teased Lonnie into a smile by pretending they were all on a trip to Yosemite, reaching back and taking a few swings at him while he bounced around saying "How much *far*ther, how much *far*ther?" like Lonnie used to do when he was a kid. But his smile dropped the second Sonny scooted into the backseat of the Toyota. "Shit," Alex mumbled. "Frankenstein returns."

They rode in silence for a while, aware of the quiet, aware Lonnie was with them again. It was hot, the car like a heater box from sitting in the morning sun. Sonny lit a cigarette. Alex unrolled the window. The breeze was hot, too. They were beginning to sweat.

"*Watch it,*" Tania screamed.

A Mack truck zipped by, a gush of wind swaying the little car.

"I saw him, I saw him."

"You're gonna kill us all."

"Keep your eyes on the road," Sonny said.

"You wanna drive?"

"No."

"Then shuddup," Alex said.

The family rode in silence for a while again, hot and cramped, uncomfortable. Lonnie stared out the window. Sonny did the same. Tania watched the speedometer and held her breath until Alex merged safely onto the freeway. They took the off-ramp near their apartment then stopped at McDonald's. While Alex was inside ordering, Tania turned around in her seat and put a hand on Lonnie's knee.

"It's good to have you home, baby."

He bowed his head.

"You don't need no goddamn psychiatrist."

He shook his head.

"We don't got those kinda problems."

"No," he mumbled.

"We work out our own problems, huh?"

"Uh huh."

"That bastard back there don't know what he's talking about." She squeezed his knee. "They mess you up, honey. Psychiatrists. They study that stuff 'cause they're messed up. I know a little bit about it myself, you know. Your momma's not so stupid."

He glanced at her hand on his knee. The skin was wrinkled, leathery, and she had taken off her wedding ring since the last time he noticed it.

"So we fight a little like everybody else." She shrugged. "Big deal. That doesn't mean anything."

At that she squeezed his knee a couple of more times and turned away. A minute later Lonnie looked up from the floorboard. Sonny pursed his lips and shook his head no, meaning not to listen to her.

The car filled with the smell of hamburgers and fries. "Ya shoulda seen the honeys in there, Lonnie," Alex said, whistling, raising his eyebrows. "'Bout your age, too. Ya oughta get a job here. Be a manager or something. The babes'll rip your clothes off." He grabbed a handful of fries, threw the bags of hamburgers on Sonny's lap, and started the car.

When they got home Lonnie wanted to walk to the door with Sonny but he lagged behind and waited for Tania. As they climbed the stairs she put an arm around him and smiled and shook him a little.

Soon everyone was full on Big Macs and cheeseburgers, fries and milkshakes. Sonny cleared the table. Mom brought out four clean ashtrays. They smoked, watching TV in the living room while they sat in the kitchen. The picture was out of focus but no one bothered to fix it. Occasionally Alex wandered to the bathroom and came back sniffling like he had a cold, only he was smiling.

It was the third week of the month and, without Mom having to remind them, Sonny and Alex reached for their wallets. Once a month they pitched in for rent, food, the other bills. Though Sonny was the oldest, Alex had been paying his share for just as long. Mom had told him that if he dropped out of high school, he had to work. And if he worked and lived here, he paid his way. No freeloading. That's the way she was raised and that's how she would raise them. Alex didn't mind, though. Home was still the cheapest place around.

What she didn't know was that he had quit his job months ago.

He always paid on time.

Standing, sighing like that-time-of-month-already? he slapped two crisp one-hundred-dollar bills on the table and announced he had sold his car. It was more than his usual contribution. Tania looked surprised and started to protest until he raised a hand for silence. No applause. He said he hadn't sold it completely out of the goodness of his heart; he was getting a good deal on another better car and just happened to have the spare cash this time around. Don't complain. Take advantage.

"That why all the people are calling?" Sonny said, grinning, tilting back in his chair.

"Huh?"

"You put an ad in the paper?"

"Right." Alex squinted his eyes at him like wait-till-later-asshole.

Mom swept some crumbs off the table and placed her elbows on the clean spot, beaming with pride. "Well? Should I tell him?"

"Go ahead."

"What?" Lonnie glanced from face to face. Nervous.

"You're gonna get smart like Sonny," Alex said.

On Monday morning Lonnie started school at Western Academy. Tania woke Sonny before she left for work, and Sonny, after setting the table, waited until a quarter to seven before rousing his brother.

"Have something to eat."

Lonnie drew a hand across his sleepy face. "I ain't hungry."

"You have to give your brain energy. If you don't, you'll be thinking about your stomach, not your work. That was Alex's problem."

"I don't care."

"You better start."

He held back a grimace. Lonnie was getting skinnier every day and it worried Sonny.

"Eat, eat."

"Lay off already."

While he choked down a few mouthfuls of dry Cheerios, Sonny lit another cigarette and finished his coffee. "Wash your face and let's go. Hey . . . and I don't mean to criticize you, but put on some decent clothes for a change. This isn't Belmont anymore."

Lonnie strolled to the bathroom and brushed his teeth

and washed his face. There weren't any towels so he dried himself on a pair of Mom's pantyhose hanging on the shower bar. Then he slipped into a clean T-shirt, slicked his hair back, and walked to the garage where Sonny was warming up the 'Vette. They drove. Lonnie felt sick inside.

"Sonny . . ."

"Yeah?"

"Can I tell you something?"

"Of course. You don't have to ask."

He started to speak but instead he looked out on the traffic and the streets and the people, listening to the swoosh of oncoming cars.

"We're brothers, remember? We talk."

Lonnie rubbed the side of his face hard. He had lots of thoughts, all kinds of different thoughts, though he couldn't seem to put any of them into words. Everything was tangled.

"C'mon, man. Open up."

He picked a loose piece of vinyl off the armrest and rolled it under his fingernail. He threw it down, picked at another piece, put it in his mouth and chewed.

"Be that way then."

"I ain't being no way. I'm jus' scared. Fuckin' scared."

Sonny pulled over to the curb, shut off the motor, and swiveled around in his seat so he was facing his brother.

"Is it school?"

"Not really."

Sonny sighed. "I told you they aren't going to do anything."

"How do ya know?"

"I know."

"I heard all kinds of shit about the ranch."

"What do you expect? Lemme tell you something, though. I talked to that guy after you and Mom left and he says if you stay out of trouble they aren't going to send you there. But you can't run off anymore."

"Goddamn it, Sonny," he whined. "You know I ain't."

"Lemme put it this way. You can't mess around even. They'll fuck you over if they can but I'm not going to let them. You have to back me, though, man." He touched Lonnie on the shoulder to get him to look up. "We're like this, huh?" Sonny crossed two fingers. "Trust me." He leaned over to see if his brother was about to cry. "Okay?" Lonnie nodded. "We'll both take off if it comes down to that."

"You mean it?"

"Hey, would I lie to you?"

Soon they arrived at the white gates of Western Academy, glass packs rumbling and tape deck blaring. Sonny opened his wallet, looked through it for a second, then pulled out a five.

"What for?"

"Lunch. Bus fare. Whatever."

"I got money," he lied.

"It's free, isn't it?"

Lonnie stuffed the five in his pocket and then sat still again. He hated school and had enough cuts and tardies at Belmont to put him in the *Guinness Book of World Records.* Now, with a new school, he had to start all over—feeling his way around, finding out who to avoid and watch out for, sizing everybody up.

"Where's your notebook?"

"You kiddin'?"

"First fuckin' day and you're going to walk in there looking like you forgot your ass back home. Where the fuck's your brains?" Sonny gritted his teeth, trying to look angry. "Here," he said, handing him a pocket book from his English lit class at LACC. "Look intelligent." Lonnie still hadn't budged. "What are you waiting for?"

A private school! What kind of bullshit was this? He looked at Sonny suspiciously.

"You're starting all over. Clean slate and everything." He popped Lonnie in the arm. "You should be happy. This is a *private* school."

"How come they lettin' me in then?"

Sonny laughed. "Whatta ingrate! Loosen up, huh? Mom's taken care of that already. Hey"—he tapped Lonnie's arm—"remember what I told you about my first week at Belmont and all those bastards got me in a circle during P.E.? My nose was bleeding all over and I couldn't see and they kept pounding and pounding on me with those fucking basketballs? The chickenshit coach just stood there watching. Like boys-will-be-boys shit, you know? Every time I tried to get out some fucker kicked me back in. I finally just went completely beserk and ran right at the biggest sonofabitch there, I mean the biggest, I mean this fucker was *huge.* He must of weighed three hundred pounds." Lonnie snickered.

"Hey, don't laugh. Well, two-fifty anyway. No bullshit. And he was about six-six, too, I mean this guy had a beard. He was shaving in elementary school. And here I am about your size but I'm *crazy* and I run screaming, *I'm gonna killl yooouuu.* I'm going straight for his eyes and he knows I'm going to rip 'em right out of his ugly face. That bastard took off and then the rest of his asshole buddies"—he raised his voice as if he remembered their faces like yesterday— "when they saw their leader was a candy-ass deep down, they ran like the bunch of chickenshits they really were. After that they knew not to fuck with me. I'll tell you something else, too. Those assholes went and dropped out or got married, I don't know, but they're nothing now. They never were nothing. They'll never be nothing.

"I come home all messed up that day, split lip, the works, and you know what Mom said? She told me I had to learn how to avoid trouble. I had to learn how to handle myself. Like it was my fault. Piss on her. When it's ten against one you're in deep shit and you better run your ass off. Those fuckers didn't want to go to school, they didn't want to learn, they didn't belong, they were wasting my time because I was *trying.* You know me. Straight A's. Shit, I tell you some bitch tore up my paper once for putting my name

on the wrong side? That's no way to teach. I had to hang
out in the library at lunch because you couldn't even walk
the halls without getting hassled by some assholes or some
Gestapo P.E. coach. You're lucky, goddamn lucky you
don't have to go to that pit anymore. This is your break. A
big load's off your chest. Now *get* already."

"I don't wanna."

"After all that? I don't understand you sometimes,"
Sonny said. "You're going. It's all set and you're not backing down."

The lecture didn't impress him. Maybe Sonny had had
a hard time at Belmont but Lonnie, as far as the students
were concerned, knew how to get along. He learned the
Golden Rule years ago: Eat no shit. He knew not to pick
fights and he knew not to back down. Although he was
small, he had worked his way up the ranks at school into
a position where he didn't have to fight much anymore. He
had already fought most of the hoods with reputations as
good fighters and had held his own. The worst was over.
Lonnie had earned a piece of respect and worked to keep
it. When he walked down the halls he carried it in his eyes,
in the swing of his arms, like a medal pinned to his chest
that said: DON'T FUCK WITH ME / I DON'T FUCK WITH YOU. It
wasn't by choice, though. Lonnie was no punk.

"Got a smoke?"

"You shouldn't smoke in the morning."

"Look who's talkin'?"

Sonny gave him the pack and told him to keep it. "Just
don't get caught smoking your first day." Then he messed
up his brother's hair and Lonnie moaned and hesitated and
finally climbed out of the car. "I'm watching," Sonny said.
"I'm staying right here till you're in there."

"See ya tonight."

"Loosen up. I have to put in my hours today, too, you
know."

Taking a deep breath Lonnie waited until a group of
students passed him and funneled through the white gates

before he made his move. It was a small school, only two classrooms, an auditorium with a small stage, two teachers, a principal, and one secretary. From outside it looked like an ordinary flat-roofed house except for the large school-type windows. But inside it was like the others: rows of desks, shelves of books, chalkboards. Western Academy went from grades one to twelve; one to six in one room, seven to twelve in the other. Enrollment, thirty-seven.

His family wouldn't tell him how much it cost, but he was sure, by the way the students dressed, that tuition was high. It was money his family didn't have. And they were doing it for him, he thought, because he was a fuck-up. That's why. That's what you are. A fuck-up. Lonnie shook his head. All this money for something that probably wasn't worth it. A school was a school. What's the difference? But maybe a private school would look good on his record, might help sway the judge a little. If that was true, okay. He'd go.

He heard Sonny gun the 'Vette and take off.

Trapped. Lonnie imagined the great white gates swinging shut and locking with the sound of a vault.

The bell rang.

Groups of students in the courtyard broke into twos and threes and walked toward the building, carrying on their conversations. Not knowing what to do, where to go, he followed them through a hallway. A secretary behind a desk asked him to wait a moment. She glanced at an opened ledger, her finger guiding her eyes down a list of names.

"Mr. Baer?"

It took a second to click. "Yeah?"

"Take the first door to your left," she said, pointing down the hall. "Class begins in a few minutes."

"Thanks."

"We're glad to have you."

Sure, he thought. Glad to have my money, you mean.

He made his entrance as planned. Quiet. Only a young girl with long black hair glanced up at him. He sat down in a chair in the back of the room and slouched. Rested one foot on the bookrack beneath the chair in front of him. Played with the cover of Sonny's novel to keep his hands busy. Now and then he lifted his head and quickly scanned the room, sizing everyone up. If it ever came down to it he knew he could take any of them, even the older guys.

At eight-oh-five A.M. a little woman walked to the head of the class and shuffled through a pile of purple ditto sheets on her desk. She wore a full-length fur coat, even if it was ninety out, and she kept a portable electric heater beside her desk at all times. Miss Rose was her name and no one knew her exact age. She had been with the school when it opened some twenty years ago and had used the same twenty-year-old picture in every yearbook since the first.

Lonnie looked down and covered his forehead with a hand, hoping she wouldn't notice him, praying she'd sit and not call him up to the front and make him do the introduction routine. His voice would crack in midsentence and he'd make a total ass of himself. The thought of it happening made his ears burn and his face change from its usual pink to bright red. But after roll call she simply handed him a battery of competency tests and ambled back to her desk. A few minutes later a chubby kid reeking of dope slipped in late and sat next to Lonnie.

"She gave me that bullshit test, too. You don't have to do it if you don't want. She doesn't read them, you know."

"I'm gonna anyway."

"Name's Eugene." He held out his hand.

"Lonnie."

"What are you doing here?"

He didn't understand.

"I mean *why* are you here? Everyone in this place has a reason."

"What's it to you?"

"Don't be belligerent, my friend," Eugene said. "You may need me." He smiled. "See that lanky young man in

the front row? The one with the unruly hair? His name is
Roy. His father is a big shit at Warner Brothers. Last week
he drank a bottle of Drano during lunch. Paramedics
pumped his stomach here in the lavatory and whisked him
off to the hospital." He shook his head sadly. "Terrible,
terrible, but he was back the next day. And that girl over
there?" He nodded at her. "The nice-looking one? Long
dress, well-bred stuff? Shy? Every school has its whore and
she is ours."

All of a sudden the students looked strange to Lonnie,
scary even. He scooted away from Eugene, wishing he
could get on with his test and get it over with. No luck.
Eugene talked nonstop.

"It's my business, well, actually, I make it my business
to know my surroundings intimately. It's the business of
being aware. For instance, in another hour or so Miss Rose
will turn on that silly heater of hers and fall asleep. At ten,
when she raises her hand to her mouth and coughs, you'll
know it's only another twenty minutes before you can do
most anything you damn well please. I've checked up on
her, and from what I gathered no one except Dr. Hotchkin,
our principal, would hire her. She has a bad heart. It's clear
she uses nitroglycerine but that isn't what puts her out. She
takes a tranquilizer, too, an extremely potent one. Demerol,
Seconal, I'm not exactly sure." He snapped his fingers.
"She goes out like that. This also has to be the most lax
school I've ever attended. And believe me, I've been to
quite a few. Quite a few. It's unlikely that you'll learn much
here, but as far as I'm concerned, and as far as you're
probably concerned, it's just one less problem to deal with.
I'm tired of pressures myself." He tapped Lonnie on the
shoulder and whispered. "Think old Rose is having an
affair with Dr. Hotchkin?"

"I don't give a shit."

"Imagine it, though, two wrinkled bitties clawing at one
another."

"Would ya shuddup?"

Lonnie bowed his head and again tried to concentrate on the test:

> If Johnny had 5 baskets of apples and each contained 24 apples, and Johnny sold 2 baskets for $5 each, how much would each apple cost had Johnny sold them individually? How rich would Johnny be if he sold all 5 baskets?

His mind suddenly went blank. Shit. Slapping his pen down he went on to the next set of problems:

$$4x \text{ equals } 16, x \text{ equals } ?$$
$$6x \text{ equals } 36, x \text{ equals } ?$$

Lonnie rubbed his forehead as he gnawed the tip of his pen. His teachers at Belmont had mostly been P.E. majors with minors in the subjects they taught. The body of the faculty had to be male, big, and in good condition to keep any semblance of order in the classroom.

"Don't frustrate yourself," Eugene said. "It isn't worth it." He took the paper and quickly filled in most of the answers, leaving a few problems blank so the results would seem believable. Then at ten-thirty Miss Rose nodded off, Lonnie slipped the test on her desk, and Eugene motioned him out the door. They went behind the stage in the school auditorium and hid in a small windowless room with a long black panel full of levers. Locking the door from inside, Eugene turned on the overhead fan and produced a joint. They smoked pow-wow style, sitting on the floor, legs crossed, blowing the smoke up toward the fan.

"Only a select few know about this room. I don't let just anyone in on it, you know. Feel privileged." He winked at Lonnie. "Now when you want to get high you have somewhere to go. But don't tell a soul or else, before you know it, half the school will find out and Dr. Hotchkin will have the lock changed. He did it on the custodian's room, my old sanctuary. This place is much nicer, though. I call it my smoking den." Eugene pushed up the sleeves of his V-neck sweater; the cuffs of his white shirt dangled loosely at his elbows. His eyes were red and glossy. "You know how the great railroad entrepreneurs like Rockefeller built the railroads? It isn't in our history texts."

"What's *entrepreneurs* mean?"

"In this case, confidence men."

"Go on," Lonnie said, though he wasn't interested. A tiny spider was climbing up the wall and he watched it, amused.

"*Opium,* Leonard, *opium.* Thousands and thousands of Chinese were imported and kept well supplied with opium. They could work long hours on a minimum of food. *And* how do you think the Egyptians managed their slaves to build those incredible pyramids? *And* just what do you think we're smoking this very second?" Eugene took a long hit, passed the joint, and smiled a stoned smile.

"Grass," Lonnie said casually. He knew opium was black and gooey and usually smoked in a pipe. "Jus' good grass."

Astounded. Red eyes wide. "You don't believe me?"

"Nope."

"Go ahead, doubt the man who befriends you."

They laughed.

The rest of the day was uneventful. After lunch they exchanged phone numbers and returned to class. Time passed slowly, almost painfully. Lonnie was still stoned and thought everyone was staring at him. He wanted out. Some fresh air. Miss Rose came and sat next to him. She smelled musty and old like stale peppermint sticks. Her words were muffled echoes, reverberating over and over in his head, but never making sense. She said something about being impressed with the results of his test and she was going to give him a challenge. He tried to shield his eyes so she couldn't see how red they were, but now and then she raised her voice and he felt he at least had to look up. He wished he hadn't smoked the grass. It made him paranoid, tense, even a little guilty for getting high during the day when there was so much left to do. Miss Rose gave him a geometry text and a history book thick as a dictionary and then slowly, being careful not to lose her balance, rose from the chair beside him and hobbled away. Her odor lingered behind for a moment as Lonnie stared at the books. Thousands and thousands of words and equations meant hours of dull labor. Opening the history book he read the first line of Chapter 3: "The American Civil War was a turning point in our nation's history." He closed his eyes, opened them, and focused on the words again: "The American Civil War was a turning point in our nation's history." What did it say? He lost it again. He was too stoned. Lonnie pushed the book away. It was useless to try to read now. When the final bell rang he was depressed as hell.

Miss Rose dismissed them in alphabetical order. As Lonnie strutted across the courtyard, the thick books under his arm, he noticed a shiny new Mercedes parked at the curb out in front of the school. One door was open and there was a girl in the backseat. Her hair was collar-length and she wore Catholic school clothes—a plaid skirt, kneesocks, saddle shoes, a white shirt. The uniform was designed to make a girl look younger and less attractive, but Lonnie thought it added a certain quality to this one. It couldn't hide her figure, and he liked the way the socks gripped her calves, woman's calves in a little girl's socks. She looked seductive but innocent. Tan and blond like one of those girls he'd seen whizzing down Ventura Highway in a BMW. He forced himself not to stare. She was probably used to it and he didn't want to feed her ego. But it was too late. She noticed and smiled, and Lonnie looked away fast and hurried on.

A minute later Eugene scooted into the backseat of the Mercedes.

"Who's that up the street?"

"Hmm?"

"That boy in the T-shirt."

"His name is Lonnie."

"I haven't seen him before."

"He's new."

"He's cute," she said.

He walked to MacArthur Park and hung around for a while, hoping some buddies from Belmont or the Boys' Club would show up. But nothing was going on. The place was dead. In the bushes, near the lake, he found a punctured basketball and tossed it around for a few minutes. It was no fun, though. The damn thing wouldn't bounce and his legs didn't have any spring today. Drop-kicking the deflated ball, he watched it sail across the park, then down into the bushes almost where he'd found it. He thought of getting Sonny and maybe going out and doing something, anything, but Sonny was probably at rehearsals by now. He thought of heading up to Hollywood Boulevard to watch the strange, made-up people for a while. That was always good for an hour or so. Instead he saved the money Sonny had given him and wandered home.

On the way to the bathroom he passed Mom's room. She sat at her dresser in a black slip, carefully penciling an eyebrow darker.

"How did it go?"

"Okay, I guess."

The smell of heavy perfumes and colognes filled the air, her drawers where she kept her different colored lingerie, even her closet. Lonnie knew she had just finished showering and that the bathroom floor would be soaked, the towels damp, the mirror fogged.

"Think you're gonna like it there?"

"It's okay."

"Just okay?"

"I guess."

"You liked it, though?"

"It was okay."

Leaning closer to the mirror, arching her back, she lightly swept her eyelashes with a thin mascara brush. "You'll get used to it," she said absently. With an old toothbrush she again swept her eyelashes to separate them and keep the mascara from clotting. "It was only the first day."

"Yeah."

He stood in the doorway staring at her burning cigarette in the ashtray on the dresser, the little bottles of cologne and perfume, the unmade bed, an open sewing box with tangled threads hanging over the sides. For a while, as Tania leaned forward and backward, peering at herself in the mirror, they said nothing. She dotted her cheeks with rouge and skillfully but hurriedly ran red lipstick over her small, taut lips. Then she reached into the dresser drawer and pulled out a plastic egg containing pantyhose. Rolling the nylon into a small ball, she slipped it over her stiffened leg, first one then the other. They bound her crotch and she swiveled her hips around a few times as she tugged at the waistband until they fit more comfortably. Her squat white legs appeared dark and smooth now. Lonnie thought she looked strange. The rest of her was pale, especially her arms.

"Is your teacher nice?"

"Yeah."

As she brushed past him on her way to the closet he heard the scratch of her nylons rubbing against the insides of her thighs and the soft rustling sound of her slip. "Hungry?" She pulled a red, low-cut dress over her head and smoothed it down with her palms and then faced the mirror again and adjusted the neckline.

"No."

"Zip me up, honey, will you?"

Mom turned around and lifted her hair off the back of her neck.

He zipped the dress up.

"Thanks, honey."

"Sure."

Before she could face forward, he had disappeared down the hall to his room. There he turned on the radio, lit a smoke, and lay across his bed. He opened the history book to chapter one and began reading, determined not to fall behind right from the start. Miss Rose had only assigned the first chapter, but he read past it and was into the second chapter when he glanced up and saw Mom standing in the doorway.

"You feeling okay?" she said.

"Fine."

"I left a couple bucks on the frig. Get yourself a hamburger or something, huh? I didn't have time to do the shoppin' today."

"Sure."

"Studying?"

"Uh huh."

"That's the way," she said, smiling. "You sure everything's okay?"

"Yeah." He pretended to read.

"Well . . . I'll see you."

"See you."

"Don't wait up for me."

"Okay."

She paused in the doorway for a full minute. He knew she was staring at him but he didn't raise his head this time until he heard the front door close.

7

Alex dreamed he walked down Hollywood Boulevard and spotted Pete in the Riviera. It was Saturday night. Traffic was thick with cruisers and tourists. Pete was with two girls, their hair windblown and their faces sunburned as if they'd spent the day at the beach. Alex broke into a run when they stopped for a red light. He planned to sneak up to the driver's side, reach through the open window, and grab Pete by the neck. Slam his face against the dash. The girls would scream. But as he approached the Riviera, ducking so they couldn't see him, the light changed and they drove off. He jumped back to the sidewalk and followed his car up to the next light. There would be no words. He intended to split the sonofabitch's head open. But the light changed again just as he was within pouncing range. Pete glimpsed him in the rearview mirror this time and laughed. Then the girls turned around and laughed and made faces at him through the back window. Alex imagined slitting their throats one by one, saving Pete for last. Suddenly he was on a dark deserted street somewhere in Silverlake. The Riviera moved just fast enough to keep him at bay. He couldn't breathe and though he screamed no sounds came forth. It was like swimming upstream underwater, struggling against a strong current, falling farther and farther behind. Alex saw himself panting and running, his face twisted in anger, his muscles wound up and tight. He lunged. The Riviera rolled just out of reach. He lunged again. It rolled again. Then, as if he were seeing himself from a long distance, maybe from a rooftop, the car spewed exhaust in his face and left him standing in the middle of the deserted street like that night in San Diego.

He bolted upright in bed, gripping the pillow so tightly his knuckles were white. His breathing came fast and shallow. The sheets were contorted into small mountains about his legs. The last thing he saw was the Riviera barreling back up the street with Pete laughing maniacally as the headlights rushed blindly toward him.

The time had come. He'd played the fool long enough. His Riviera was probably sitting stripped under some freeway overpass by now but he didn't care. Pete was who he wanted, and when he found him, he'd make the bastard pay in blood. Nobody fucks with Alex. Not anymore. He threw his legs over the side of the bed and jumped up. Thin bars of sunlight shot through the venetian blinds and fell across his wide muscular back. Placing his palms together and pressing hard, his favorite muscles, the huge lumps on his shoulders, bulged forward.

Alex stood in the kitchen in his red jockey shorts, scratching his stomach.

"How come you're up so early?"

"Business. Lots of business to do."

"Keep your voice down."

"What for?"

"You'll wake Mom."

He made a face like oh-no! Didn't want her clamoring around, bitching. So early.

"Lonnie asleep?"

"I'm going to wake him soon."

"He like that school?"

"I don't know yet."

"Bet he's already got his eye on some nice bitch, eh?"

Sonny shrugged. He placed a cast-iron pan on the stove and turned on the fire. "Did Mom and Lonnie have a fight before he took off?"

"Yeah."

"Why didn't you tell me?"

"You were at work."

"You could've called."

Alex raised his voice. "How was I supposed to know what he was gonna do?"

"Keep it down."

"I can't read the fuckin' future."

Sonny laid strips of bacon into the hot pan. "They were fighting about . . ." he said, waiting for Alex to complete the sentence.

"The same old shit. Who knows?"

"You really are stupid, aren't you?"

"I'm stupid, huh?"

"That's right."

"If you're so fuckin' smart then, how come he didn't come crying' to you? I'll tell you why. He's sick of your preachin'." He threw a hand into the air. "You're always laying this almighty big brother shit on me and him all the fuckin' time like you think your shit don't stink. Well, it does. And I'm tired of it." It was quiet for a few, long seconds. The bacon popped and crackled. Then Alex sighed and said, "Hey, man, I'm sorry. I didn't mean it. Lonnie listens to you like you're a god or something." He started to put a hand on his brother's shoulder but changed his mind. "Can I borrow the 'Vette?"

"I have an interview today."

"I can see it now," he said, leaning back and drawing his hands through the air, framing it. "The Grauman marquee. Sonny Baer in lights. Can I have your autograph, please?"

"Lay off."

"Can I borrow the car?"

"Tomorrow."

"When you gonna give it up? You can't act."

"Fuck you."

Alex held out his hand and shook it impatiently. "C'mon, c'mon. Gimme the keys. I always go outta my way for you." Sonny jabbed the bacon with a fork, stepping back so the hot grease wouldn't splatter him. "How come you only talk to me when you want something?" he said. Alex glared at him. He dumped the drippings into a coffee can on top of the stove and pushed past his brother to the refrigerator.

"Hey."

"Shh. How many times I gotta tell you?"

"Don't walk away when I'm talkin'." Alex stabbed the air with his finger. "Yes or no?"

"Sorry."

"Damn it, man. I'm askin' and I'm askin' politely."

Sonny was most dangerous when he was silent and that's the way he was now. Alex stood close to him, too close. He smelled the fragrance of his brother's clean hair, felt Sonny's heat against his arm and bare stomach, felt his hot breath. He imagined grabbing him around the waist and binding his arms so he couldn't lash out. Control him, fight or no fight. Ram Sonny up against the refrigerator. Why worry? He was bigger; almost a head taller, stronger too. He could take him by the neck, between forearm and bicep, and crush the air from his lungs. But when his brother turned to reach for a pot holder, Alex only flinched and stepped out of his way. Stepped quicker than he meant to. It looked bad. Never act scared. Never. He glanced around the kitchen for something to grab in case Sonny whirled around suddenly and flung the hot pan in his face. You couldn't trust him, he thought. Like once when they were kids he wrapped the telephone cord around Alex's neck and didn't let loose until he was blue in the face. The fucker was crazy.

Sonny slid the bacon from a paper towel onto his plate

and walked past him as if he wasn't there, calm, humming a tune from *Midnight Cowboy*. Alex, stunned, stood motionless while his brother sat himself down at the kitchen table and began to eat.

He took the phone book from the top of the refrigerator and stomped off to his room, brushing close to Sonny, tempted to slap him in the back of the head as he passed. He pushed the clothes in his closet to one side and knelt and removed a section of baseboard covering a small hole in the wall where he stashed his cocaine and paraphernalia.

His hands shook as he poured coke from a brown vial onto a mirror, quickly crushing the granules with a rusty razor blade until it was all a fine powder. He stretched the pile into two big lines and snorted through a plastic straw. Winced. Wiped water from his eyes. The stuff burned like a sonofabitch. It was probably cut with methamphetamine, he thought, or else the wash was bad. But it was still clean enough to cut again if he ended up using more than his profit margin allowed. He'd already broken the half-ounce with mannite. Weighed it into grams. Half-grams. Quarter-grams. Dimes. By the time his product made its way up customers' noses he knew it couldn't have been better than twenty percent pure. But nobody was complaining. The phone had been ringing off the hook since he returned from San Diego. It was as good, or bad, as most of the stuff being sold around town lately.

In a few seconds his head tingled, his heart beat faster, his palms began to sweat. He felt alive again. Opening the telephone book, turning to *M*, he scanned the long list of McCarthy's. All he had was Pete's number. He'd never been over to his place. But he matched the number with the name and came up with 1436 Geyser. It wasn't far from Silverlake Lanes. Alex smiled to himself. This was it. The sonofabitch was going to pay.

At the bus stop he threw one hip out and stood poised beside the bench. On display. He wore an imitation satin shirt that made satin look dull, and black slacks with per-

fectly ironed creases. A pretty girl drove by and he cocked
his head back and grinned. He had another snort. Soon the
84 bus pulled to the curb and he dropped his money into
the glass box and squeezed by an old woman searching for
her senior citizen's card. Inside it was crowded with
women in white smocks, and men in chambray shirts and
khaki pants or jeans. There were kids too, on their way to
school maybe, and old people who didn't look dressed for
work. They were probably getting an early start on the
day's shopping. Glancing down the long aisle, seeing no
empty seats, Alex reached for the handrail overhead. For a
while, to keep from meeting anyone's eyes, he read the
advertisements on the bus walls. Marlboro Man, Ellen
Feather's Self-Improvement Seminar, Computer Program-
ming Training, and a picture of a fat, poorly rolled joint
beside some reds and whites and a hypodermic needle with
the caption "Dope is for Dopes." He'd seen it so many
times before it didn't even amuse or offend him anymore.

Whenever the bus stopped to pick up or let off riders,
whenever it pulled away from the curb, Alex swayed with
the others. In the seat beside him was a bald-headed man
with a lunchbox, staring out the window at the passing
buildings or cars, or maybe at his own reflection. Alex had
seen him before. He worked somewhere near Silverlake
Lanes. Pitiful bastard, he thought. Nothing in him anymore. Just sits there, hands folded. The guy probably
worked his whole life for what? Two weeks off a year? Paid
vacation? A fucking gold watch or something? By the time
the old man retired and could take a couple of trips he's
been dreaming about for twenty, thirty years, what's left
of him? Nothing. The old man goes and buys one of those
nice new trucks. Cab-over camper, four-wheel drive, snow
tires. Nice machine. He's been eyeing it for how long? But
now that he's got it he's too worn out to drive it much
farther than the goddamn grocery store. He's all crippled
up. What can he do? Sit around until he dies, that's what.
Fuck that shit. Alex wished he'd quit his job sooner, wondered why he even took one in the first place. Extra cash?

That was a lie. For all the long hours he put in he never made enough to call what he brought home *money.* Pocket change, maybe. At minimum wage, after deductions, he figured he would've been better off panhandling the tourists. There were better, easier ways to get along without busting his ass from eight to five, five days a week, in some ugly bowling alley. In one night of dealing he could take home more than that old man netted in a month. And he didn't have to pay income tax or state tax or social security or state disability. What he made was his—like it should be, damn it. Hustling for yourself was the only way to get ahead in this fucked-up world.

Alex looked out the window when the bus stopped in front of Silverlake Lanes to let the old man off. The sight of it made his legs weak. He could almost hear the balls smashing pins, drilling his ears to deafness. He remembered how the time clock sounded when it stamped his card and how, after he put the card back in its rack with the others, there always seemed to be something false and unfair about it all. At the end of the day he felt nothing but relief, a relief that soon turned into a gnawing emptiness, as if his freedom had been stolen and there was no way to regain it.

He sighed and sat down in the seat the old man had left. A train was crossing up ahead. Sometimes, alone on his shift, he'd sneak out to the parking lot and watch them pass and dream about someday hopping one to New Orleans for Mardi Gras. Once he counted a hundred and nine cars with two cabooses. Soon the train was thundering past the bus. There were two young hobos standing in the open doorway of an empty boxcar. Alex waved to them through the window. They waved back. He smiled, surprised they had noticed him. For a moment he wished he was with them, on that train, rolling, going.

The lobby smelled of piss and dirty diapers. Laughter from a TV game show flowed from behind a closed door. Alex rolled his shoulders, shook his arms loose, and clenched his fists a couple of times to make sure his knuckles closed flat and evenly. Scanning the mailboxs on the wall in the hallway, he found the name McCarthy. Apartment fourteen. He climbed the stairs, gripping the handrail tightly, imagining how he was going to kick the door open like in the movies. Like a cop. Throw Pete up against the wall.

At first he knocked lightly, waited a second, then put his ear to the door. Silence. He got down on his hands and knees and looked through the crack. All he could see was carpet. Standing up, brushing his pants off, he knocked again. No answer. He placed his hands on his hips, wondering if he should go outside and wait on the corner. That way he could follow him upstairs when he came home and catch him off guard. If Pete was there now he might ask who it was before opening the door. What could he say without his voice being recognized? He should have thought of that earlier. Alex started down the hall and then suddenly he spun around and ran back and pounded on the door with both fists. *"You dirty bastard."* He took a few steps back, bent at the knees, and was ready to hurtle himself against the door when a black woman from the next apartment stomped into the hallway in her bathrobe.

"You crazy?" she hollered. "I got a sick baby tryin' to sleep."

He stood up straight, blushing. A small whimper came from the woman's apartment, followed by another whimper, and finally a full-scale scream blasted through the hallway. Alex winced.

"Now see what ya gone and done?"

"Sorry."

"Sorry don't stop that child's bawlin'."

She turned to go inside.

"Hey, lady. Wait a second. You know when Pete McCarthy gets home?"

"He got long, ratty hair?" she said, putting her fingertips to her shoulders.

"Yeah."

Before slamming the door in his face, she said, "You wastin' your time, honey. That boy done move outta here a week ago."

Later that night Alex went to the Y and worked out. Battered the bag, pounded and kicked. His fists ached and he was nauseated with exhaustion. But when he wanted to quit he imagined Pete's face in front of him and let go with another flurry. Ducked and feinted. Shot one to the belly and followed up with a sweeping left that came high over his head and landed smack on Pete's chin. Swinging around, he connected with an elbow, a forearm, kneeing the bag hard into the bastard's crotch. When he'd finished Pete beyond recognition he threw off his gloves and lay down on the bench press. Two hundred and thirty pounds. Three sets of five repetitions. Warm up. He went for his maximum, three hundred fifteen, while another body-builder spotted him. The guy looked like a Sumo wrestler without the fat. An ex-Mr. Hollywood. Standing over him behind the bench press, his crotch inches from Alex's sweaty face, he shouted "No strain, no gain. You can do it, baby. Get angry. Pump it, pump it, pump it." He grunted and arched his back and pushed until his arms felt frozen. It was like trying to move a brick wall. The Sumo wrestler placed one hand under the bar, lifting just enough to keep him grunting and straining, grunting and straining. "Pump it, pump it." But it was hopeless. He heaved the weight back on the stand so it wouldn't crush Alex's chest. "You'll get her next time, baby. You'll get her." He had someone sit on his ass while he did donkey raises; on his legs while he did sit-ups. Then he worked his biceps—curls; lats—pull-ups; triceps—dips; shoulders and triceps—forward rows on the free bar; biceps—reverse curls. Finally he rubbed himself down and flexed as he admired the size and definition of his shiny muscles in the full-length mirrors surrounding the walls of the weight room.

Alex's arms were so pumped up by the time he left the Y that he could barely scratch the back of his neck. He did more coke and soon he was bouncing and strutting along the sidewalk like a rooster, head up, feeling powerful and cocky. When he got to Pearl's he ordered a beer and swaggered over to the jukebox. Get some music in the place. It was empty except for the cook and two men sitting at the counter. Bad way to run a business. Who's going to come here, he thought, when it's so goddamn quiet?

He deposited some coins, punched some buttons. Doing steps to the music, he headed back to where the pool tables and pinball machines stood, grabbed a stick from the rack, and rolled it across the table to see if it was straight. He chalked his hands and the cue, and played a few quick games, taking turns with himself as if he were two different people. It was Alex against the Fat Man for ten thousand dollars.

He ordered another beer. Another and another.

On an empty stomach, right after a workout, it hit him hard. And about every twenty minutes, when he felt the coke wearing off, he cut more lines on the glass face of a pinball machine and snorted them up through a rolled dollar bill. The cue felt like a toothpick in his hands, and if Pete happened to walk in that moment he thought he would've busted the stick across his face without a word. He called out a corner pocket to himself, forgot and aimed for a side pocket, and still missed by a long shot. Suddenly he felt dizzy. The cue ball looked fuzzy. Lining it up for a simple bank shot that would do the Fat Man in, he scratched and ripped the green felt.

One of the men at the counter chuckled. He wore a wide-brimmed plantation owner's hat pulled down low in the front. "I didn't see it," he said.

Alex grinned.

"Wanna beer?"

"You buyin'?" Alex said.

"Give the man a beer," the other man hollered to the cook.

"Coors." Alex hung the cue in the rack and sat on a stool beside them. The cook placed a beer and a glass on the counter and went back to the kitchen. Alex pushed the glass away and tilted the bottle to his lips.

A lady swished by outside. The man without the hat had a mangy goatee and he tugged on it, commenting—nice ass. Alex bought them a round. They bought him two more rounds. They talked a while, small talk to fill the silences. It was that frantic time of night—too early to go home but too late to move on to another bar. Finally one of the men turned to Alex and, tipping his hat, said point-blank, "Sharing your coke tonight?"

"Huh?"

"He knows what you mean."

"We look like narcs, A?"

"Another beer for a line," the man with the goatee said.

"We aren't narcs."

He shrugged like he didn't know what they were talking about. The cook came out and announced last call. "Thanks for the beers," Alex said, rising. His heart fluttered.

"Thanks for shit," the man in the hat said.

Alex pretended he hadn't heard that last remark as he strolled casually toward the door. When he turned the corner, away from the windows of Pearl's, when he knew they couldn't see him anymore, he walked a little faster. Occasionally he glanced over his shoulder. Once he swore he heard footsteps behind him and spun around. Nobody. He peered down the street, squinting until his eyes watered. His hands shook from the coke and his head swooned. Take deep breaths, he thought. Breathe the damn alcohol out. But it only made him dizzier. Sick. A patrol car cruised past him and he forgot about the men and concentrated on his steps, looking down, trying to walk straight but swaying. The sidewalk was sparkling black and each square was engraved with a gold-bordered pink star. Some had names in them like Greta Garbo or Bette Davis or Cecil B. De-Mille. Some were empty. Some cholo wrote Jose-con-Sandy in one star with a black felt pen. Alex remembered a game he used to play as a kid and laughed and avoided all the cracks, and when he came to a curb and stepped off he wasn't paying attention and his ankle twisted and he nearly fell. On the next block the sidewalk squares were just gray concrete and the game wasn't much fun. He gave it up and took a short cut through an empty parking lot.

There was the swish of shirts and footsteps, a slight breeze behind his ears. A sudden warmth enclosed him. In the next instant his arms were locked tight behind his back. Something ice cold was shoved under his throat. He caught only a glimpse of a face—shiny, skull-like under the shadows of the dull parking lot lamp. *Don't move or you're a dead motherfucker.* It was a whisper, hot and stale, reeking of beer. *Be cool, be cool.* He jerked as he felt hands pulling at his pockets, his pants leg rising, the cool air there on his skin. The face in front of him shoved the barrel up harder. His neck made an eerie cracking noise. *Blow your fucking head off?* He winced, tensing his bladder. The barrel was shoved still deeper into his neck and now he could hardly breathe. His ears rang. *Blow your fucking head off?* Alex listened to himself wheeze, no longer aware of the pain in his neck or the pounding of his heart. *Fucking hurry, A.* The man behind him struggled with his boot. Wrenching it off, he found the gram vial. *Look, A, he got no sock!* They laughed. He heard his boot hit the asphalt and knew it had been thrown. The barrel left his throat and then something hard, he didn't know what, probably the gun butt, landed on the side of his face and knocked him to the ground. A sharp kick in the ribs caused him to double up and moan.

Then they were running, their footsteps trailing off across the parking lot. Alex heard a roaring in his head and tried to stand but he was stunned and couldn't get his balance. He touched his mouth, and when he looked at his hand he saw blood, lots of blood, so much it startled him. A second later a lump the size and color of a Santa Rosa plum sprang from his cheek.

Stormin' Norman, a.k.a. the Mad Tattooist, was popping wheelies on his Enduro Stingray when Alex strolled into the alley behind the apartment. It was morning but the roaring in his head was still there.

"Hey, Norman. C'mere."

He shot by at a terrific speed. Cards in the spoke rims clattered loudly.

"C'mere, c'mere," Alex shouted. "I ain't gonna hurt ya."

Norman spun around, picked up speed, and skidded to a halt in front of him.

"What happen to your face?"

"I got hit."

"By a Mack truck." Norman giggled. "You look ugly."

"Thanks."

"Any time."

"You still got that gun?"

"What gun?" Norman said, looking puzzled.

"The gun you stole from Old Man Wheat's garage."

"I didn't steal nothin'."

"Don't bullshit me."

"I ain't. Honest."

He was poised to jump down on the pedal as if it were a motorcycle kick-start and zoom off.

"Take ten for it?"

"*Ten?*"

"Twenty?"

"Twenny! You're outta your fuckin' mind. It's worth a hunnerd."

"Watch your mouth or I'll tell your old man. Twenty-five or nothin'. Take it or leave it."

"I'll leave it."

"Okay, ya little prick. Forget it. You just lost twenty-five bucks."

At that he turned and began walking, confident Norman
would change his mind. Twenty-five bucks was big money
to a punk kid, even now, he thought. But it was soon obvious he wasn't going for it and Alex, infuriated, whirled
around and lunged for the bike. Norman fell off and tried
to scamper away like a little mouse. He grabbed his foot
and dragged him back screaming.

"Lemme go, ya asshole." Norman swung blindly.

Twisting his chocolate-stained T-shirt into a knot, he
lifted the kid off the ground and pinned him against the
stucco wall of the apartment house.

"*Daaaddd.*"

"Shuddup." Alex slapped him. "Jus' shut the fuck up."
He pulled back his fist, holding Norman up with one hand
now. "One . . . two . . . *three* . . ." Norman barred his face
with his arms.

"Okay, okay."

"Where is it?"

Between sniffles he said he had it buried in the empty lot
up the alley.

"Show me."

Alex let him down. His T-shirt was balled up around his
neck. Alex made him walk the bike as he led the way up the
alley and over a chain link fence.

Norman pointed to a big rock on the ground.

"Here?"

"Yeah."

"Start diggin'."

"Me?"

"Who the hell you think I'm talkin' to?"

He rolled the big rock aside and clawed at the dry ground
while Alex stood watch.

"Whatta ya want it for anyway?"

"Protection," Alex said. "Keep diggin'."

In a few minutes a bit of wood appeared at the bottom
of the hole. He pushed Norman away and reached down
and pulled up an old cigarbox covered with mildew. Open-

ing the box, he let it drop to the ground. In a paper bag was the gun, an old .38 snubnose, wrapped in several layers of plastic. It was dark blue and well oiled and looked in excellent condition. Alex stared at it for a long time. He liked the weight of it in his hand, hefty and solid. Steel. A real gun. No toy. He flicked the chamber. It spun easily. The barrel was short, compact. The grip felt just right. He slid the gun in his pants waist and jumped the fence, Norman scooting after him down the alley.

"Where's my twenny-five bucks?"

"Too late now."

"Gimme my money."

"You blew your chance."

Norman ran up and kicked him in the ass. He turned around, pulled out the gun, shut one eye, aimed.

"It loaded?"

"I don't know," he said, jumping backward. "But don't be messin' around like that. Ya ain't suppose to mess with guns."

"Right between the eyes."

He threw his hands up in front of his face. "*No.*"

Click.

Alex grinned. "You got lucky again," he said. The grin vanished. "Now get the fuck outta here before I beat your head in."

Geometry was a drag. Now and then he might glance at another student's paper, and if he saw he was falling behind, he felt pressured to hurry and catch up. If he was ahead he felt pressured to stay ahead. And if he was even with the next student he felt pressured to stay even. Soon his mind would freeze over and he couldn't concentrate. "The volume of a cone equals ⅓ times pi times r^2 times h." Solutions? Sometimes nothing made sense to him. But at home in his room he could think better and problems didn't seem as hopelessly complicated. He thought if he worked hard he might even catch up to where he was supposed to be, where most of the other students were now, by the end of the semester. That might mean something to the judge.

Lonnie sat up in bed. The pillowcase was stained a dark circle with pomade and hair oil where he laid his head. On the dresser was a trophy he won for shortstop when he played for the Police Athletic League one summer. It was dusty now and the bat the gold man held had been broken and lost a long time ago. Three walls of the room were surrounded by bookcases that Sonny had built out of old pallets and crates. They went clear to the ceiling, the shelves sagged in the middle. There were hardbacks from Twice Read, paperbacks, a set of *Britannica Great Thinkers* that Sonny was still making monthly payments on. There were all kinds of novels, nonfiction books on all kinds of subjects, plays, old books with ancient leather covers and brittle yellowed pages that gave off a strange musty odor when you opened them. Once Lonnie waved a hand around the room and asked his brother how many of them he had read. "About two-thirds," Sonny said, like it was no big deal. Lonnie wagged his head, amazed. He didn't see how anyone could read so much, so fast, and know as much as Sonny without acting or talking like some jerk who thought he was an intellectual. Not until he was thirteen, until Sonny gave him a copy of Nelson Algren's *The Neon Wilderness*, had he read a book cover to cover. Until the age of seven he could barely read or write. He saw letters upside down, or backward, he couldn't tell which. Every day after school Sonny sat him down in the kitchen in front of a small chalkboard propped on a chair and drilled him for two hours. Just trying to *see* often made Lonnie so frustrated he often ended the sessions on the verge of tears. But by the end of the school year he raised his English grade from D-minus to B-plus and passed to the second grade.

In the corner near the closet were two rusty cages that once held a hamster and a rat named Willard. They still stunk although they had been empty for over a year. Lonnie knew he should take them out to the garage. Another thing to do. How many times had Sonny asked him? So do it. He started to rise and then sat again on the edge of the bed, elbows on knees, fingers laced, his head bowed.

Sometimes he forgot about the hearing, and when he remembered it seemed like only a distant memory, like the hearing had come and gone and they'd done what they had to and now everything was okay. Those moments were brief, though. He knew it wasn't the truth. It was as if a grudge were being held against him with no way of appeas-

ing it. What could he do? Say he was sorry? Cry? He'd pay
for a new ignition lock on the Volkswagen. All he used was
gas in the Camaro, no damage.

Here he was, his days more or less back to normal, going
to school and living home, not doing anything wrong—all
for what? Why, if they were just going to put him in the
ranch? He could take off right now and they'd never catch
him. Last time he messed up. *If you didn't stop at that fuckin'
gas station . . .* He'd still be going. He could change his name
when he got to some city and get a job and take things from
there. Shit, he could do that easy. One kid in a big city!
Nobody would know the difference. Maybe come Christmas or Thanksgiving, when he was settled, he'd phone
Sonny and Alex. They could all get together. It would be
good. Of course they'd have to let Mom know he was okay
but she didn't have to know where he was. That was a small
problem, though. It could be worked out later. The point
was he'd have a good job, be making his own way, and
Sonny and Alex—even Mom—couldn't help being proud
of him. Fuck school. He'd be bringing in good money and
he and his brothers could be sitting around getting a little
drunk and talking at Lonnie's place. *Lonnie's place.*

But that was another dream, another goddamn dream. It
would be stupid to take off before he knew what the bastards planned to do with him.

The 'Vette was jacked up in the garage. Sonny, wearing
dirty frayed coveralls, worked beneath it. "Hand me that
wrench, would you?" Lonnie did and then squatted and
looked under the car. His brother strained his chin toward
his chest, the veins in his neck bulging. "You look depressed." He smiled at Lonnie. "Lonnie the old man. The
only guy I know fifteen going on forty-three."

"Whatta you doin'?"

"Trying to get the starter off."

"What's the matter?"

"The engine isn't turning over."

"Your points openin'?"

"Yep."

"Battery good?"

"Just bought a new one," Sonny said. "Hey, I called a wrecker to see if I could get that strip of chrome for the door and put it on while I was doing this today, and you know what he said when I told him what kind of car I had? The man asks if I have *gold* in my pockets. Can you believe that?" He chuckled. "It isn't cheap owning an old Corvette." Lonnie scooted under the car beside his brother. It was cramped and their sides touched. The motor was pleasantly warm and smelled of grease and gas and oil. "Push up on it a little. The bolt's binding."

Lonnie pushed and soon he felt the starter grow heavy in his hands. Sonny rested the wrench on his chest and together they shimmied the starter off. Then, with one quick turn of the shoulder, he rolled out from under the car.

"So what's bothering you?"

"Nothin'."

"C'mon, you can tell me."

"I ain't got nothin' to tell."

"Okay, be that way," Sonny said. Joking. "But if you have something on your mind you should talk about it. Don't let it build up inside."

Soon they had the rebuilt starter bolted in. Sonny hopped in the car and turned the key. The motor roared. They smiled at each other. Lonnie sat on the hood of the 'Vette, bumping his dangling feet together while his brother stripped out of his coveralls. "We ought to be mechanics," he said, pulling two warm beers from a paper sack, handing Lonnie one. "It's for damn sure I'd make more money than I would acting."

Lonnie jumped off the car. "That's a great idea, that's a fantastic idea." Popping open the beer, he took a big swallow. "We could goddamn do it, too."

Sonny smiled. "I've never seen a forty-three-year-old

midget so excited about anything in my life."

"It's a great idea."

"First you're dying of depression and now look"—he slapped his forehead—"a monster."

" 'Magine it, though. Me and you startin' our own shop and everything. *Ours,* man. *You* and *me.*" Lonnie clenched his fist and shook it. "What's union? Fifteen, twenty bucks an hour? Huh? We could work for nine or ten and kick ass we'd be so busy."

"What do we do for cash? It takes cash to get a business going."

"Work outta the garage." He shrugged. It was simple. "We got the tools."

"They'd shut us down in a week flat."

"Who?"

"The city. You need a business license."

"So we get it."

"They aren't cheap."

Complications. Lonnie thought for a while. Suddenly his face lit up again. "I got the answer." He smiled deviously. "Uncle Ernie."

"Uncle Ernie?"

"He got a shop, don't he?"

"Yeah, in *Gilroy.*"

"It's better'n L.A., man. This place sucks."

Sonny made a face like it's-not-so-bad.

"Anyway, like I was sayin', he got a shop. Maybe he could give us a start." Lonnie slapped his knee. "Damn, don't it sound great? Me and you goin' off and gettin' outta this city. Workin'. And shit, you know, if ya wanted me to keep goin' to school and everything I could go in Gilroy. They got schools there. Whatta ya say?"

"Look into it."

"Damn right I will." Lonnie nodded. "But would you do it?"

Sonny turned his back and dipped his hands into a jar of grease remover.

"I mean I'm talkin' in case they don't send me away or nothin'."

"They won't."

"Well, if they don't . . ."

Sonny hesitated a while longer. "Sure," he said, finally.

"Really?"

"Really."

Lonnie dashed out of the garage.

"Where you going?"

"Phone's ringin'."

He ran upstairs to the kitchen and picked up the phone.

"Hello, Lonnie?"

"Yeah?"

"This is Eugene."

"What's up?"

"You want to double-date tonight?"

He set a family record for the longest time in the bathroom. There was the beginning of a monstrous pimple on the tip of his nose and he didn't know whether to squeeze it or leave it alone. If he popped it now it would only grow more red and ugly, but if he left it alone it might come to a head sometime during the night. Nothing looked worse than a big whitehead on the tip of your nose. So he popped it. Immediately he wished he was dead. Now he looked like a clown. The only thing to do was rub in a little fleshtone Clearasil for camouflage and hope it miraculously disappeared within the hour.

While he was in the shower Alex pounded on the door. "What the hell ya doin' in there? Jerkin' off?" Twenty minutes later he came back again. "You know other people gotta use the bathroom, too." Lonnie ignored him. Eventually Alex gave up and went downstairs and pissed against the side of the garage. After washing his hair and showering, Lonnie shaved the few small hairs from his chin, then the peachfuzz over his upper lip. Used Sonny's body powder. Sprayed deodorant under his arms. Doused himself

with cologne. Brushed his teeth. Gargled. Put on a clean
T-shirt. Slid into a pair of black slacks cuffed perfectly at
the bottoms. Spit-shined his PR fence climbers. Slicked his
hair back with Pomanade. Ready.

He went to the living room and looked at the clock on
the wall. A half hour to go. He looked around the room.
The place was a mess, his Mom's taste in furniture gaudy
—bright orange velveteen armchairs and matching couch,
a velvet seascape from Mexico on the wall, big ornate table
lamps with the shades still covered in plastic. What if he
had to invite them in? It would be better to wait outside at
the corner.

He'd just lit a smoke when he spotted the Mercedes, the
same one he saw out in front of Western Academy, rolling
toward him up the street. Eugene, his sister, and another
girl sat in the front seat with the windows down. The
stereo pounded out The Eagles. Crushing his cigarette beneath his shoe, Lonnie took a deep breath and stepped off
the curb.

The theater was packed with college students from
UCLA. It was an arty place where they served hot apple
cider and organic cookies, where people lounged around
the lobby during intermission and discussed "films," not
movies. Lonnie strutted and swaggered like a hard ass as he
followed Vicky and Eugene and Eugene's date down the
aisle. Vicky wore a skirt with a slit up the side that showed
a lot of her leg when she walked. It was hard for Lonnie
not to stare. He made sure he sat in the inside seat beside
the stranger and kept a mean eye out for anyone who might
be trying to put the make on his date.

"This should be good."

"I heard a lot about it."

"Do you like Bertolucci?"

"He in this?"

"He's the director."

"Oh yeah," Lonnie said, like it just slipped his mind.
"That's right."

He wished the movie would start, that the lights would go out so she couldn't see his pimple. She seemed to be staring at it while she rambled on about how Bertolucci was a master of this and that and how trashy most American films were. Except, of course, for early Orson Welles. She said *American* with a tone of spite in her voice. Even though he didn't understand most of what she said, Lonnie figured if she liked this guy, for whatever reasons, then he had to be pretty damn good. He'd like him if she did. He was ready to watch this movie like he'd watched no other movie before. She might question him afterward and he didn't want her thinking he was too stupid to get it.

But twenty minutes after the curtains parted Vicky put her hand on his knee and he couldn't follow the action on the screen. Feeling himself grow hard, he shifted in his seat and squeezed his legs together, trying to hide the bulge in his pants.

They piled out of the Mercedes while Lonnie stood staring at Eugene and Vicky Van Pattens' home in old Los Feliz, fantasizing about the great parties he and his brothers could throw if they lived here. The house was painted white, there were large hollow pillars on the porch like on a traditional Southern mansion, and the front lawn was so spacious it could've been a park. He'd seen pictures like this place in magazines. He'd seen the big houses on Sunset in Beverly Hills when he hitched to the beach. And once a long time ago, on Halloween, Sonny drove him to Bel-Air to go trick-or-treating. But he'd never been in one of these homes before.

The girls took their sweaters off in the foyer and then they all went down a long staircase that led to the living room. They sat on big pillows in the den, listening to Eugene's jazz collection, staring at each other. The music was too loud to talk. While Eugene was changing a record Vicky suggested everyone go to the game room and play pool. Her brother said no. Vicky rose from the pillow and nodded at Lonnie to follow her. There in the game room she flipped on the light and Lonnie, chest expanded, swaggered around a competition-size pool table. "Nice place you got here," he said. The wallpaper was black-and-white tic-tac-toes. There was a half-kitchen in one corner, an antique walnut bar in another corner, a complicated stereo system on a shelf above a Ping-Pong table.

"It's okay," Vicky said, shrugging. She fumbled with the lock on her parents' liquor cabinet behind the bar.

Lonnie put his finger on one of the small faces of an old class photo hanging on the wall. "This guy looks like somebody I got in a fight with," he said, rolling his neck a couple of times. "Pulverized him. The punk was messin' with my buddy's old lady." He remembered a line from Alex that he'd been wanting to use for a long time. "Don't get me wrong, Vicky. I don't start trouble but I know what it looks like, if ya know what I mean." He grunted for effect. "Yeah, I don't start trouble but I know what it looks like."

"You said that already."

"Sorry."

She poured half the contents of two cans of Coke into the sink and refilled them with vodka while Lonnie set up the balls on the pool table. Just as he was leveling down on the cue ball, stick between fingers on the edge of the bumper, sliding it back and forth, a woman appeared in his sights and he froze. Her nightgown showed white beneath her robe. She was a big-boned woman, a tall woman. Looked mean as a witch. He stood up straight, letting his free hand fall to his side. The woman said she was Vicky's mother and, without giving him a chance to introduce himself, motioned to Vicky with a curl of her finger. Vicky hesitated, then sighed and followed her mother out of the game room, handing Lonnie a Coke as she passed. He heard them down the hall arguing, and though he couldn't make out their words, he knew it was about him. Taking a long swallow off the Coke, he felt his mouth swell and he gagged.

She returned a few minutes later.

"Guess I should be goin'."

"Notice how she doesn't bother Eugene and Marisa? Only me. They're probably fucking right now."

"It's gettin' late."

"Who cares?"

"I don't wanna get you in trouble."

"She won't be back for another hour," she said. "I know her."

"I better be gettin' anyway."

Vicky took the Coke from his hand and rested it on the pool table, smiling a smile that scared the hell out of him. His body stiffened. "Relax," she said.

Lonnie glanced at the door. "You sure she ain't comin' back?"

"Positive," she said.

He heard his zipper. "I don't wanna get you in trouble." She swung him around and sat on the edge of the pool table and then placed his hand between her legs and grinned. No panties. He was paralyzed. She shimmied his pants down to his ankles, exposing his pale white ass. "I think I hear footsteps. Don't you hear footsteps?" She tried but he was like rubber. "Why don'tcha turn off the light?" Again she tried. Nothing.

Sliding her hands up his neck, she massaged the tense muscles there, saying, "Relax, relax, we're alone" in a soothing, cooing voice.

Lonnie felt himself grow hard against her teeth, her lips, even though she was scraping him every other stroke. The pain. He wanted to beg her to stop, yet he didn't want her to. Wrapping one fist in her blond hair, he put his other hand on the pool table to steady his dizzy head. Closed his eyes. "You better stop." Her head bobbed faster. *"You better stop."*

The next day he moped around the garage. Five times in three hours he picked himself up and went to the bathroom, locked the door, double-checked it without rattling the knob, and masturbated. Then he wandered back to the garage and wondered if he was impotent. He wasn't if he could come. Right? But that didn't mean anything unless he came in Vicky. Right? So what was the matter with him? He'd fucked before. Once. Behind the 7-11 in Alex's Riviera. Her name was Crystal. He was drunk. She was homely and overweight but he didn't have any problem getting hard. Maybe if he'd finished the Coke he could've done better. Vicky rushed him. She probably had had a lot of guys. She was probably laughing like crazy at him right now. Probably burst into laughter the second he left. The idea of her going down on another man infuriated him. She must've thought he was incompetent. Gay. He'd do it right next time. If she gave him a next time. And what he lacked in experience he thought he'd make up for with gentleness and desire.

He was considering locking himself in the bathroom again when the garage door flew open.

"How'd it go last night?" Alex jumped and grabbed a rafter overhead. He chinned himself a dozen times. "Get a piece?"

"A little."

"How much is a little?"

"Shuddup."

"Not much, eh?" He dropped to the floor and slapped his hands clean. "That's the way it goes."

Later that night Lonnie and Sonny lay on the floor watching the original version of *Invasion of the Body Snatchers.* But it could've been a commercial and Lonnie wouldn't have cared or known the difference. He was thinking of Vicky. Even at Belmont there was that line you didn't step over. Certain girls were out of your league. You could talk about them with friends like yourself who lusted after them the same way, admire them from a distance, dream of them at night when you couldn't sleep, but it was tacitly understood you never approached one for a date without

expecting to be turned down and laughed into silence.
Vicky was pretty and rich, and everybody knew pretty rich
girls could have any man they wanted.

Lonnie went to the kitchen. The linoleum creaked under
his weight. He picked up the phone. The receiver smelled
of perfume and stale tobacco and he held it away from his
face as he dialed.

"Yes?"

"Eugene?"

"Lonnie?"

"Yeah. Is Vicky there?"

"She's at her piano lesson."

"Damn."

"How you doing?"

"Okay. Did she say anything?"

"What do you mean?"

"You know."

"*Oh,*" Eugene said.

"Well?"

"Not really."

He'd bored her. She was out of his league. He was right.
She'd never go out with him again.

"Nothin', nothin' at all?"

"She had a good time, I know that."

Yeah, yeah. A good time. So what? It meant nothing.

"That all?"

"Let me think."

"Think, think."

"She did say you were cute."

"Honest?"

"Yes."

"Think she'd go out with me again?"

"I couldn't say."

"But she had a good time?"

"That's what I said."

"And she said I was cute, too?"

"Right."

"You're a friend, man."

"Sure."

"Oh Eugene . . . don't tell her I called, okay? 'Specially don't say I was talkin' about her."

"Right."

"Bye."

Lonnie strutted back to the living room, feeling a great sense of relief. "Hey, Sonny, whatta you know about this guy Bertolucci?"

9

Tania didn't feel right. It was the beginning of a cold, or flu, something. But she'd promised last week to make Dan and his kids dinner tonight and she didn't have the heart to call it off. While she and Dan were shopping she stopped to lean on the cart a couple of times, closed her eyes, and rubbed her forehead, feeling woozy and funny inside. Here she had her coat completely buttoned and she was still shivering. Everyone else was walking around in thin blouses or short skirts. Kids half naked. And Dan didn't even notice. It irritated her. But he was like that and she knew she shouldn't get flustered. Sometimes he reminded her of a fat little boy who wasn't responsible for anything he did, and when she thought that she smiled to herself and quit acting sick. Half of sickness was in your head, anyway. When they got back to his place she pumped herself full of aspirin and they had a few drinks. Soon she felt better.

A big pot of spaghetti boiled on the stove. An old T-shirt of Dan's was stuck into the waist of her jeans for an apron. She had just finished slipping four parfait glasses of orange Jell-O, a dab of Cool Whip, and a green maraschino cherry on top of each one, into the refrigerator. Now she stood

over the sink staring out the steamy kitchen window, a
little light-headed from the drinks. She wondered if she
should start washing some of the dishes, so there wouldn't
be so many later, but she didn't feel up to it.

Occasionally a drop formed on the window and slipped
down to the sill, making a clear streak. Putting her finger
to the glass, Tania drew a big round face for Dan's kids over
at the park across the street. It was an apelike face with
floppy ears and a dot for a nose, a cute face that seemed to
draw itself. She cleared a spot on the window with the ball
of her hand, thinking of waving to the kids to let them
know dinner was almost ready. They were busy, though,
and she knew they wouldn't see her.

Through the window she watched Tim pull up grass by
the handfuls and chase after his sister. Carla was eight and
Tim was nine. He was chubby like his father and had had
to wear horn-rimmed glasses with thick lenses since he was
three to keep his eyes from crossing. Carla was small and
frail with bright red hair. She ducked under the slide of the
jungle gym, and Tim, screaming at the top of his lungs,
faked to one side; she peeped out the other, and he threw
two handfuls of grass in her face. It fluttered to the ground
like confetti. Picking up chunks of bark, she heaved them
at him, harder than fooling around.

A minute later the front door burst open. Carla came
crying to Dan, who was sitting in the living room writing
a check for the electric bill. Tania heard him tell her don't
tattle on your brother, go help set the table, dinner will be
ready soon. Panting, out of breath, Carla walked to the
kitchen. Blades of grass clung to her red hair. She went
about putting placemats and plates, silverware, and nap-
kins on the table, being careful not to get in Tania's way.
Except for an occasional sniffle, she was silent. Tania stared
absently at her small face, flushed, spotted with orange
freckles. They exchanged awkward smiles. Carla blushed,
dropping her eyes.

It was important, Tania thought, for the kids to like her.

Of course she felt like a stranger to them and knew they felt the same about her. But that would pass in time. She'd have to make them dinner more often. Maybe they could all do something together sometime—go to Disneyland or have a picnic or something. It didn't have to be a big deal. What worried her was that they might be jealous of her, that they might think she was trying to be someone she wasn't. That would be selfish and cruel, and she hoped they knew better.

Their own mother had divorced Dan years ago to run off and live in a trailer house in Montana with an old high school lover. Some truck driver. She never visited her kids anymore. Never phoned. And according to Dan she hadn't sent Timmy or Carla Christmas or birthday cards in two years. The slut. If she was so hard up she couldn't afford a little gift, she should at least take the time to send a lousy card. But kids loved their mother no matter what. It was instinctive. She remembered a woman who used to live in the next apartment with her five-year-old boy. Would you believe the bitch was caught burning him with cigarette butts? He was a darling thing, too, quiet and handsome. A perfect little gentleman. They put him in a foster home but a month later he escaped and ran back to her. Poor kid. It happened again, only this time there were cops, an ambulance. She burned him so bad he wound up in intensive care.

No, Dan's kids had no reason to be jealous. They had no reason to dislike her.

Carla stared up at Tania, waiting. She was a funny-looking girl. Not ugly, just funny-looking. Buck teeth, braces, kind of plain. She didn't take after her father, not with that red hair, anyway. She could've looked like her mother. The mother must not have been very pretty. A person couldn't always go by that, though. Sometimes two handsome people had hideous-looking kids. Still, Tania wondered if his ex was prettier than herself. Sexier. Had more personality.

Why was it men always went wild over women they *knew* were going to screw them up and down and then dump them when things started looking a little rocky? For all she knew he might still love her. Two people who spent years and years together could hardly forget each other overnight. Those things took a while and some-times, most of the time, a person never got over them completely. It bothered her when Dan talked about his ex, even though he didn't speak highly of her. A person shouldn't dwell in the past. You have to keep on like other people and discard the heartbreaks. At least Dan and his wife *decided* to split up, or she did, anyway—he never really said. She would've liked to known the truth but she didn't think it was any of her business to snoop and ask. Dan was a responsible man, a man who would live with his mistakes forever despite himself, happy or unhappy. Hell, that was in the past. It was different for her. No choice had been involved.

She had been caught off guard. First she hadn't believe what the cop told her, wanted it to be a lie. A mistake. Some other worker. When the shock wore off, the pain set in like concrete. Then the funeral. The condolences, the well-meant words said too many times for too many others. Afterward she felt naked inside, and everybody and every-thing seemed distant, vague. When someone you loved was dead, all of it seemed ridiculous. She was dead, too, felt her mind pale and gaunt like her face, like a white ghost, her heart hollow inside. And it scared her to think she was capable of not caring about anything or anyone ever again.

But there were the boys. She had to keep caring, for them. It was enough to make her shudder to look at Sonny certain mornings when the sun filtered through the dusty venetian blinds, catching his profile at a certain perfect angle, his thick hair rumpled from the night, his eyelashes long and delicate like his father's.

"Can I go now, ma'am?"

"Carla?"

"Yes, ma'am?"

She bent over and placed a hand on Carla's shoulder.

"Honey," she said. "You don't gotta call me *ma'am* anymore."

A half hour later they'd had dinner. The kids excused themselves from the table. Tania sat back in her chair, full on spaghetti and red wine, proud of herself. The meal was a success. Then suddenly it hit her. A temperature of a hundred and one. Must be the flu. She was supposed to take Lonnie to see his probation officer tomorrow, but it looked like she wouldn't be going anywhere, except for back and forth to the bathroom from between the damp sheets of her bed.

The room went from black to gray to light as the sun rose. From his bed, he watched the changes in silence, arms crossed behind his head. The alarm clock on the dresser read six A.M. He'd never felt more tired in his life, but he wasn't sleepy.

"Get up."

"Lemme alone."

"Get up."

He pulled the covers over his head and breathed hot air. "I don't wanna." The voice was muffled, strained. "Lemme alone."

"Hop to."

"Go away."

Sonny waited a second for him to stir. When nothing happened he slapped a lump under the blanket. It could've been a foot. No movement. Drill sergeant time. "Let's go. *Up, up, up.*"

He grabbed the blankets and yanked them back. Cold air. Lonnie was curled up into a ball. "Lemme alone," he whined, sitting forward fast, pulling the covers back over his head. His bare ass poked out from beneath the sheet.

"You asked for it, you asked for it." Grabbing the blankets again, heaving Lonnie up with them, Sonny pounced. They squirmed and wrestled, the headboard banging against the wall, the box springs squeaking, until he gave him a chin-chiller in the spin and Lonnie, laughing and giggling despite himself, screaming, *"Stop . . . stop . . . stop . . ."* tumbled off the side of the bed all tangled in the sheet. He popped up with a pillow and Sonny ducked and it hit the dresser mirror. "Whoooaaa," Sonny said, eyes wide. "Lucky it didn't break." Retrieving the pillow, he tossed it on the bed on his way out of the room, hollering behind him, "Go on now, get dressed."

"Yeh, yeh," Lonnie mumbled. What was he doing screwing around anyway? He dragged himself into a pair of Levi cords, pulled on a clean T-shirt, and went to the kitchen. Sonny was poised against the stove, drinking a beer. Smoking. Lonnie opened the cupboard.

"Whatta you looking for?"

"The Cheerios."

"I ate them last night."

He slammed the cupboard shut. A shiny cockroach dropped to the counter on its back, legs waving frantically. Crushing it with his thumb, he opened the refrigerator and reached for the milk. It felt light. He shook it. "Who put it back empty?"

"Alex."

"Fuckin' Alex."

He crushed the carton into the trash and grabbed a beer.

"Nope."

"You're drinkin'."

"I had too much coffee. I'm nervous."

"I'm nervous."

"I'm older."

"What's that gotta do with it?"

"Just put it back." He pushed himself away from the stove and peered into the refrigerator with Lonnie. "We have eggs. Want me to fry you a couple of eggs?"

"I ain't hungry."

Sonny rolled his eyes. "I'll do the shopping tomorrow," he said. "Why don't you put on another shirt?"

Lonnie looked down at himself. "What's wrong with this?"

"Do I have a T-shirt on today? Do I?" He put his fingers to his chest. "I have a nice shirt. You know why? Because today it's important that you look good. Shit, if I didn't watch your ass you'd go in there with liquor on your breath." He pinched the collar of Lonnie's T-shirt and pulled it and let it snap back. "Where's your head, man?" His voice dropped to a whisper. "Look at it this way. At least Mom isn't taking you. Huh? Am I right?" He bent at the knees until they were eye to eye. "Look at me." Lonnie turned away and headed for his room to find another shirt. His brother hollered after him. "And wash your face while you're at it."

A building was being demolished a block from City Hall. It was a gray morning, overcast and humid, the air thick and muggy like the inside of an attic. Lonnie watched the great steel ball, suspended from a crane, swing back and forth as it built momentum before its release. There came a crash; dust rose from the wreckage below. A string of boards dangled from the second floor by electrical conduit. Sonny hid his tape deck under the front seat and locked the 'Vette. Together they walked in silence. In an hour he'd be back outside, Lonnie thought. Simple. Get it over with. But he could only think like that for a few seconds at a time and then the fear rose again, stronger than last night. The building appeared cold and ugly to him, not because of its design, but because he knew it was a place for people like him, people in trouble.

Sonny stopped just outside the main doors. "Let me tell you something, Lonnie. Don't be acting cocky. This man can put in good words for you. Call him *sir*, always *sir*. Show respect. Today you're a prince, all right? A prince." He punched him lightly in the arm, trying to cheer him up. "It's just a meeting, anyway. Think of it like that."

"Jus' a fuckin' meeting, huh?"

"Don't be cussing either . . . *sir.* "

"Sorry."

"Let's go."

They found the PO's name in the lobby directory and then rode the elevator to the fourth floor and walked down the hall to a door set with opaque glass that said MR. THOMAS in bold black letters. "Comb your hair." Sonny handed him a comb which he dragged across his head once. "Tuck in your shirt." Lonnie did. *As if it was going to matter.*

Sonny tapped on the glass, then stood back. They waited. Waited. He tapped again.

"Guess he ain't in."

"He has to be."

"Maybe he forgot," Lonnie said.

"You mean you wish he forgot."

He knocked again.

Another minute passed.

"No use hangin' around," Lonnie said, smacking his lips. "He ain't in."

Just as he turned to leave he saw the PO hurrying toward them, briefcase in hand, wearing a blue jogging suit with white stripes on the cuffs and lapels. Lonnie's palms began to sweat. He swallowed dryly. The PO unlocked the door, saying he was sorry, that he hoped they hadn't been waiting long. "Have a seat."

"You want me here?" Sonny said.

The PO shook his head.

"I'll be outside then, Lonnie." He gave him the okay sign with his right hand as he backed out of the office, shutting the door behind him.

The PO shuffled through some papers in his briefcase

while Lonnie sat quietly, hands folded in his lap, waiting. On the desk was a small plaque that said THINK, on the wall hung a cartoon picture of goblins laughing with the caption YOU WANT IT WHEN? Stupid stuff, Lonnie thought. The PO wiped his forehead with a handkerchief and told him there was no special reason for them to get together today, nothing major, just talk. Sit back, relax. He told about his run this morning, how quiet it was around the lake, how he really felt in shape lately.

Lonnie listened for a few minutes as if he were interested, wishing the man would quit trying to be friendly and get to the point, whatever it was. He didn't care about the PO and he knew the PO didn't really care about him, either. This was just a bullshit routine they both had to go through. But he'd play along, act nice, show respect, like Sonny said. Lonnie sighed. It wasn't easy to respect a man who combed his hair over his bald spot. The PO leaned across the desk and, suddenly looking concerned and serious, asked Lonnie if he'd been going to school, not cutting. "No, sir," he said. "I'm in a private school now."

"Where?"

"Western Academy."

"That's a good school, a very good school." He asked how his grades were. "You don't need a tutor, do you? Any reading problems? Any math problems? I can arrange it." Lonnie shook his head no.

The PO offered him a cigarette, which he took, thinking the PO would smoke, too. But when he didn't light up with him Lonnie knew he'd just fallen for another buddy-buddy tactic and was pissed at himself. The cigarette tasted stale, dry, anyway. Not worth it. The pack had probably been in his desk for a year. He probably offered a smoke to every punk who walked in here.

"Do you play any sports?"

"No, sir."

The PO raised his eyebrows like he couldn't believe what he'd heard. "No baseball, even?"

"No."

Pushing himself up and down in his swivel chair, he started a long story about a kid who got in trouble for arson. Burglary. The works.

Lonnie, facing a set of windows, stared off over the man's head. Across the way, in another building, he could see a woman sitting at a typewriter with her back arched. And in the distance he saw the top story of the building that was being demolished. The steel ball was hidden from view but the cable and the tip of the crane were visible. "That kid," the PO said, "now pitches for the San Diego Padres." By the swaying of the cable, by the dust that rose moments later, Lonnie knew when the steel ball had hit. Occasionally he heard the faint boom of a good blow, and once he felt himself slouching and sat up straight. He heard the PO, too, although the words weren't registering. If he was asked if he was listening he could've recited back exactly what was said. But he couldn't have responded in words of his own.

"You're going to be more careful, more thoughtful in the future, aren't you?"

"Yes, sir."

"You won't let me down?"

"No, sir."

"You won't let your family down?"

"No, sir."

"Tell you what," the PO said, smiling. "Get involved in one of the clubs at school. Fill your time. That's what the judge likes to hear. Get *involved*. Understand?" Lonnie nodded. The PO paused to glance at the calendar on his desk. "Your hearing is three weeks from today on the twenty-first." A drop of sweat slid from under Lonnie's arm and rolled down his side, stopped, and then slid down to his belt line. "You'll meet with your mother in this building in Court D at one o'clock." He printed the date and time and court room on a pad of paper. Tore the sheet, handed it to him. "I want to see you and your mother here, in this office, one hour before the hearing."

Again Lonnie nodded.

"You got that?"

"Yes, sir."

The PO stood, extended his right hand, and they shook. Lonnie felt queasy inside, nauseated, with a slight fluttering below the ribs. Another minute, he thought, another minute and he'd be outside, away from this place. When he walked out of the office he spotted Sonny and slipped his hands into his pockets and quickly glanced down the hall to the elevator. The PO stopped in the doorway. "You want to talk to me?" Sonny said. The PO, looking beyond him, waved his hand. "Your brother has it all." A kid and his parents rose from their seats in the waiting room. The man's nose was riddled with broken blood vessels. Smiling, the PO led the kid and his parents into the office. The door closed.

They walked to the elevator at the end of the hall and watched the panel overhead. One lit up—two lit up. It stuck on three.

"What did he say?"

"Nothin'," Lonnie mumbled, bowing his head.

"You looked at each other for a half-hour?"

"He wanted to know how I was doing."

"You tell him you're enrolled in a private school?"

"Yeah, I told him." He jabbed at the button. Impatient. "C'mon, already." The three went dark, a bell rang. It was crowded inside and they had to squeeze close together. The elevator stopped at the first floor and they funneled out with the others and walked side by side through the sterile lobby in silence.

At the 'Vette Sonny unlocked the passenger's side and then straightened up and put his arm around his brother. "Smile, man. You're my Frankenstein. I won't let anything

happen to you." Lonnie smiled but it was weak. "You call
that a smile? Go on, get in the car." Sonny faked like he was
booting him in. They drove up the boulevard. "I wish we
had time to go somewhere and talk but I have to get down
to the theater. My play opens tomorrow. Take the wheel
a second, huh?" Lonnie steered while Sonny reached
around for his wallet. He pulled out a twenty. "Get yourself something to eat." When Lonnie didn't move he leaned
over and stuffed the bill in his shirt pocket.

"Listen," he said. "I know what you're thinking. As soon
as this damn play is over I'll have more time. Maybe we can
go up the coast for a couple of days. Camp out. Do some
fishing, some talking, just you and me. How's that sound?"
A few seconds passed. No response. "Well, don't get too
excited. I wouldn't want you to have a heart attack." He
poked Lonnie in the ribs, trying for a smile. It didn't work.
"Look at that." Two queens were swishing along the sidewalk. One was over six feet and bleached blond, the other
was short and fat. "Laurel and Hardy."

Sonny pulled out in front of another car and took up the
slack in the road. Clear board. "I ever tell you that story
about Dad? He liked cards, you know. Alex was either
three or four, you weren't even born yet." Sonny laughed.
"The old man was good. He'd have a pile of money on the
table, I mean a big pile, and Mom—Miss Banker—she'd
wake me in bed and say 'Listen . . .' Before he got too drunk
and lost it all, I'd creep into the kitchen in my pajamas and
ask him for five or ten, like I didn't know the meaning of
money. He knew what was going on, so he'd usually give
it to me just to keep her quiet. It was a game." A Ford was
tailgating them. Sonny slowed down until the driver got
the hint, turned into the next lane, and barreled past them.
"Asshole," he muttered. "Anyway, ten minutes later I'd go
back to the kitchen. I used to think he forgot, at least that's
what Mom told me. 'Your daddy's drunk, he don't remember.' Well, he might've been drunk but he didn't forget. He
was only humoring her. So this time, if he still had a pile

of money, I'd ask for ten or twenty. You had to catch him
at the right time, though, because when he started losing
—forget it. Once he blew his entire check and Mom locked
him out of the bedroom." Sonny shook his head, grinning.
"Man, was he mad. Poor Alex was so scared he was nearly
shivering to death. Me, I was all brave." He stuck out his
chest. "I got up from bed to see what was going on. Mom
was in her room bawling, he was in the hall screaming for
her to open up. It went on like that for an hour. Know what
he finally did? One blow! One blow! He hit the doorknob
and the whole damn door tore off the hinges like a fucking
earthquake. I thought he was going to kill her but he just
sat on the bed and stroked her hair, saying how sorry he
was."

"Could ya pull over?"

Startled. "What?"

"I feel like walkin'."

Sonny frowned. "It's still a long way."

"I wanna walk."

He pulled into a bus zone.

"You feeling okay?"

"Yeah."

"You sure?"

"Yeah."

"Are you going home or what?"

"Probably."

"There's two beers in the refrigerator."

"Good."

"Why don't you drink them and take it easy. Get some
rest. You look tired."

Lonnie stood at the curb, waiting for his brother to leave.
Instead Sonny leaned over and unrolled the passenger's
window.

"Want to drive the 'Vette the rest of the way?"

"I better not."

"The deal of a lifetime."

Lonnie cocked his head and smiled like it's-okay-I'll-pass.

Sonny hesitated a few moments longer before putting the car in gear. When it was clear he tapped the horn good-bye and made a U-turn. Halfway up the block Lonnie crumpled the piece of paper the PO had given him and popped it over his shoulder.

11

Opening night.

"Think he's mad Mom ain't going?"

"Sonny don't care."

"She probably caught it from her boyfriend."

"You ever see him?"

"Naw."

"He came here one time," Alex said, laughing. "The guy weighs a fuckin' ton."

"Shh, Mom'll hear you."

"Ah, she's out of it. Or else she's doing a good job faking so she don't gotta go to the play."

"You don't gotta go either," Lonnie said. "Just drop me and Vicky off."

"I'm going, don't worry. I just ain't too excited about watching a bunch of dummies play make-believe all night. His last play was boring as hell. Admit it." Alex rose from the living room couch and unbuttoned his shirt. "I'm gonna take a shower." Lonnie followed him into the bathroom, wondering why he was always downing Sonny. "Shut the door if you're gonna stay." He stared at himself in the mirror over the washbasin as he undressed. Lonnie couldn't understand why his brother wore those faggot red jockey shorts.

"Sonny's a goddamn good actor."

"He's a has-been, a never-was-been."

"You really hate him, don'tcha?"

"C'mon, he's my brother, too. I love the asshole. But how many years he been hustlin' trying to be an actor? Where is he? Huh? Fuckin' nowhere, A." Turning the hot-water handle, he held his hand in the stream of water, waiting for it to grow warm. "Poor old Sonny couldn't act his way through a one-liner if he rehearsed ten years. He ain't no god like you think. Sonny's for his own ass like everybody else."

Lonnie threw open the door and started down the hall.

"Go on," Alex hollered. "Run off like you always do."

"Up yours."

A rented spotlight rocked back and forth outside the theater, drawing a swarm of moths. Neighborhood kids stood on the corner, smoking joints, staring at the beam as it rolled across the sky. No one was in line at the box office and it was quiet except for the motor that moved the big light. Inside people sat in small clusters, single sheet programs in their laps. At five after eight the curtains parted. On stage was an overstuffed chair, an unmade bed covered with clothes, and a bookcase with two books in it. A woman of about twenty-seven lay perfectly still across the bed. Her face was heavily made up with rouge, yet she looked pale. A knock came from backstage.

Sonny entered, dressed in blue jeans, tennis shoes, and a yellow polo shirt.

Lonnie cupped his hand over his mouth and whispered, "That's him."

Vicky nodded.

Alex sighed, sinking into his seat.

"That guy there."

Vicky nodded again.

He stared at her but her eyes were concentrated on the stage. She looked great there in the dark, her hair up, her long dress folded in her lap. Her shawl had slipped down a little and he could see the smooth, well-rounded curves of her shoulders. Lonnie settled into his seat, feeling proud with Vicky beside him and his brother onstage.

The actress seemed stiff and mechanical, but Sonny moved and spoke as easily as he did at home. His mannerisms, his voice, his casual movements—they were all different. They all seemed natural and controlled but they weren't Sonny. He even looked different, dressed and carried himself different, combed his hair different, and had a kind of poise on stage Lonnie had never seen in him before. Alex was dead wrong. Sonny was great. Now and then he'd pause in midsentence, almost as if he'd forgotten his lines, and then suddenly he'd explode with the rest of it like a crazy person and shock everyone. But it wasn't done for shock. It was done like it would've happened outside the theater and it worked. And when he cried it was subtle, not overacted, stifled but *there*, causing a chill to shoot up Lonnie's spine.

He didn't dominate the other actors and yet it was apparent he understood more about the character he was playing than the others in the cast knew about the characters they were playing. His movements were precise and his voice carried well and powerfully without sounding like the trained voice it was. And when he had no lines he filled in the blanks with some small gesture or expression that didn't draw attention away from the other players but hinted at his thoughts and moods.

The second the curtains closed Lonnie jumped to his feet and clapped like a madman.

A long makeup dresser ran the length of the wall. Costumes lay over the back of wooden chairs. Willie Nelson played over an outdated phonograph normally used as a stage prop. Lonnie stood in one corner of the dressing room, drink in hand, with Vicky and Alex. He wanted to congratulate Sonny, but he was surrounded by a group of actors and actresses on the other side of the crowded room.

"Who's that over there?" Alex said. "I seen him somewhere before."

"Who?"

"The guy in the corduroy jacket."

"He did a couple of 'Kojaks,' " Vicky said.

Lonnie drained his drink. "So what?" Alex hadn't stopped talking to Vicky since the play ended.

"You meet Lonnie at school?"

"No," Vicky said. "My brother introduced us."

"Yeah?"

"Uh huh," she said, unconcerned.

"How old are ya?"

"Sixteen."

Alex leaned back, amazed. "Is she lyin', Lonnie?"

He pretended not to hear him.

"I'm nineteen. Probably more mature'n most guys you know."

"I wouldn't say so."

"I don't mean age, I mean *mature.*"

"How old is Sonny?" she asked.

"Him? Fuckin' too old, A."

"He's very handsome."

"Put a monkey on stage, people'll love it."

Lonnie narrowed his eyes at Alex.

"Do either of you have a light?" Vicky said, raising a cigarette to her lips.

They shot their hands into their pockets, Alex coming up first. Lonnie frowned while his brother lit her cigarette. "Watch my purse," she said, exhaling smoke. "I have to use the bathroom." As she crossed the room, he caught Alex staring at her ass. Shaking his head in disgust, he headed through the crowd to get himself and Vicky another drink. Asshole Alex could get his own.

On the way back, balancing two plastic cups filled to the brim with vodka and orange juice, he felt a hand come down on his shoulder from behind. A little of the drinks spilled on the floor.

"Michelle, this is my brother Lonnie."

"Hi."

"He's a doll," she said.

Sonny put his arm around him. "Takes after me, huh?"

"I can't keep my eyes off him."

"Careful of her." He shook him lightly. More drink spilled on the floor. They all pretended not to notice. "She's putting the make on you."

"In a few years . . . mmm."

Hilarious. Great fun, he thought. Sonny and the actress laughed while he stood there, wanting to leave, but not knowing just how. She kept shaking her hair back like a Clairol commercial, shifting her weight from one leg to the other, posing. They carried on about the play as if he wasn't there. Politely, subtly, Lonnie tried to slip out from under his brother's arm but Sonny only held him tighter. He thought the actress was trying to look pretty and sexy when really she wasn't very pretty or sexy at all. Too much eyeliner, too much rouge. Her blouse was lowcut and her jeans were so tight he didn't know how she moved. She had to be at least ten years older than Sonny, too. She annoyed him; the way his brother spoke to her annoyed him. It was a different voice, not the voice of the character he played tonight, but not his own, either. It was a voice Lonnie had heard him use before, one he disliked, one that Sonny only used around his actor friends. A phony voice. A kind of light prissy voice full of airs. Why did he do that? He didn't have to, he never did at home. And his laugh, his goddamn laugh, it was fake.

Scanning the room, he spotted Vicky standing beside Alex again. "S'cuse me." He elbowed Sonny lightly in the ribs. "C'mon, let loose. I gotta go." He sidled his way through the crowd and handed Vicky her drink. Alex swaggered to the table where the liquor was kept, looked around once to see if he was being watched, grabbed a fifth of Canadian Club, and motioned Vicky and Lonnie outside to the parking lot.

The big light in front of the theater was gone. Alex unlocked the Toyota, turned the radio on low, and then offered Vicky the seat. "We'll have our own party. It's stuffy in there, if you know what I mean." He chuckled, passing the bottle. Lonnie drank, winced, wiped his mouth on his sleeve.

Vicky looked at each of them one at a time. "You're all a handsome family," she said. Lonnie felt his face flush red and he bowed his head. Alex grinned, placing a hand flat on the Toyota's fender, pushing. A tricep popped up. He wiggled his fingers, making the muscle twitch. "But Sonny is very talented," she said. The tricep stopped twitching.

"I ain't into that ego shit," he said. "I hustle."

Vicky laughed.

"What's so fuckin' funny?"

"Oh, nothing," she said. Lonnie sighed, wishing his brother would disappear. Take off. As it was, he and Vicky weren't going to have much time together. He doubted they'd be able to make love tonight, that he'd be able to make up for last time. Ah, it wasn't that important anyway. What he really wanted was to just sit and talk to her, alone. Maybe not even talk. Just hold each other. She looked good, smelling of perfume, wrapped in a shawl, her dress at midcalf. Her feet were in sandals and he stared at them, noticing her toes. They were delicate, like the fingers of a child. The tops of her feet were tan like her arms, soft and smooth like her shoulders, and her arches were sharp and strong. He wanted to take her sandals off and hold her feet under his shirt against his belly to warm them.

"You said you hustle?" Vicky said to Alex. "Hustle what?"

Lonnie sighed again, flicking his cigarette butt into the sky. It hit the asphalt, sparks flying.

"Hustle," Alex said. "Business, A, business. I do. I don't pretend."

"Wanna go for a walk?" Lonnie said.

"I don't think so."

"C'mon, get the blood going." He hopped around. "Stretch those legs." He breathed deep. "Fresh air."

"Let her relax." Alex handed him the bottle. "Go ahead, guzzle it. It's about dead."

He didn't feel drunk until he walked back to the dressing room for more liquor. It was as if he was standing still and the ground was moving beneath him. Close objects looked distant. Voices and laughter sounded loud and shrill. He knew he saw Sonny still talking with the actress, and he did fix himself another drink, and he did make it outside again. But after that it was all foggy. How long he lay in the backseat of the Toyota before Alex and Vicky decided to leave, he didn't know. The engine roused him a bit, between consciousness and dream. He felt the road rumbling beneath him, tires whirring, heard the radio, felt the warm air from the broken car heater blowing gently across his face. His eyes were closed but he sensed the light of street lamps pulsing on his eyelids. Colored specks floated about his head. Lonnie curled up into a ball as he felt the car turning. The engine wound down and then grew loud again as the speed increased. When it reached a steady, constant hum, he knew they were on the freeway. And then it seemed they had stopped, though he wasn't certain. He thought he heard someone say something, someone touch his arm, his brother maybe, but he lay there, not sure he'd been touched or spoken to at all. His arm fell from across his face and he saw soft shades of gray and black and orange like he had held his eyes shut for a long time and then opened them to the sun.

"Lonnie . . . you asleep?" Silence. "Lonnie . . . ?" Alex swiveled around in his seat and smiled at Vicky. "He's passed out."

"Thanks for the ride."

"No problem."

She picked up her purse from the floor of the car.

"Wait."

He leaned over and they kissed. A minute later she put her hands on his chest and pushed him away. She stared him straight in the eyes.

"You're a real prick."

Alex sat back, stunned. The dome light flashed on. Vicky quickly stepped out of the car. Lonnie mumbled.

Inside the house she locked the door and then placed her eye to the peephole. The Toyota was just leaving. She hurried downstairs to the living room where Eugene sat watching an old Bogart movie and threw her shawl across the couch.

"Next time Lonnie calls tell him I'm not home."

"Oh shit."

"I'll explain later."

"What did he do?"

"Lonnie didn't *do* anything."

Jay Petty was known in Boyle Heights as an all-around general fuck-up. He and his nine brothers had a total of eighty-seven arrests, ranging from disturbing the peace to assaulting an officer with a deadly weapon. It was Jay who bought the Riviera for two hundred dollars after his prize Chevy was repossessed. Delinquent payments. He was a member of Summer Knights, a car club in East L.A. During the week Jay worked as an apprentice machinist at Lockheed where he had lost the tip of his middle finger operating the drill press once when he was high. He'd been reprimanded twice in the last six months for tardiness and threatening to crack his foreman's head open with a crescent wrench.

Evenings Jay Petty divided between his family, working on his car, and an auto body class at East L.A.'s adult education program. But come Sunday night he'd be out cruising Whittier Boulevard with his club in some of the finest machines in California. All of them had the same polished chrome wirewheels and chrome Summer Knights plaque suspended from the rear window. All were lowered and worth thousands of dollars. Jay had had the Riviera painted a few days ago. He was working on the upholstery when his wife came into the garage and told him they'd run out of Pampers. Rather than argue, he'd hopped into the Riviera and headed for the twenty-four-hour Safeway on Mission.

As he pulled into the parking lot, Alex and Lonnie were making their way up Mission in the Toyota.

Lonnie woke when the car stopped.

"We home?" he asked, groggy.

"I'm gettin' beer."

He sat up and looked around. The side of his face was imprinted with dots from the vinyl seat. Suddenly he realized something was wrong. "Where's Vicky?"

"You passed out on us."

"Huh?"

"I hadda take her home."

Panic. "Where's a phone?" He fumbled with the latch on the backseat.

"You'll wake the whole fuckin' house."

"I gotta apologize."

"Forget it."

"Was she mad?"

"Mad ain't the word."

"Goddamn it," he moaned.

"A bitch is a bitch. Don't take 'em serious."

"She ain't a bitch."

Alex opened the car door. "Wanna go in with me?"

As they walked toward the fluorescent lights of Safeway, Alex stepped away from Lonnie and looked him up and down. "Whatta you weigh now? Ninety-eight? One-oh-three? You might be a good wrestler if they got wrestlin' at that candy-ass school of yours." He made a muscle. "Look at that gun, huh? Go on, hit it. Hit it. It's rock, man. Fuckin' rock."

"I don't wanna."

"Go on."

"No."

"Hit it."

"No."

"Hit it."

Lonnie reared back and let go with a punch but it glanced off his brother's arm and stung him square in the jaw. He took off running, Alex after him, hollering, "Ya little bastard, ya little bastard," while Lonnie weaved and feinted until he got behind a car. Alex was at one end, Lonnie the other. "Ya little bastard." Every time he ran around one side, Lonnie ran around to the other. Finally he took a chance and threw himself across the hood of the car and caught him by the shirt. They both tumbled to the asphalt.

"Truce, truce," Lonnie screamed.

"Now you call truce," Alex said. "Little bastard." He climbed off him. "You know," he said, "that's the trouble with Sonny. Like he means good and all but sometimes he got his head up his ass. He don't know how to have fun. You take after him that way and it ain't good. A guy's gotta keep loose so he can roll with the punches. Know what I mean?" He held out his hand to help him up but Lonnie waved it away.

"I ain't stupid."

"Don't even trust your own brother," he said, shaking his head. "Goddamn, if I . . . ." Suddenly he fell silent. Lonnie got to his feet and brushed his pants off.

"You gonna stand there all day?"

He took a step and stopped. Squinted and stared. Took

a step and stopped. Squinted and stared.

"Hey, this way," Lonnie said, nodding toward the Safeway.

He reached into his pocket for his knife, then knelt on one knee.

"Whatta you doing?"

Holding the blade between thumb and index finger, Alex scratched at the paint below the lock on the trunk. "Putty," he said, a few seconds later. He chipped off a piece and held it in his palm under the parking lot lamp for Lonnie to see. "This is my car."

"You're crazy. That's a lowrider."

"Look at that, goddamn it." He shook the knife at the dent that had been puttied over. "Mom backed into me here."

"Naw."

"Hell, she did."

"So what if it's yours? You sold it."

"I lied, man. It was stolen."

"You better call the cops then."

"They don't do shit."

He glanced at the doors to the Safeway. "Can you get it going?"

"Call the cops."

"Since when you so righteous?"

"I don't want no trouble."

"The fucker'll be comin' out soon." Alex checked the car door. It was unlocked. "Don't waste time."

"Forget it."

"No way."

He pulled him over to the car, then dashed to the Toyota and returned with the toolbox.

"You sure it's yours?"

"I'm sure."

"Gimme the wire cutters."

He opened the box and handed him the cutters. Lonnie

lay on his back on the floorboard, cramped between the pedals and the seat, his legs hanging out the open door. His brother held a flashlight for him while he reached up under the dash and yanked down the wires running off the back of the ignition lock. Clipped them. Stripped the ends bare. "Somebody's comin'," Alex whispered. Lonnie straightened up fast, bumping his head on the steering wheel, dropping the wires, ready to run. Alex grabbed a tire iron from the box and held it behind his back, muttering, "C'mom, fucker. C'mon." The man was getting closer and then, just when Alex spread his feet for leverage, he hopped into an MG a few cars away and drove off. He exhaled and squatted again, holding the tire iron in one hand, the flashlight in the other. "Hurry the fuck up." Sweat beaded on Lonnie's forehead and rolled down, stinging his eyes.

"This is bullshit."

"Jus' shuddup and do it."

"Hold the light steady."

"What's takin' so long?"

The light was weak. His hands shook; his arms ached from holding them up.

"Hurry, goddamn it."

Lonnie gritted his teeth. "You wanna do it?"

"I'm sorry, I'm sorry."

Ten seconds later he crossed the hot leg with the ignition line, twisted the ends together, and touched them to the starter wire. A spark. The engine groaned—clicked—groaned—clicked. A touch of gas; it roared. He pulled the starter line and twisted the other two accessory wires to the ignition and battery leads and then scooted out from under the dash. Taking the keys from Alex, he grabbed the toolbox and sprinted across the parking lot. At the Toyota he stopped and looked behind him. The back end of the Riviera hit the driveway and made sparks as his brother barreled into the street.

Lonnie heaved the box into the cab. Tools spilled across

the seat. With his lights on high beam, he backed calmly out of the lot so no one could read the license plate.

The electric doors slid open. Jay Petty wandered out cradling a box of Pampers. He patted his pockets for his keys and turned in a circle, looking around the parking lot as if he were lost. He walked out into the street, around the block, and partway up another block. "I'm not high," he said slowly, clearly. "I'm not high." Dazed, he stumbled back to the Safeway, set the Pampers on the ground beside the phone booth, and called his brother.

"My ride got ripped off."

"Fuckin' A!"

"We gotta find the fucker, Bobby."

"Don't worry."

When he hung up his brother called the Knights. The Knights called the Dukes. The Dukes called the Comrades of Montebello and they called the Styles and the Escorts and the Playboys of Echo Park. The message was the same —a sixty-nine Riviera with a cherry red metal-fleck paint job, a new chain steering wheel. And one gold pinstripe from the hood to the trunk.

12

She moaned too much and hissed dirty words into his ear. Once he asked her to be quiet, and she was for a while; then she began hissing again, and he gave up and concentrated on coming. But he was drunk. Couldn't keep it hard. Eventually they both grew too tired to continue. When their sweat evaporated he pulled the sheet up over them and soon the actress fell asleep. Sonny crossed his arms behind his head and lay there, tired though still horny, thinking about the play. The *Times* review might already be in the racks. He thought about how drunk he was at the party and how every goddamn time he vowed not to drink, or only to have one or two, he ended up getting drunk and making an ass of himself. He said things he knew he wouldn't say sober. It had to stop.

In the morning he wanted to leave quickly but he stayed for a cup of coffee. The actress looked homely without her makeup, sort of bland, sallow, dressed only in a kimono. He already regretted last night. Now when they met at the theater he'd have to avoid her without being obvious about it, hoping she wouldn't feel too put off. If he gave in to his sympathies she'd cling to him like a child. The whole affair would slip into something false. He had too much on his mind to be bothered with that. The apartment reeked of her. All the little knickknacks, the Japanese prints on the walls, the plastic geisha dolls on the coffee table, a Japanese tea set that only gathered dust. He had to get free.

A half-hour was polite enough.

His eyes felt heavy with liquor in the glare of the morning sun. The sky was smoggy. He stopped at a bus stop beside which stood rows of newspaper machines, bought a copy of the *Times,* sat on the bench, and scanned the headlines. "Father Kills Daughter." "Pile-Up on San Diego Freeway." A minute later he flipped over to the entertainment section, hoping the review would pop out at him naturally, as if he wasn't looking for it.

The reviewer said the play was worn out and dated, that the best performance was given by the other lead, not Sonny, that Sonny overdramatized his scenes. The play was compared to a high school production. Closing his eyes for a moment, he pinched the bridge of his nose. He reread the article, hoping the words had somehow changed, that there had been some mistake, but it was all there like before. At the bottom, at the goddamn bottom where no one ever read . . . *Sonny Baer.* He stared and stared. The only thing good about the review was his name in print.

So the man was a fool.

He didn't know what he was talking about.

It didn't matter.

Who cared, anyway?

He cared, damn it.

Living and working when you had big dreams, dreams of being somebody someday, weighed on his mind and made his days seem long and meaningless. He needed approval, not condemnation. Sonny walked slowly down the street to his 'Vette, unlocked it and climbed in, sat back and sighed. He was a dreamer. A foolish, fuckin' dreamer. Alex was right. He couldn't act worth shit. If only there was something tangible to fight—a person, a thing—he was sure he could fight it and win. It wasn't that way, though.

He was older now, no longer a child actor. Being Mr. Personality, knowing how to memorize lines quickly and accurately, wasn't enough anymore. Unlike his first commercial, he landed the second one by shaking hands with the casting director, then carrying on a cute "adult" conversation. He landed the other job for Kellogg's Corn Flakes, playing a tough kid dressed in knickers, because the casting director knew exactly what he wanted. And it wasn't another Hollywood child actor. Acting tough wasn't an act then. The other kids, bratty kids with pushy young stage mothers coaching and pawing at them, could never have played the part convincingly. It was two years, though, between his first job and the second. During that time he was up for a lot of different parts, TV and commercials—all rejections. He changed his strategy and acted like the other kids who were getting work, but by then it was too late. After the second commercial he outgrew child roles and entered another league where talent and skill came more into play. He had the talent, the skill, but no connections. He was starting cold. He needed a break. If he screwed it up he'd at least be able to say he'd had his shot and done his best. It wasn't failing that scared him; what kept him awake nights was the constant fear of growing old and never having been a contender.

Shove the review.

He threw the paper on the floorboard and started the engine. Damn if he wasn't a good actor. And that was being modest. When he was on stage under the lights, bending and molding a character until it was real, he knew he was talented. Alive. *You're gonna win* . . . Sonny raised his fist like he wanted to bust the windshield, making an angry face in the rearview mirror, pointing a finger at himself. *You're gonna win* . . .

At home he parked in the garage and went upstairs to the apartment. Mom was asleep on the couch in her bathrobe in front of the TV. The morning paper was heaped beside her on the floor. Wrinkled tissues and a bottle of Vicks

Vaporub rested on the lamp table. Her nose looked red and chafed enough to make Sonny's eyes water.

He crept past her to the kitchen.

A note, written on a piece of newspaper, was stuffed in the dial of the phone:

> Sonny,
> Call Donna. 555-3280

The secretary answered: "Schwartz and Associates."

"Is Donna in?"

"May I ask who's calling?"

"Sonny . . . Sonny Baer."

"One moment."

One moment undoubtly meant ten minutes. He turned the mouthpiece of the receiver up toward his head, plopped into a chair, drummed his fingers on the kitchen table. A couple of minutes later Donna came on the line.

"How are you?"

Shitty. "I did the play last night."

"Good. Are you free this afternoon?"

"I have to work."

"Call in sick," she said. "Have a pen?"

"Yeah."

"Can you hang on?"

Before he could answer he was on hold again.

He phoned the Standard station where he worked. Ray, a freshman at Hollywood High, answered.

"Let me talk to Mr. Hill."

"Just a second."

Sonny pinched his nostrils shut.

"Hello?"

"It's me." He coughed into the receiver. "I'm not feeling so good."

"Not again. We're shorthanded today."

"I think I got the flu."

"You mean you got an audition, don'tcha?"

He went into a coughing fit. "I can't even get out of bed," he moaned, clearing his throat, sniffling. "I swear."

"This is the last time, Sonny."

The part was for a TV movie about street life on Van Nuys Boulevard. Donna said the show was originally intended to be a straight documentary, a kind of exposé, using nonactors in a series of casual interviews. Two hundred teenagers auditioned for the parts before the director decided that nonactors were too dull. The movie would fail. A quick story line was worked into the script and the search for trained talent began. Actors were needed, but unknowns, unrecognized faces, professionals who could make the film interesting while maintaining the flavor of a documentary.

Think. From the second he walked into that office, he'd need an edge. Creeping past Mom on the couch, he headed for Alex's room. A WRONG WAY/DO NOT ENTER sign his brother had lifted from a freeway exit was nailed to the door. Sonny knocked lightly and then turned the knob and poked his head into the room. "Alex?" No answer. "Alex?" He slipped inside, leaving the door open. A life-size poster of Marilyn Monroe, holding her skirt down against a burst of air, stared at him. Two dumbbells lay on the floor in front of the dresser mirror. A tie-dyed parachute hung suspended from the ceiling over the bed. The paint on the wall beneath the window was cracked and peeling. Sonny rummaged through the dresser drawers—underwear and T-shirts, an ashtray full of roaches, a pack of studded condoms. Crazy Alex. But maybe some women liked them. He considered taking one but knew he'd be too embarrassed to ever use it. Look at that. A blue velour sweater hung in the open closet. Brand new, never worn, even the price tag was still on it. But he needed a shirt, not a sweater, and it had to be exactly the right one for the part. You know the first thing he'd do if he got the job? He'd tell Mom to put on her best dress and then he'd take her to Ma Maison or the Polo Lounge where the waiters stumbled over themselves to light your cigarettes. Pure luxury. After dinner he'd sweep her off to an expensive clothing store, no Zody's or Sears, but Bonwit Teller in Beverly Hills where Mom had once stood looking through the windows, wishing and dreaming, too proud or embarrassed to even consider going inside to browse. "Go on, get yourself something nice for a change," he'd say. "It's on me." Then he'd stand back, smiling, acting like it was nothing. All the guilt, the doubt and the fear of being looked on by Mom as a bum, another dreamer, would be replaced with pride. Respect.

Look. Sonny laughed to himself, holding up a pair of bright green pinstripe slacks. Did Alex actually *buy* these or steal them off a pimp? And look. His old work shirt from Silverlake Lanes with his name on the pocket. A white dress shirt? "That's mine," he muttered. He had wondered where the hell it went. Sonny pushed the hangers to one side, one by one, pausing now and then when a piece of clothing interested him. An orange satin shirt? No, he thought, too flashy. A purple one with doves? Definitely not. Too gaudy. Fishnet T-shirt, fluorescent red? He continued sliding clothes to one side of the closet until he came across a shiny black shirt, European cut with a wide collar. Hoody but stylish. Sophisticated. He liked that. A sophisticated hood, an intelligent hood.

It fit loose in the shoulders, a little long in the arms, but he liked it that way. A tailored fit would look too studied, too self-conscious. He sucked in his stomach as he tucked in the shirt, staring at himself in the dresser mirror. He backed up until his shoulder blades touched the wall. Throwing his hips out, crossing his legs, he looped his thumbs in his pants waist and cocked his head. The stud. Cool, sly, like James Dean. Some pleated slacks might look good, too. All the young cholos were wearing them again. Maybe he could even scrounge up a pair of PR fence climbers like Lonnie's.

"Whatta ya doing in my room?"

He spun around.

Alex leaned in the doorway, arms crossed over his chest.

"I'm admiring your decorating."

"Cut the shit."

"You have good taste."

Alex wasn't laughing.

"Actually I'm preparing for a role."

"Not in my shirt, you ain't." The top dresser drawer was open. Alex raced over and slammed it shut. "What you doing fuckin' with my shirt?" He grabbed a chair and used it to stand on so he could count his hat collection on the shelf above the closet.

"I'm sorry."

"Want me to go fuck with your shit?"

"I apologize, all right?"

"You oughta."

"Hey, relax."

"Gimme my shirt."

"I need to borrow it."

"Go to hell."

Sonny thought for a second. "I'm up for a part, a big part," he said. "And I need your help, man. I have to look like a hood."

"You callin' me a hood?"

"You weren't listening."

"You think my clothes look like a hood?"

"Let me finish."

Alex jabbed a thumb in his chest. "You're callin' me a fuckin' hood."

"Hold it," he shouted, pausing until he had his brother's attention. "You get around, right?"

"Huh?"

"I mean you know what's happening."

"Whatcha gettin' at?"

"There's some people who know what's going on and there's some that don't. The smart ones know and you're one of them," he said. "You plan to interrupt again?"

"Go on."

Sonny smiled. "Let me put it this way. Say you're at a party you know is going to be busted, or, better yet, say you're dealing to someone you don't know well. You have doubts. That doubt, man, is what is called instinctive intelligence." He held up one finger for emphasis. "You have to follow your instincts. There's people who'll sell to somebody they doubt because the deal's so good they're afraid to let it pass. They may be smart but they don't know how to use it. They end up being busted and saying 'Shit, I knew it all along.' That's one kind of loser. The other kind is even worse. He'd sell to a six-year old. He'd be at a party where the cops warned them to turn down the music and he'd throw a bottle at the car when they're leaving. Everyone gets busted. This type is so lost he doesn't know trouble until it hits him in the face and *then* he doesn't even realize how he fucked up. The sorry bastard never stood a chance from the day he was born. The only trash lower is a narc. But you, Alex, you have this." He patted his head. "Intelligence. You know how to take care of yourself. You can spot a fuckin' narc a mile away."

"Easy."

"See? I don't have that good of an eye."

"Sure ya do."

"Not like you."

"You know something?" Alex said. "You're right. I always did know what trouble look like." He was still standing on the chair. "It's for sure I ain't never been busted."

Sonny patted his head again. "Either you have it or you don't."

"Instinctive intelligence."

"That's right."

"Instinctive intelligence." He said it again, more slowly. *"Instinctive intelligence."*

"Tell me what you think." Sonny went through his bad-ass routine again. When he finished he looked up at his brother. Alex jumped off the chair. "You got it all wrong. If you're trying to be all bad and shit then ya gotta put more *style* into it." Grinning, he took a fresh pack of Marlboros from his pocket, popped it open, flipped one into the air and caught it filter end between his lips. "Watch." Shifting his weight from one leg to the other, he did a kind of shuffle, only keeping his feet on the floor. He rolled the cigarette from one corner of his mouth to the other, eyes darting side to side. "You gotta keep movin' all the time. Nobody hassle ya for loiterin'. Think you're walkin'. Keep your hands outta your pockets. Gotta be quick. No fuckin' around. Know what I mean? Stay loose but don't relax. Quick draw, A. *Fast.*" He whipped his hands into the air, thumbs cocked, aiming at Sonny. "*Boom.* Waste the cocksucker." Alex laughed. "Wait a second . . ." He undid two buttons on Sonny's shirt. "Show some chest for the ladies, *ese.* Now try it." Posing in front of the mirror, Sonny did it Alex's way. It worked better. "Not shabby . . . for an amatuer. You gotta polish your footwork, though." Alex demonstrated again. "Use more hip. Be loose." Sonny swiveled his hips. "Now lean back like you got time."

"How's that?"

"You're gettin' it."

"Know what I need?" he said absently, staring in the mirror, pushing his hair back and holding it there. "I need grease." He hurried down the hall toward the bathroom where Lonnie kept his pomade.

"My shirt," Alex hollered.

"Thanks."

He exploded. "You want my shirt, take my shirt. Here, take this too." Alex whipped the shirt off his back and threw it down the hall. "Want my fuckin' shoes?" he screamed, hopping on one leg, struggling. Sonny slammed the bathroom door just before it hit.

"*What's going on?*" Tania hollered, scurrying up from the couch.

*   *   *

Groomed and ready. Sonny coughed to cover the sound as he opened the kitchen cabinet. Slipping a pint of Mom's vodka into his jacket, he rushed outside. On the way downstairs he noticed the door to Stormin' Norman's apartment was open. Norman's leg was in midstride over the threshold. Suddenly it was sucked backward. The door slammed. Stormin' Norman's father cursed. There was a thud, body against wall. The stair railing vibrated in Sonny's hand. For collecting disability for a bum back, he thought, the old man was in pretty good shape. Tossing his kid around like some Tonka Toy.

As he bent over to lift open the garage door, he spotted Lonnie coming up the alley, holding a couple of Dr. Peppers at his side.

"What'd you do to yourself?"

"My new image." Sonny raised his chin, turning his face. A grand profile. "Like it?"

"C'mon."

"I'm dressed for a part."

"I figured something like that."

He blinked a couple of times. "Aren't you supposed to be in school?"

Silence. Lonnie popped open a Dr. Pepper. "Want some?" Sonny shook his head. "Today's a holiday."

"Since when?"

"Washington's Birthday."

"That's in February."

"Memorial Day?"

"Not funny, man."

Bowing his head, Lonnie kicked at the ground. "Mom forgot to wake me."

"You're an adult now. That isn't her job anymore. Anyway, you have an alarm clock. Use it."

Lonnie rolled a cold Dr. Pepper across his forehead and sighed. "I won't do it again."

"It isn't my problem." Sonny shrugged, pretending not to care.

"One day don't matter."

"For you it does."

"I said I'm *sorry.*"

"You can't afford to fuck off. I told you that a hundred times." He heaved the garage door open. "What the hell's this?" The Riviera, which hadn't been there when he drove in this morning, was now parked dangerously close to his 'Vette. It was a large garage, but it wasn't meant for two cars.

"It's Alex's," Lonnie said, wincing. Sonny inspected the side of his 'Vette for damage. Alex was just the spiteful sonofabitch to fling open his door and call it an accident.

"When did he get it?"

"It's his old car." Lonnie said, kneeling behind the trunk, pointing to the dent. "'Member this?" Sonny did, vaguely. "They painted it is all." He scratched the metal with his fingernail. "See the old brown. They didn't even sand it down."

"Yeah."

"Crazy, huh?"

"That's not his license plate."

"So they changed it."

"You sure it's his?"

"It's his all right."

"Where'd they find it?"

"Some lowrider had it."

"I can see that."

"It's obvious, huh?" Lonnie said. "I mean that a lowrider had it."

"Yeah."

"Well . . ." He slapped his thigh. "I got a lot of homework to do."

"Where'd they find it?"

"*Where'd they find it?*"

"That's what I said."

"You wanna know where they found it?"

"Are you getting hard of hearing?"

"I'm jus' hung over. Last night, you know." He laughed.
"I forgot to say I really liked you."

"Thanks."

"You were great."

"Lonnie . . ."

"You know that part when you cried?"

"*Lonnie.*"

"You don't gotta holler."

"Then answer me."

"Okay."

Silence.

"So?"

"Yeah?"

Sonny exhaled like he was exhausted. One thing his
brother couldn't do worth a damn was lie. "Where'd they
find it?" he said softly. Lonnie crossed and uncrossed his
arms and then slipped his hands into his pockets and nib-
bled his lower lip. "It was at the Safeway, I think."

Sonny stared him in the eyes. "You think," he said, "or
you know?"

"It was at the Safeway."

"They get the guy?"

"Not exactly."

He leaned inside the Riviera through the open window.
The ignition wires had been yanked down from under the
dash and cut. Anyone who stole a car, who fixed it up, who
invested in a custom paint job, wouldn't leave the leads
dangling in plain view for a meter maid to spot. Cops
wouldn't wire it; they'd tow it. And he knew Alex couldn't
change a spark plug if his life depended on it.

Lonnie gulped, cupped a hand to his ear. "Do you hear
the phone?"

"Mom'll get it."

"I'm expectin' a call."

"She'll take a message."

Lonnie stepped to the left. "You better talk to Alex."

Sonny stepped to the left. "I'm talking to you."

Lonnie stepped to the right. "I don't know nothin'."
Sonny stepped to the right. "How'd you get the car?"
"I don't gotta take this shit."
Sonny grabbed him by the back of the neck. Pressure point. As he wrestled him over to the Riviera, Lonnie bucking up and down, their legs tangled and they almost fell. Sonny wanted to rub his brother's nose into the hood of the car. *"What's that? Huh? What's that?"*

Lonnie tried to shake loose but Sonny squeezed harder, forcing him to stoop until his head was below his hips, his face bright red.

Sonny clenched his teeth and his words dropped to a mean hiss. *"Who wired it? You wired it, didn't you?"* Lonnie dropped to his knees and sprung up like a missile. Throwing his head back, he turned into Sonny as he leaped sideways, breaking the grip, and dashed out of the garage.

Sonny bolted after him, stopping a few seconds later short of breath. His brother was too fast. Cursing, he swung at the air. He shouldn't have blown up. He shouldn't have touched him.

Running back to the garage, he hopped into his car and sped down the alley, slamming on the brakes at the cross street. There he was, two blocks away already, walking heatedly down the sidewalk. Sonny made a right turn and caught up with Lonnie and rolled down the passenger's window. "Hey," he hollered. "Let's talk." Lonnie kept walking. "Goddamn it, listen to me." He continued to cruise alongside his brother, looking for a place to pull over. The curb was lined with cars. Traffic was backing up. A man in a Fiat behind him honked. Flipping on his emergency lights, he waved the traffic to go around him. "Get your ass in this car before I get *mad.*" People on the sidewalk stopped and stared. He opened the passenger door to the first catch. The man in the Fiat honked again. Lonnie quickened his pace. His neck was mottled where his brother had grabbed him, his hair was disheveled, and his face was contorted like he was trying hard not to cry. "I didn't mean to hurt you," he shouted. "If we're going to open a shop, we have to learn how to get along. Am I right?" The man in the Fiat honked. This time Sonny nearly jumped out of the window, half his body suspended in midair. He flipped him off Italian style. *"Blow that fucking horn again I'll ram it up your ass, mister."* When he turned around and looked back to the sidewalk, Lonnie was gone.

He had just disappeared. Poof. Sonny spent the next half-hour cruising the neighborhood. Finally he gave up in disgust and drove to Beverly Hills. Parked at the Ralph's Supermarket on Wilshire, he drank from the pint of vodka. Then he popped three Certs into his mouth, combed his hair in the reflection of a store window, and hustled to the interview. He gave the best reading of his life but left the office not knowing or caring what they thought of him. He didn't return to the apartment. He didn't look for Lonnie. The routine of working and coming home, of being responsible, responsible all the goddamn time, had been tearing him apart until he ached inside. But he knew the pain would soon pass. It always did. At least it kept him lean and slightly crazy. And that craziness, he thought, was what kept him alive. It was when he lost it, when the aching stopped completely, that he knew he'd be in trouble.

An hour after the interview he sat drinking in a strange bar, tying on a magnificent drunk, wondering who he was and where he was going. Later he passed out in his car, and when he woke he bought a pint of bourbon and nursed it until the bars opened again. Not until last call the following morning, when he ran out of cash, did he head home.

13

Hollywood Boulevard. Poster shops and paraphernalia shops. T-shirts with iron-on pictures and slogans. Overpriced souvenirs. Import stores. Lonnie pushed his way up the sidewalk through the crowds of tourists. He could still feel Sonny's grip on his neck, squeezing, reminding him of the scene. A red halter top caught his eye as he passed a clothing store and he backed up to look at it more closely. Clothes were risky gifts, though. He didn't want to get Vicky something she wouldn't wear, or would wear just not to hurt his feelings. It was sort of skimpy, anyway. She might think he was weird, that he was hinting at something he wasn't. What could you get for twenty bucks? A couple of records? Naw, he thought, that's a bad idea. She wouldn't like his pick, she'd know how much he spent, she'd think he was cheap. A record wouldn't mean anything special. He wished he had more money. It was a bitch being broke all the time.

He browsed through the women's department at The Broadway, avoiding looking at the mannequins in panties and bras, feeling awkward around only ladies. Perfume? That's what he always bought Mom for her birthday when he couldn't think of anything better. Perfume was boring.

And even if Vicky did like it, after she used it up that would
be it. Out goes the bottle. He needed something she
couldn't use up, something she'd be proud of, something
she'd keep for a long time.

Lonnie wandered out to the street and continued walking.

$14.95 FREE ENGRAVING WITH PURCHASE

In the showcase of Woolworth's, on a white blanket of
cotton speckled with glitter, lay five neat rows of silver and
gold ankle bracelets. An ankle bracelet was small and could
be worn discreetly. He could have it engraved. An ankle
bracelet was delicate. An ankle bracelet was perfect. Dou-
ble-checking his wallet, he stuffed his hands in his pockets
so the clerks wouldn't suspect he was a thief, and strolled
inside to the counter where the bracelets were kept. A
woman opened the case from behind the counter and
handed him the silver one he pointed to. The chain was
thin like thread with a small oval plaque attached to it. He
imagined Vicky at the beach in a bikini with the bracelet
loose around her slim ankle, shining, as he lay beside her
on the towel. Somehow they'd have the whole beach to
themselves. There would be a slight breeze, the air would
taste salty but sweet, she'd be smiling.

The clerk asked if he wanted it engraved. He stammered
and shifted his weight, looking down at the floor, embarrassed.

"Yeah," he mumbled. "Vicky."

"With an *i* or a *y?*"

"What?"

"V-i-c-k-*i* or V-i-c-k-*y?*"

"I."

Lonnie strolled down the aisle while waiting for the
engraving to be done, absently picking up a can of hair-
spray or a bottle of shampoo, pretending to read the contents. When the clerk finished she let him inspect the brace-

let and then he paid her and she wrapped it in a gift box
for him. On his way out he spotted a phone booth across
the street and made a dash for it.

He had the whole scene pictured in his mind. They'd sit
outside on the spacious front lawn of her house in privacy.
He'd apologize for the other night. She'd forgive him. As
smoothly as the apology went he'd slip the box out of his
pocket and hand it to her with a smile. If she put the
bracelet on he'd know it was the right time to pop the big
question. Do you want to go steady? He couldn't balk on
something like this. One second they'll love you, and the
next, forget it.

"Hello?"

"Is Vicky there?"

It was her mother. "She's not home yet."

"Do you know when she'll get in?"

"It won't be until late tonight."

What was she doing out late? "I'll try again."

"She'll be going straight to bed."

Damn. "Could you tell her Lonnie called?"

"Sure."

"Tell her it's important, okay?"

"Bye now."

"I'll be up real late if she wants to get ahold of me."

"Bye."

An ashtray rested on his bare chest. The apartment was
dead quiet. He lay in bed watching the red ember of his
cigarette smolder, wondering where Sonny was, wishing
he'd come home so they could talk. Make up. Lately their
hours had been different. Either he was asleep when Sonny
came in or Sonny was asleep when he came in. He liked
when they could lie in bed and talk as they grew drowsy.
It seemed like they could talk more easily and openly then.
He missed those conversations. Secure, warm beneath the
covers, he could see his brother's face across the room in the
darkness—his lips, the slope of his nose, the inside of his

pale arms locked behind his head. He was beautiful. The most handsome. Big soft brown eyes. He'd stare at the ceiling, thinking, always thinking about something, it seemed. Christ, he missed him. What they said at night always seemed more true, more meaningful, no regular day-to-day bullshit. The darkness freed their thoughts like a liquor. Then sometimes they might not speak at all, sometimes they might just lie there listening to each other breathing, sometimes that was enough. Christ, he missed him. They never did anything together anymore. There was never any time. No time for nothing.

Taking a last drag off the cigarette, he stubbed it out, set the ashtray on the dresser, and turned the radio on low. The whine of an alto sax filled the room, high-pitched and brassy, moaning like some kind of intimate confession. As it ended he slipped into his boxers and wandered to the kitchen. His schoolbooks were spread open across the table where he'd been studying earlier in the evening. The radio in his room was faint, barely audible. Lonnie picked up the phone and dialed the first number, kept his finger in the hole for a second, let the dial circle around and click.

It rang twice, three times, four . . . five . . .

"Hello?"

"Vicky?"

"It's one o'clock in the morning." Her voice was harsh. "If you're having fun, great. Because I'm not, Lonnie. *Don't* call again."

He wanted to tell her this wasn't a joke, he wasn't having fun, that he wanted to apologize for the other night, but he couldn't speak. Her words had stunned him. She slammed the receiver down. He stood in the kitchen shivering, listening to the phone buzz, wondering why the hell he'd called. What the hell he'd done.

Miss Rose moved Eugene to the other side of the room after a third warning to stop talking. Alone, Lonnie grew bored. The day dragged. During lunch he caught Eugene

leaving campus and hinted around about Vicky to see if
she'd said anything about him. Eugene lit a cigarette and
played dumb. He took up where Miss Rose left off in her
lecture. Filling in, he said, what she so conveniently neg-
lected to mention. Old Kennedy wasn't the complete angel
the text and Miss Rose would've liked you to believe. Ad-
visers in Vietnam. The Bay of Pigs, for Chrissakes. Every
time Lonnie tried to change the subject, Eugene only raised
his voice.

Two hours later the last bell of the day rang. He spotted
the silver Mercedes as it rolled up outside the school, gathered his books, and sat back until Miss Rose dismissed him.
Trying to keep a straight face, he swaggered out to the car
and tapped on the window. Vicky turned, looking at him
blankly. She wore her Catholic school uniform but had
changed out of her black-and-white saddle shoes into some
raised sandals. They lifted her so that her toes slanted
downward and turned up slightly, posing her ankles, shar-
pening the arches of her feet, making her calves firm and
round. A strand of blond hair was curled behind one ear
and her mouth was open just enough to show a bit of white.

The window slid down silently. Lonnie leaned in, elbows on the frame, smiling wide. "How you doin'?" he
said. To the chauffeur he nodded, tipping an invisible cap.
Vicky narrowed her eyes as she leaned away from him.
"Why did you call last night?" Standing back, frowning, he
put his fingertips to his chest like me?-call?

"You woke my mother."

Lonnie rolled his eyes. "What can I say? I was walkin'
down the street last night when these three bloods from
Roosevelt jump me. I'm gettin' two of 'em good and then
this guy whips out a knife." He jumped back as if the
person was in front of him. "All of a sudden I see five more
comin' up behind me. *Five.* " He spun around. "I ain't no
genius but I ain't dumb, you know?" He held his chin up,
running in place. "I get to this phone booth, right? They're
pushin' and kickin' on the door but I got my foot up like

a jack so they can't get in. I ain't no Hercules, though. There's what? Eight, nine of 'em? I can't hold it forever." Paused to gulp some air. "So they're all over the booth, kickin' and everything, and I'm screamin' these numbers at the operator. I guess I jus' must of give her you by accident." He shrugged. "I don't know." Vicky wasn't smiling. "I'll leave you dyin' in suspense a second," he said, holding up one finger, reaching into his back pocket. Eugene came out then and, lowering his head, hurried around to the other side of the car.

"I got you something."

"No, thank you."

"Go on, see what's in it."

"I said *no, thank you,* didn't I?"

Lonnie grinned, smacking his forehead with an open palm. "Sometimes I don't know, like I forget my manners. I'm sorry about the other night. All right?" She stared at him. "Apologies accepted?" He held the present closer, shaking it. "C'mon, take it." Silence. "It ain't a weddin' ring or nothing." The window slid closed. The chauffeur started the motor. Lonnie tried to keep smiling. "Hey." He tapped on the window as the Mercedes lurched forward. "Don't you wanna know how I got outta the phone booth?"

He strolled out of the liquor store with a pint of Jack Daniels hidden inside his notebook. At the park he drank, shooing the pigeons, trying to figure it all out. Some old friends from Belmont sat on the bench under the trees but Lonnie turned and took another path. He kicked at the ground as he walked around the lake, disgusted. Paper cups and plastic sandwich bags, cigarette butts and beer cans floated on the brown murky water. Oil streaks like rainbows lapped at the bank. The walls of the building where they rented paddleboats were covered with spray-painted *placa.* Jesse loves Lily. Diablos rule. The sidewalks were grimy and spotted with bird droppings of the same gray color. A bum was passed out on a bench. Even the pigeons looked old and diseased.

As he rounded the last block home he looked up and saw there were no lights on in the windows of the apartment. Good. The place was his. He didn't have to worry about putting on a phony smile or talking to anyone. Shutting the door softly, he went to the kitchen. The sink was full of dirty dishes. A greasy frying pan rested on the stove with bits of yellow egg in it. Lonnie took a pad of paper and a pen from the drawer and sat at the kitchen table to write a letter. It was dark, he couldn't see well, but he didn't want to turn on the light. Not now. There was something secret, something private about being here like this that lights would ruin.

He planned to ask his uncle if he and Sonny could live with him. But when he saw the words he crumpled the paper and started over. It was too much to ask. Maybe a summer. Maybe when they were there Uncle Ernie would see they were good workers and offer to keep them on.

Dear Uncle Ernie,

How are you? Everybody is fine here. Alex got his car ripped off but he got it back. It's a lowrider now. Ha, ha. Sonny is doing a play. Mom is seeing this guy all the time. I think it's serious. Remember last Christmas you said Sonny and me had a job if we want? School will be out soon and I think I want to take you up on that. We could work just for summer if that's okay. I could clean shop and stuff if you want. I want to learn more about cars. I already know a little. I'm almost sixteen and I don't want to waste a summer again if you know what I mean? You don't got to pay me or anything. Mom talks about you all the time. I think she would say okay if you say okay. I guess I'm just trying to say I want to get out of L.A. I guess you heard I got in trouble. I have to go to court but don't

worry. I'll let you know. Sonny thinks it's going to be
okay. If you say no I understand. Okay? Let me know
as soon as you can.

Lonnie paused, wondering if he'd forgotten to mention
anything as he signed and addressed the envelope and
slipped the letter inside, when he heard a sound somewhere
in the apartment. He stood, and as he passed Mom's room
he saw her door was open. He froze. She was lying in bed,
the covers rumpled.

"Sonny?"

"It's me."

"C'mere, honey." Her voice sounded thick, congested.
"C'mere." The room was warmer than the rest of the apartment and smelled damp with sickness. His mother's face
looked gaunt in the pale moonlight that fell through the
window across her perspiring forehead. Suddenly he felt
dizzy. "You been drinkin'," she said. "I can smell it." She
reached for him. He sat on the edge of the bed, feeling it
give, her hand hot and clammy on his arm. There was a
breeze outside and he felt a draft on his legs and face. In the
distance he watched the leaves shake on the wild orange
tree in the empty lot that grew oranges too sour to eat. "Lie
down, baby." The voice was less throaty now, weaker, soft
even. She tugged on his arm and he lay beside her as best
he could without them touching. The heat and smell of her
was strong. She stroked his hair. "Why you drinkin', baby?
Don't drink. You make Momma worry." His body was all
balled up inside, his neck muscles tensed. "Lie down." She
continued to stroke his hair. "I never get to see my baby
anymore."

"I gotta go."

"Why don't you stay home tonight?"

No answer.

"A girl?" She propped herself up on an elbow. Moonlight shone on her shoulders. Her hair was mussed. "Tell
me her name." He stared at the shadows on the floor that

the blinds against the window made. "Where you gotta go?"

"I gotta go out."

"I didn't mean nothing, baby. Momma didn't mean nothing. You know that." She squeezed his arm. "You go on." It wasn't until he was outside that he realized he'd been holding his breath and that his legs were trembling. Exhaling, taking a long drink, he capped the bottle and tucked it under his jacket. He intended to mail the letter and come straight home. But after he dropped it into the mailbox he kept walking. Faster. Until he was running.

A line of light ran beneath the Van Pattens' front door. Raising his fist, Lonnie sighed and let it drop back to his side. Another drink first. One more sip. The whiskey burned its way down his throat. He shook his head, rolled his shoulders loose, and raised his fist again. Just as it was about to land, he changed his mind and jerked it back, hurrying down the stairs. He hid in a clump of bushes, staring through a web of bare limbs, studying the silver snail tracks on the ground. Why he had come here tonight, or if he should leave, he didn't know. Vicky would probably call the cops if she found him. She was probably in the living room watching TV with her parents; maybe even out having a good time with some jerk. On the way over here he had thought about what he would say to her, how when he knocked on that door no one was going to stop him from coming in, how he and Vicky would have a talk and straighten this shit out once and for all. But now that he was here he felt like he didn't care what happened. It was all idle hope. Lonnie broke a twig off the bush and began snapping it into tiny pieces when the sprinklers sputtered and coughed. He dashed out into the open.

"Who's there?" Eugene barked, peering into the darkness. He was in his bathrobe and pajamas, barefoot, gripping a three-foot-long water key. Slowly he grinned as he turned the sprinkler system off. "Hang on. Let me get dressed." While he changed Lonnie strutted around the lawn, wiping drops of water from his face with the back of his hand, sipping the whiskey to make it last. A live band played loud reggae at the mansion on the hill above the Van Pattens' place.

A few minutes later Eugene came outside, six-pack in hand, and they headed up the hill toward the music. The street was lined with Mercedes and Porsches, BMWs and Cadillacs, and a few not so expensive cars. They stopped to watch a man in a red tailcoat open a tall, ornate wrought-iron gate for a young woman in a chiffon dress. She climbed into a kind of golf cart, gathering her skirt into her lap and holding it there as she was shuttled up the long steep driveway to the mansion. People spilled out into the front yard, drinking from stemmed glasses, laughing and talking in small groups. "A guitarist for the Stones used to live there. Now the ambassador to Iran owns it. He was quiet compared to this man." Eugene laughed. "Father could kick himself in the ass for not buying that place when he had the chance. For the peace alone, mind you." They continued up the hill, Lonnie dragging his feet, staring at the ground. "Cheer up," Eugene said, patting him on the back. "Vicky's a confused little tease. She did to you what she did to another friend of mine just last week." He flipped the finger. "That's how dear we are to each other." But Lonnie didn't want to hear about her, even think about her; he wasn't listening. "Consider yourself lucky. My sister never went with anyone longer than a month. Get the picture? The girl doesn't know what she wants."

A middle-aged couple stepped out of a powder blue Cadillac. Lonnie watched the valet hop in and drive up the block. When he parked the car, though, he paused momentarily to reach under the seat before returning to the iron gates. Soon they had passed the party and the music faded. Tall trees obscured the lamplight, casting the street into darkness. Lonnie opened the door of the powder blue Cadillac. "Are you crazy?" Eugene said.

The keys were on the floor mat under the driver's seat, just as Lonnie thought. He strolled to a Porsche 911 and found the keys on the floor there, too. "Which one you want?" The next one was a vintage Rolls but it was locked tight.

"None of them," Eugene said.

Then there it was. His dream. A red Jaguar. Twelve cylinders, stick on the floor, leather upholstery. Lonnie wiggled his ass around, testing the seat for comfort.

"Get out of there."

"C'mon."

"No."

"C'mon." He patted the seat. "Hop in."

"You're crazy."

"You gonna stay or go?"

He shut the door, wagging his head, saying, "I'm going to regret this, I'm going to regret this" as they pulled away from the curb. It handled so beautifully it was like learning to drive all over again, minus the fear. All twelve cylinders pumped up and down, humming in perfect rhythm. "I'll have some of your whiskey." Lonnie gave him the bottle and they laughed together as they sped up the hill and turned onto a street that led to Griffith Park.

The entrance gate was locked but he jumped the island divider and shot through the exit lane past the darkened Greek Theatre. The road was narrow, twisting. "Slow down," Eugene gasped, clutching the dashboard. He maneuvered the Jaguar into a bend, letting the wheel swing wide for a split second, then pulling it hard right at the sharpest point of the turn, huddling the mountainside. A great rush of adrenaline flowed from his head to his arms, his fingertips, his chest and legs. He accelerated. The Jaguar burst out of the bend into another, its body swaying from one side to the other, finally leveling itself when they hit straight road.

They stopped at the top of the mountain at the observatory parking lot. Eugene removed his hands from the dashboard and collapsed in relief. "Look," Lonnie said, opening a beer. The smog had mixed with the moisture in the air and settled across the huge sprawling valley below. It was a view so clear and sharp he thought he could almost see the soft gray glow of TV sets in the windows of the houses and apartments dotting the hills and flat lands by the thousands. Smiling to himself, he stared across the valley, remembering the time years ago on a hot afternoon when he and Sonny drank a bottle of wine behind the green dome of the observatory. It had been quiet, a weekday, no one around. Sonny had furrowed his eyebrows, cigarette slanted white across his unshaven chin, his head cocked. Jimmy Dean in *Rebel*. He had mouthed the lines from the scene shot here until their stomachs ached from laughter. Ah, that was a good time. A good memory. Lonnie never felt drunk if he was depressed, only if he was happy, and his head was reeling now for the first time that night.

Clamping the beer between his thighs, he started the Jaguar and they weaved down the mountain to Los Feliz and caught the freeway. He glanced in the rearview mirror as he picked up speed—seventy, eighty, eighty-five—until the billboards and motel signs alongside the road blurred into each other like a crazy neon collage. When they approached a group of cars he slowed down, and when they passed them and he saw there were no black-and-whites in the pack, he picked up speed again. The Jaguar cruised at about ninety; the motor purred. They passed the whiskey back and forth, drinking and smoking, talking and laughing. Soon they were almost to Anaheim. Lonnie spotted the peak of Disneyland's Matterhorn poking into the sky and pulled off the freeway. Throwing the engine into neutral, he turned to Eugene and grinned.

"*No.*" Eugene pronounced it slowly and carefully.

"Why not?"

"Because it's closed."

Lonnie looked at him like he was dense. "How many times you been here?"

"Millions of times."

"And it's always full of kids. Right? You can't even move. That ain't no fun." He laughed. "We get hassled, jus' say we're early."

Before he could protest Lonnie was sprinting across the empty parking lot toward the ticket booths. He leaped over a turnstile like a professional hurdle runner, scaled the chain link gate, then dashed under a train bridge and crouched down low. He could see the plaza and all its shops and stores, the tip of the big castle in the distance, and he listened for footsteps or voices. "Quiet." Eugene banged his way over the turnstile after failing to squeeze through. He teetered at the top of the fence, looking down at the ground, groaning. "Shh," Lonnie hissed. Slowly lowering himself to the pavement, Eugene staggered under the bridge and slumped against the wall, wheezing, clutching his chest. Some ducks paraded by, chests up, squawking angrily. Lonnie scanned the area again, slinking forward, staying close to the wall, eyes shifting fast from side to side.

"Let's get out of here," Eugene moaned. "I don't like it here. I don't like it here at all." They crept up Main Street. The lights in the stores and shops were still on, though, and it was too bright. Too dangerous. Turning down a side street, they headed for Adventureland, where it was darker.

"Now, my friend," Lonnie said, bowing, extending his hand. "I shall take you on a grand tour of Disneyland. To your right is the Swiss Family Treehouse, to your . . ." He disappeared into Fantasyland.

Eugene spun around. "Lonnie?"

"Over here."

"Where?"

"Here."

He sat in a giant teacup, resting his head on the rim, staring up at the stars, relaxing like he was in a hot tub, blowing smoke rings at the full moon while he scanned the sky for the Big Dipper. "We have to stick together," Eugene said, panting, his face pale. "We don't want to get lost, not here for Chrissakes."

Holding the whiskey up to the moon, checking its level, Lonnie took a swig and jumped out of the cup. "Cheer up." He patted Eugene on the back. "We're having a good time."

Eugene gagged. "A good time? Sure, Lonnie, sure." They wandered up the street, hiding in the shadows of the buildings, stopping to peer around each corner before stepping out into the open.

At the Matterhorn Lonnie found the powerbox behind the control podium and tugged on the small metal door until his fingertips were sore.

"Let's get out of here," Eugene moaned. "I don't like it here."

Lonnie tried wedging his Buck knife into the crack of the door; he looked around for something like a crowbar to pry with. No luck. "Check your laces. We gotta go on foot." He spoke like a guide giving a pep talk to his troops. "Stretch out." He did some deep knee bends. Touched his toes.

"I'll wait here."

"Ah, c'mon."

"Sorry."

"Chicken?"

"I'm not budging."

"We'll go up the tracks."

"I still couldn't make it."

Lonnie shrugged and jumped on top of a bobsledlike cart. He looked up. A flag fluttered at the mountain's peak. Black tunnels burrowed into its sides. Thousands of crevices, painted white like snow, were etched into its surface. Arranging his feet on the rails, he slid one foot forward, then the other, as he made his way up toward the mountain. "Goddamn it," Eugene groaned, scampering onto the tracks. "Wait up." With his arms out to his sides, he slowly inched his feet forward. His stomach jiggled beneath his shirt, his legs quivered, he looked down. Fifty feet. Gulping, he double-timed it until he was safe inside the Matter-horn.

"See, you made it, no hassle." Lonnie punched him lightly in the arm.

"*Don't,* " Eugene screamed, groping for anything solid to grab hold of.

Lonnie stepped off the track and hopped up and down on the tunnel floor. "It's safe. See? Take it easy."

The sun had been beating on the mountain all day and it was warm inside. There was the smell of metal and grease and burned wire from an old fire. Portions of the tunnel walls were scorched black with smoke. "If I get killed," Eugene said, "it'll be on your conscience." The track zigzagged up through the Matterhorn like a spiral staircase. Sometimes the track was firm on the tunnel floor, sometimes it led outside and wrapped around the mountain, supported only by bracing. "What if one of those sleds happens to come on? I'll haunt you, Lonnie. I'll haunt you forever." The higher they went, the closer Eugene squatted to the tracks. Suddenly it dropped downhill. They heard the slap of water far below. Cables from the Skyway ride ran through the tunnel overhead. A small breeze blew across Lonnie's face.

"This is the place you turn like you're gonna go straight over the cliff." He could see Tom Sawyer Island, the People-mover, the Haunted Mansion, the Dumbo Flying Elephants, the Rocketjets. Everything. "*Look.* " He spread his arms. "*Look.* "

Reluctantly Eugene crept to the edge and peered over the side. "Nice, very nice," he said, crawling back inside. Just then Lonnie leaped and grabbed the bar protruding from the concrete wall above them. Pulling himself up, he gave a high-pitched scream, letting it fade as if he were falling, followed by dead silence. Eugene spun around awkwardly and scrambled to the edge. Lonnie swooped down laughing and caught him by the neck with his legs.

Eugene yelped. "Goddamn you." That did it. "Goddamn you." He turned right around and headed back down, cursing all the way.

Lonnie followed him down Main Street.

"Where you goin'?"

"Home."

"Ah, c'mon, it's still early."

"The hell it is."

"I didn't mean to scare you."

"You could've killed me."

"I'm sorry."

Suddenly they saw the spark of a match in the distance and froze. A janitor leaned against his canvas pushcart, lighting a cigarette. They shot to one side like a couple of jets doing maneuvers. Lonnie heaved the whiskey shattering to the ground and they raced back up Main Street past the glassblower's shop, past the souvenir stands, across wooden sidewalk planks that made their footsteps sound hollow and loud like a herd of horses. He held his chest out, chin up, his arms and legs pumping wildly. Ducking between two buildings, he hopped a gate into a yard loaded with broken bobsleds. A few seconds later Eugene came tumbling over, holding his aching sides, panting. "Shit," Lonnie groaned. The fence ahead was ten feet high with no footholds. He thought of hiding inside one of the broken bobsleds but that was too risky. He ran the length of the yard looking for another way out. There was none.

"We're dead," Eugene whimpered, holding his ribs. As Lonnie started back for the gate he heard footsteps approaching on the other side. Whirling around, taking short fast steps, he leaped and grasped the top of the fence by his fingertips and hoisted himself up. They heard the janitor fumbling with his keys.

"*You boys are in trouble,*" he hollered. "*The harder you make it on me, the harder it'll be on you.*" Eugene ran full blast into the fence and fell to the ground, dazed.

"Get up," Lonnie said. Glancing at the gate behind him,

Eugene rose to his feet and ran again. This time Lonnie caught his hand. His back muscles felt as if they were about to tear. "Don't twist." Lonnie pulled, strained, his face bright red. "Grab the fuckin' fence."

Eugene wiggled like a porpoise. "*I can't.*" His hand was slick with sweat, he was heavy, Lonnie couldn't hold him much longer. "*Don't leave me.*" He heaved again.

"Your *other* hand," Lonnie said. "Your *other* hand." Catching hold of his wrist, Lonnie threw his weight backward and they dropped to the other side with a dull thud. Lonnie blinked and looked through the slats of the fence just as the gate swung open. A gray-haired man burst into the yard with a sawed-off broomstick.

Scanning the area quickly, Lonnie spotted an open door and pulled Eugene inside. Darkness. They climbed down an iron fire ladder onto a narrow catwalk. Keeping their backs tight to the wall, they shuffled along the catwalk, feeling their way through the darkness with their feet. Eugene held fast to the back of Lonnie's belt, muttering and sobbing, wiping his eyes with a fist. Suddenly lights flashed on. Music played. They froze, momentarily blinded. Water in a channel beneath them started to roll. An ugly face stared Lonnie square in the eyes. His heart jumped. It had a smirk on its lips, a knife in hand, a bandanna covering long greasy hair. All kinds of faces stared at him. Eyes everywhere. Big men. Fat men. A man with a peg leg. A woman. He backed up. "Watch it," Eugene screamed. They teetered near the water.

"*I know you're in here,*" the janitor hollered, slowly climbing down the iron ladder. "*There's no use hiding.*" They jumped onto an island where two pirates sat on a keg of gunpowder. One had its mouth open in mock laughter. "*This place is worth thousands of dollars. You break anything and you've had it.*"

Lonnie pulled Eugene down behind a treasure chest full of jewels and gold doubloons and locked his arm so he couldn't bolt. Closing his eyes for a moment, he felt his heart beat fast and powerful, as if the sand was pushing at his chest, as if the sand was alive and trembling, not him. They heard the jingle of keys again. Footsteps. He held his breath, squeezing Eugene's arm.

The janitor tapped the broomstick along the wall. *"You're not fooling anybody."*

Lonnie dug the balls of his feet into the sand and strained his body flat. His neck throbbed, his lips were parched. Tap. Tap. Tap. He felt the vibrations on his belly and knew the janitor was close. *"Come out."* The voice sounded as if it were on top of them. The tapping stopped. All he could hear now was the swoosh of the water in the channel and Eugene's heavy breathing. A long thirty seconds passed. Peeking from behind the treasure chest, he spotted a pair of khaki pants and black shoes. A human silhouette stood above them on the catwalk.

The corners of Eugene's lips quivered. He sobbed. The janitor stepped forward and stopped like a blind man, head cocked, listening. Lonnie eased his hand up to the back of Eugene's head and ground his face into the sand. Ten seconds... twenty seconds. The janitor started away. Eugene began to struggle. Lonnie pushed harder. Five more seconds. Squirming loose, Eugene gagged. The janitor spun around and raised the stick. They jumped up and half-clambered, half-ran across the island. A pirate popped out of nowhere and Lonnie smashed into it, Eugene smashed into him, and they slipped and splashed into the cold, rushing water. The pirate's sword tangled in Eugene's shirt and he shrieked and tore wildly to free himself as the current forced him along, bobbing up and down, coughing and spitting up water.

They swam and pushed off the bottom, bouncing back and forth against the sides of the channel while the janitor ran along the catwalk screaming, *"Stop . . . stop,"* lunging and waving his stick. Lonnie bucked through the water, chest rising and falling, rising and falling, his feet catching on what felt like metal tracks. Eugene followed, sobbing and coughing. They pushed and swam. When the channel branched off the janitor lunged once more and then stomped the ground and threw the broomstick at them.

At the berths Lonnie grabbed the edge of the channel and pulled himself out on his stomach and shot for the main entrance. Hit the fire bar. The doors flew open. *"Eugene,"* he screamed, spinning around. The silhouette of the janitor raced down another catwalk toward them. Eugene lay on his back on the concrete floor beside the berths, gasping for air like a beached whale, his stomach jiggling and contracting. The sword was still tangled in his shirt. *"Get up, goddamn it, get up."* He rolled to his feet and they ran through New Orleans Square to Main Street, over the fence and through the turnstiles.

Two trucks were parked in the lot, huge vacuums attached to the beds. The sky was growing light. On Katella Avenue Lonnie slowed to a walk and tried to steady his breathing. The headlights of a fast-moving car sped toward him and he bowed his head, praying it wasn't a cop. A moment later his wet pants cuffs flapped in the rush of air and then it was dark again. He sighed. Farther up the block he spotted the Jaguar, its windshield silver with dew. A plane, blinking red and green, flew silently overhead.

He crossed the street. Eugene lagged behind, soaked and shivering, carrying the sword by its handle now. "Where are you going?" he said, pointing to the Jaguar with the blade.

Wrinkling his nose, Lonnie glared at him. "It's too hot now." The rooms in the Disneyland Hotel were all dark except for the lobby. A little kid in Superman pajamas stared at them from a small window over the cab of a camper idling in the driveway. Eugene waved to him with the sword as they passed. The kid's mouth dropped open and he ducked from view.

"Did you see his face?"

"Why don't you get ridda that thing?"

"What for?"

"It don't look good."

Eugene flipped and caught the sword by its blade a couple of times. "I like it." They staggered up the street until they came to a bus stop. Lonnie's T-shirt clung to his chest, his nipples showing dark through the fabric. He let out a long, deep sigh as he collapsed on the bench. The Matterhorn looked miles away in the distance. It seemed impossible that they were ever there. He wished he was home; he wished he'd stayed home. The whiskey and beer had worn off a long time ago and now he was groggy and hung over.

Touching finger to cheek, he said, "You got sand on your face."

"I wonder why."

"You know why."

"What if I'd smothered? Did you consider that?"

"Lemme alone." He struggled to stuff his hands in his pockets but his pants were too wet. Another car passed. The driver slowed to look at them. "Get ridda that sword, huh?"

A few minutes later the first bus of the day pulled to the curb, brakes squealing. Quickly dropping some coins into the box, he headed for the back of the empty bus, his shoes squeaking with water. Eugene sat up front behind the driver with the sword in his lap. "Would you like to know what we did tonight?"

The driver chuckled, sipping coffee from a Styrofoam cup. "Maybe you shouldn't say," he said. The bus jerked forward. Lonnie shot Eugene a dirty look. Raising his eyebrows, he swayed to the back of the bus.

"Whatta you doin'?"

"You actually think he cares?"

"Don't talk about that shit to jus' nobody."

"What's he going to do? Bust us?"

"You mouth off too much, man," Lonnie said. "Sometimes you mouth off too much."

Eugene held the sword out and, grinning, tapped him on the knee. "May the Force be with you." Lonnie batted the sword away. One eyelid twitched almost imperceptibly. Eugene grinned wider. "I've nothing to hide. *You* stole the car, my friend, not me." He reached over his shoulder and scratched his back with the sword, moaning luxuriously. Lonnie's eyelid twitched faster, his ears burned, he gritted his teeth. "If we were busted my father would've had me out within an hour. I wasn't scared. In fact, I wasn't scared at any time tonight." The bus stopped. When Eugene turned to see who was boarding, in that split second, he was completely off guard. Lonnie knew he could've nailed him clean, but he only stared out the window at the buildings and streets slowly growing light, filling with people and cars.

A couple of men in suits sat down together. Eugene returned to the front of the bus. "As I was saying . . ." he began, acting out how they were trapped, how they had to lie low. Occasionally he glanced back to Lonnie, using the sword to point, and said, "Isn't that so? Isn't it?" Lonnie sank into his seat. Go fuck yourself, he thought. Tell Vicky to go fuck herself, too. I don't need you. When his exit finally came he rang the bell and headed for the back doors.

"Oh, Lonnie," Eugene shouted, clear across the bus. "Vicky said Alex . . ." He paused to grin that grin. "I better skip it. She made me promise not to tell."

Sonny was passed out in his clothes. His feet lay on the pillow, his head rested at the foot of the bed, and he reeked of liquor and too many cigarettes. One arm dangled over the side of the bed. Lonnie stood over him for a moment, wanting to touch him, hold him, but afraid to. Unlacing his brother's shoes, he pulled them off gently and placed them on the floor. "You're gonna catch cold," he whispered. He draped the bedspread over him, slipped out of his wet clothes, and climbed into his own bed. For a while he lay watching his brother, listening to him snore softly and rhythmically. Outside he could hear the trashmen banging cans in the alley. The people in the apartment next door were walking around now; the floorboards creaked and groaned. A cold chill came over him. He tugged the blankets up to his ears, wrapping his arms around his legs so that his knees pressed his chest, wishing he could crawl inside himself and hide.

14

Dark circles had formed under his eyes. His complexion had grown sallow. He'd lost weight, and now his body wasn't much more than skin drawn taut over bone. Each abdominal muscle protruded like the sections of a wasp, rounded and hard, smooth like polished stone. He hadn't slept six hours in the past three days but he didn't feel tired. After rolling out of bed and dressing, he reached beneath his dresser for a violin-shaped case and snapped open the latches. Inside was a triple-beam scale. He set it on top of the night stand, carefully zeroed the arm, then went to the closet for his dope. One ounce. Profit from the first half-ounce enabled him to reinvest in a full one. This time it came from a local, more reliable dealer. Anything Alex wanted, this man had, or could get within a couple of days.

The coke rose and fell in small mounds around his fingers as he pinched it through the plastic baggie. Nice. All his. Lots of rock. Solid rock shiny in texture like abalone. It was good enough to fix if a person wanted. A couple of lines and he could go like a machine. If he started to come down, if he started to get depressed, he'd just do a little more and he was speeding again.

Another bag, half the size of the other, contained methamphetamine.

Alex opened the writing tablet:

$$28.5 \text{ grams} = 1 \text{ oz.} \qquad 14.3 \text{ grams meth}$$
$$14.3 + 28.5 = 42.8$$

$$
\begin{array}{r}
\$120\,\text{gram} \\
\times 43 \\
\hline
\$5,160
\end{array}
$$

Subtract 5 grams uncut personal

$$
\begin{array}{r}
\$5,160 \\
-600 \\
\hline
\$4,560
\end{array}
$$

Not bad. He could sell this stuff in a week, maybe two. That was nearly two thousand dollars profit. Figure it out. Nobody makes that kind of money working in a bowling alley. Alex scooped five grams into a small bottle for himself, capped it, cut pages of an old *Playboy* into three-inch squares, then blended the remaining coke with meth until the shades of white blended consistently. Weighing it into grams, half-grams, quarters, he dumped each portion onto a square of paper and folded it into a tiny envelope. When he finished he snorted a long, thick line, turned his stereo on, then dropped to the floor and did fifty army-style push-ups, clapping hands on the fall.

Sonny stumbled out of bed, head throbbing. Hung over. He gazed at the clock on the dresser. Six-thirty A.M. Fumbling for his cigarettes, he stuck one in his mouth, lit a match. The first drag made him dizzy and he had to brace himself against the wall for a moment. As he slid into his work shirt, he noticed Lonnie curled up in bed, a ball of rumpled hair peeping from beneath a gray blanket. He crossed the room to sit gently on the edge of the mattress. Hip touched spine. His brother's warmth radiated through

the covers. He studied the smoothness of his face, clear and
fine, cheeks a soft pink, his lips thin like Mom's. Like his
own, he thought. But his eyes—they looked old, worn, as
if they belonged to a worried man twice his age. Already
there were wrinkles, like hairline cracks in glass, straying
from the corners. He was squinting, jaws clenched. What
was he dreaming about?

Sonny softly stroked his brother's hair. You know, he
thought, it was getting harder and harder to get through to
the kid as he grew older—instead of easier, like it should've.
The younger, the less reasonable. Sensible. The older, the
more reasonable. Shame it didn't always work that way.
Stifling a cough into his fist, glancing around the room for
an ashtray, he spotted Lonnie's clothes on the floor. Soaking wet. What the hell was he doing? Where had he been?
There was a lot to straighten out and although he needed
time to think, to find the right words, gentle but stern
words, he couldn't put it off any longer. He had to work
today and tonight and tomorrow. They might not be able
to talk again for another week. That was too long to wait.

Something clicked in his head. He dashed his smoke in
the ashtray on the dresser, grabbed his shoes, and followed
the music he heard down the hall to Alex's room. He rattled the knob. It was locked. He pounded on the door.

"Who is it?"

"Me."

"Whatta you want?"

"I want to talk."

"What about?"

"Your car, asshole."

Alex turned the stereo up. "Fuck off."

Suddenly the bathroom door flew open. *Boom.* A cloud
of steam rolled into the hallway. *"Where the hell you been?"*
Mom bellowed, her voice no longer congested. She stood in
the hallway in jeans and T-shirt, hands on hips, steam
flowing about her legs, her hair wrapped in a pink towel.
"I want an answer."

"Out," Sonny said.

"Don't get smart."

"I stayed over a friend's."

"Your friend don't got a phone?"

"I'm nearly twenty-two, remember?" He heard Alex cackle in the background. Sonny hollered at the door, "Shut your mouth."

"Don't talk to your brother that way."

"That's right. You listen to her," said Alex.

"Just wait," said Sonny.

"I ain't afraid of you," said Alex.

Sonny rattled the knob. "Then come out."

"Stick it, fucker."

"Alex . . . ?"

"Yeah, Mom?"

"You cuss in my home one more time and I'm gonna kick your ass." She grabbed Sonny by the arm and shoved him down the hall. "I'm fed up with your shit. You hear me?"

"I hear you, I hear you," he whined, pulling away from her. "Don't get pushy." She stormed to the kitchen sink and fished the coffeepot out from beneath a clutter of dirty dishes, banging pots and pans, making as much noise as Sonny thought humanly possible. He winced, his head pounding, as he sat at the table to put on his shoes.

"Your agent called. 'Course I didn't know where you was. You don't tell me." She dumped the pot of water into the Mr. Coffee on the counter. The silver burner was stained black with layers upon layers of coffee residue. "How do you think it sounds to people? Huh? What kinda mother do they think I am? Two o'clock in the morning and I don't know where the hell my boy is? Huh? You could be dead for all I know." She pursed her lips, narrowed her eyes. "But you don't give a damn, do you? No, you don't give a damn about anybody but you."

He cradled his head, elbows on knees, rubbing his forehead. "When did she call?"

"When what?"

"My agent."

"Don't raise your voice to me." She pulled her hand back as if she were going to slap him. "You live under this roof, you live by *my* rules or get out. Wanna pack up and go?" she hollered, pointing to the door. "You know the way."

I move out, he thought, and what are you going to do? You don't make enough hustling nickels and dimes at Denny's to buy your own liquor. But he didn't say it. Mom might talk tough but it only took a few well-placed words to break her. She'd run to her room crying and then he'd feel like an asshole. The next hour would be spent apologizing.

Sonny went to the phone and called his agent.

"Schwartz and Associates."

"Let me talk to Donna."

"This is her service. Can I take a message?"

Damn. It was Saturday. He left his work number, name, and hung up. As he tied his shoes, he glanced at the Mr. Coffee on the counter. Water dripped into the pot, hot and clear, steaming. Mom had forgotten the coffee. Fuck it. He'd get a cup on the way to work.

Lonnie rolled over in bed. If they quit fighting right now, maybe, just maybe, there would be no major explosion. It seemed someone always slipped and said something low and vicious. Always a cheap shot. Always someone was hurt. This time he thought his brother was in the wrong, that he should've called when he knew he wouldn't be home. But Mom was wrong, too, for overreacting. He gripped the pillow. The sheets were damp with sweat and he shifted, searching for a cool spot. Any second now he expected Sonny to raise his voice, shout back, but he hoped he'd remain calm. "Hang on," he mumbled. "Mom'll blow herself out. You know how she is."

He wondered if other families fought as much as his but he didn't see how it was possible. They argued constantly. Why couldn't they get along anymore? Lonnie remembered when they lived with Uncle Ernie and how there were hardly any fights. If Sonny or Alex stooped to a cheap shot Ernie gave them a look that shamed them into silence. There was a sense of closeness and respect among them then which was definitely missing now. And that was sad. Family was all you had. What scared him was how, after a fight, Sonny or Alex or Mom could go for days without speaking. They'd hold their anger inside, in their eyes, fixing each other at exactly the right moment when a cold stare hurt for all it was worth. The atmosphere was tense, delicate, like a time bomb waiting to explode. A person couldn't live like that. *Family was all you had.* He nodded, confirming it. *And if you couldn't goddamn get along you sure as hell couldn't call yourself much of a family.*

Covering his head with the pillow, he tried to drown the voices out, wishing he could turn them off like the TV and split. He pretended that he didn't care what they said to each other or how long they carried grudges and that the fear he felt for his family didn't exist. But it didn't work, it never worked. He threw the pillow on the floor. No matter how hard he tried to act tough, spit and shrug it off, the fighting still worried him. Mom's voice penetrated the room again. Suddenly the apartment door slammed and he knew Sonny had left. Putting his finger to the wall, he let it slide down slowly, leaving a faint trail of oil and dirt, gray on white. How long did it take a letter to travel from L.A. to Gilroy?

"What'd you say?"
"I told him to talk to you."
"That all?"
"He knows it came from Safeway."
"What else?"
"Nothing."
"No lie?"
"No lie."
"Good boy."

"I did you right, huh?" Lonnie patted the Riviera's fender. "You couldn't have got it going without me."

"Whatcha want?"

"A favor."

"Depends," Alex said, shrugging.

"Don't tell him I wired it."

"Whatta you care?"

"Just don't, okay?"

"It was my car, A."

"That ain't it."

"You didn't steal nothin'."

"Tell that to Sonny."

"Fuck Sonny."

"Say you found it wired. For me. Okay?"

"Relax, I'll handle the asshole." Alex reached for his coveralls hanging from a nail on the garage wall. Battery acid had eaten holes in the sleeves and the cuffs were spotted with light green mildew. The smell was sour, wretched. "Sonny thinks he's a fuckin' cop or something. Know what I mean?" He threw the coveralls at the big garbage bin outside the garage. They landed a few feet short, knocking over an empty beer can, sending it clattering down the alley.

Alex didn't need them, anyway, Lonnie thought. When something went wrong, when the engine began making strange noises, he'd turn the radio up and keep driving. Not until the car broke down completely did he even consider opening the hood. He didn't put in oil or water, either, unless the idiot lights in the dash flashed on. Whoever had the Riviera last, Lonnie thought, at least took good care of it. The motor had never sounded better.

"Wanna take a ride?" Alex said, slipping a stick of Juicyfruit into his mouth. "There's something I gotta ask you."

Lonnie hesitated. "I was going to see Sonny at work today."

Alex snapped his gum a few times. "C'mon, keep me company. Don't let that prick get you down. Look at you,

A. All bent over like a old man. Keep your chin up." He placed his hands on Lonnie's shoulders and pushed. "Stand straight. Walk tall, *ese*, walk tall. That's what it's all about." He slapped Lonnie on the back. "Hey, check it out," he said, strutting around the Riviera. "Chain steering wheel, shag on the dash." Leaning inside the cab, he flicked the pair of foam dice suspended from the rearview mirror with his finger. "Is this shit outta date or is this shit outta date? Look here. Dingo balls, too. Fuckin' watch this, A." A grin stretched across his face as he pressed a button beneath the dash. The body of the car rose. "Now it's normal." Pressed again. The body sank until it was four inches from the garage floor. "Now it ain't. Magic, huh?" Lonnie stood silent, slouching, unimpressed. It was a lowrider with hydraulics. So what? Hadn't Alex seen one before?

"C'mere, I'll cheer your ass up." As Alex threw his arm around him, Lonnie caught a powerful whiff of Juicyfruit and cologne. "Try some of this." Alex reached into his boot and handed him a tiny envelope and a plastic straw. "It'll put your head in the right place." Lonnie stared at the envelope apprehensively for a moment, then opened it just enough to slip the straw inside, and sniffed. It burned his nostril, his eyes watered, he stifled a ferocious sneeze. *"Goddamn."* He shuddered. *"What is this shit?"* Alex hustled him into the Riviera and started the engine. "You can go fifteen with Roberto Duran in a minute," he said, laughing, as they pulled out of the alley.

They cruised at twenty miles an hour in a thirty-five zone. Cars zipped by. Annoyed drivers glared at them. Alex turned the radio up loud, rolled down his window, sank into his seat, and threw his head back. "Step on it," Lonnie said, feeling foolish. "I could fuckin' crawl faster." His brother gave him a sly look, eyes half-mast. "Low and slow, *ese.* That's what it's all about." There were people and sights to see and Lonnie's thoughts were clipped, passing and changing as quickly and indifferently as the scenery. Occasionally he sniffled and tasted the coke/meth as it slipped down the back of his throat. An electric high, not dopey, not slow like marijuana or liquor. A plastic statue of the Virgin Mary vibrated on the dashboard as he drummed in time to the music, speeding, high, no worries.

They made one delivery in Studio City, two in Hollywood. Another in Laurel Canyon. "That's where Frank Zappa used to live." Alex pointed to an old house modeled after a rugged log cabin. Across the street was the mansion where Harry Houdini once lived. Nearby another house lay in ruins at the foot of the canyon. It had slid down the hillside in the last major rain storm. Beams, ceiling joists, studs, and plumbing jutted from the walls like broken bones.

They worked their way east, toward Echo Park.

"Could you drop me off at the station?"

"Quit worrying about that asshole."

"I ain't worrying."

"So what's the problem? He don't own you."

"I just wanna talk to him."

"Wanna talk, talk to me. I'm your fuckin' brother, too. The thing is I treat you like a man, he treats you like a kid. Whatta you wanna be? A kid or a man? You gotta make up your mind. You're gonna be sixteen soon." He leaned over and punched him in the arm. "Know what I was doing at your age? Fuckin' working. Pulling my own weight. So maybe I screwed up in school but I always knew I had a good head. A business head. That's what counts. I got intelligence, *instinctive intelligence.* Fuck that school shit. I'm gonna be rich." Stopped at a red light, Alex reached for his wallet, flipped it open, and flashed a thick pile of bills. "Know what I started with today? *Two* fuckin' dollars, A." The light dropped to green. They drove on, top speed twenty miles an hour.

"I got a proposition to make," he said, smiling. "Those punks at your fancy-ass school got money. I know they do. And I know me and you could rake it in. Whatta you say? I'll split with you seventy-thirty jus' for leg work." No

answer. Lonnie stared silently ahead. He flipped open his
wallet again. "Did you see this or what? Don't be an ass."
He shook the money under his brother's nose. "If you got
an opportunity, take it. Ain't no second chances in this
world. You help me, I help you. Teamwork, A. We'll fuckin' deal this whole town." They turned onto Mohawk Avenue and parked in front of a run-down apartment complex.
Glancing around once, Alex reached inside his jacket and
pulled out the .38. "Nice, huh?" he said, stroking the cylin-
der.

Lonnie's eyes widened. "Whatta you carrying a gun
for?"

"Protection, A."

"You're crazy."

"You mean smart."

"Bullshit."

"Everybody with any sense got one nowadays."

"Get rid of it."

He held it out to him by the barrel. Lonnie wagged his
head, waving it away, disgusted. "Open your eyes, man,"
Alex said. "You'll see what I mean." He winked, grinned,
then shoved the gun back inside his jacket. "Nobody fucks
with Alex. And if they fuck with you, they fuck with me.
Look at it that way if it makes you feel better." He hopped
out of the car. "Be back in a second. Think about what I
said. You could get a 'Vette in a couple years maybe."

Slumping into his seat, he watched his brother climb a
set of stairs, arms swinging freely at his sides as he crossed
an open hallway lined with doors. The screens on most of
the windows were missing or badly torn. A barren rock
garden spanned the front of the building. Someone was
cooking somewhere and the smell of grease was in the air.
Up the street a pack of kids played football, shouting, half
of them stripped to the waist. Skins versus Shirts. Another
bunch huddled around the mailbox on the corner. A lanky
black kid with a long face carried a big AM-FM thirty-watt

radio-cassette player-tape deck strapped across his shoulder. Music blasted through the neighborhood.

The door opened and he saw his brother disappear inside the apartment. He shook his head. What was this town's fascination with coke? It was ridiculously expensive, and most of the time it only made him nervous. Tense. Alex was looking pale and skinny, and he thought if he lost much more weight he might get sick. He lit a cigarette, then turned the car radio up full blast. The lanky kid swung around. Squinting one eye, Lonnie shot him a mean look. Hood, he thought. Think you're bad? Well, you ain't.

The Playboys of Echo Park ran out of beer. Paranoia struck. They were going to a dance at Sacred Heart later tonight and not one of them had the nerve to step on the dance floor unless he was drunk. A collection was taken. Rudy, the only Playboy over twenty-one, was elected to drive to the 7-11 and pick up another case of Coors. His car was the last of eight shining Chevies parked in the driveway of the Playboys' clubhouse, a garage in back of the president's parents' home.

Rudy's Chevy had long chrome side pipes that grumbled deep like a speedboat, smooth like a saxophone. He spent the afternoon washing and waxing the body, polishing the chrome, until it sparkled inside and out. After the dance tonight the Playboys would form a motorcade and cruise Whittier Boulevard or Hollywood like peacocks strutting their colors. At the end of the main drag they'd loop around and cruise it again. And again. Round and round in circles. About midnight they'd stop at the Jack-in-the-Box and hang around the parking lot and have a smoke and a few beers. Talk cars. Watch the pretty Chicanas tease their hair, snap their gum, straining butterfly-colored eyes along the main drag, whistling and wooing the finest lowriders. And when the Playboys left, they left together, all at once like an army. It looked better, felt better. It showed style, class,

organization. It was safer. If a cop waved down one Playboy, they waved down all the Playboys, and not many cops
were that ambitious.

As Rudy cruised for the 7-11 he spotted the Riviera
parked on Mohawk and slowed down to take a good look.
He noticed every lowrider on the road, parked or moving,
and compared it to his Chevy. The Riviera was so-so. It had
potential but it was still light-years away from being a
master machine. Halfway up the block he realized what
he'd just seen and hit the brakes.

A second later Alex hustled downstairs and jumped into
the Riviera. "The guy wants another half," he said, turning
the radio off. "We'll come back tonight." They rolled down
Mohawk, headed toward home, when he reached across the
seat and grabbed Lonnie's arm. "Keep what I told you
under your hat." Lonnie jerked his arm free. "It's between
you and me, *not* fuckin' Sonny."

Rudy dashed to the phone booth at the Shell station
across from the Palms Apartments. He tapped on the glass
door. The old man inside opened it a crack. His face was
grizzled and he wore a long wool overcoat with the collar
turned up. A shopping cart loaded with groceries rested
against a parking bumper nearby.

"What do you want?" he growled.

"I gotta use the phone."

"So do I."

"It's an emergency."

"Go away."

The old man shut the door, turned his back to him,
slipped a dime in the slot. *"Hey,"* Rudy shouted, grabbing
the grocery cart. The old man stumbled out of the booth,
waving his hands over his head, hollering in Spanish. Rudy
led him on for a few yards and then, just as the old man
caught up with him, he veered to one side and gave the cart
a swift push. The old man gasped, staggering after it. The

cart rolled off the curb and toppled over. A head of cabbage bounced into the street.

Rudy trotted back to the phone booth.

Jay Petty and his brother were watching a cop show on TV when the phone rang. He hollered at his wife to answer it. The baby started bawling. Jay gritted his teeth.

"Jay there?"

"Hang on." She held the receiver to her bosom. "It's for you."

"Who is it?"

"He didn't say."

"Find out."

"Who is it?"

"Rudy."

"Rudy," she hollered.

Jay dragged himself to the phone. The elastic band of a black hairnet was angled across his forehead like a widow's peak. "Get me another beer while you're up," his brother said. His brother's shirt sleeve was pinned to his shoulder; his right bicep was round and thick as a calf's thigh. He had lost his left arm in a motorcycle wreck six years ago at the age of seventeen, racing a Transam down the coast highway, high on PCP. Eighty-five miles an hour without a helmet. He was two months in a coma. Suffered minor brain damage. When he came out of it he had to learn how to speak all over again. Even now he sometimes strained to remember common words. Simple arithmetic baffled him. He drove an old primer gray Chevy Impala, and worked off and on as a lumper for a cousin who owned a small trucking firm.

When Jay picked up the phone, Rudy said, "I found your ride." Rudy gave him exact directions.

"I'm on my way."

"I'm going, Jay."

"Sure."

"I don't want nothin' to do with it."

"Don't worry."

"Fine."

Click.

Jay swung around and bumped into his wife who had been standing behind him listening. He glared at her. The baby continued to bawl. "Shut that fuckin' kid up." She winced, stumbling backward. "It's fuckin' driving me crazy."

The Playboys were mad. It had been over an hour. No Rudy.

"Maybe he got jumped."

"Naw."

"We're gonna be late."

"Leave it to Rudy."

"The jerk."

"We shoulda went with him."

"Ten more minutes and we go."

Six nodded, one dissenter. A quorum.

"That's it."

"But maybe he got in a wreck."

"Somebody shut this guy up."

A raised Dodge, yellow flame painted on the hood, skidded to a halt behind the Standard station. Sonny looked up from the tire machine, drawing an arm across his forehead, wiping sweat. A red rag hung from his back pocket. Inside the Dodge were two boys and three girls, drinking Boone's Farm wine, giggling. The kid driving wore a Fairfax jacket with medals pinned to the letter.

"Ray around?"

"*Ray?*" Sonny shouted. "*Your ride's here.*"

"*Comin'.*" He grabbed his street shirt from the coat rack as he passed through the garage. "I didn't get a chance to clean the bathrooms."

"That's all right."

"You workin' tomorrow?"

"Not unless you want to take my shift."

Ray laughed.

"See you later. Have a good time."

"Come over when you get off. We bought a keg of Lowenbrau. Lots of ladies'll be there." Ray raised his eyebrows lecherously. "They love older men." The kid in the Dodge revved the engine. Thunder.

"If I'm not there by eleven," Sonny said, "don't look for me." Ray hopped into the backseat with one of the girls. She kissed him, then raised the bottle of wine to his lips as the Dodge sped off, leaving rubber on the asphalt. They were going to get sicker than dogs drinking that sweet shit, he thought, shaking his head.

He stepped on the pedal and the machine hissed, exhaling. Removing the iron bar, he spun the clasp off the rim and inflated the tire. He was getting too old for this job. Been here too long. All the other attendants were four or five years younger than him, about his age when he first started working here. Four years at a gas station. Was he fucking crazy? The only person who had stayed on longer than himself was a Vietnamese immigrant, and he left shortly after he learned to speak English fairly well.

Cradling the tire, he squatted, then heaved it into the rack overhead without a bounce. Two down, one to go. Sonny stood in the doorway of the garage, resting for a moment. The big Thrifty store sign across the street shone bright. A breeze cooled the sweat behind his ears. Saturday night. Damn, he wished he was someplace else.

A woman in a Ford drove over the cord in the driveway. The bell rang. Tucking in his shirt, Sonny hurried out to wait on her. Another credit card customer. Why couldn't people use cash once in a while? He gave her her copy of the receipt and returned to the garage, eyeing Mr. Hill through the office window, feet up on his desk, drinking coffee while he read the evening paper. "Lazy sonofabitch," Sonny muttered. Mr. Hill could've waited on that one. He wrestled another tire onto the machine and then bent over, hands on knees, suddenly faint. Rolling his head around, stretching his neck, he glanced at the Pennzoil clock on the wall. Eight-forty-five P.M. He'd been here ten long hours and had to work again first thing tomorrow morning. Another car rolled in. The bell rang. Mr. Hill passed him on his way to the pumps. "I'm going to Thrifty's for an ice cream," he said. "Can you handle it alone?" Sonny nodded without looking at him. What difference did it make? Look at the man's hands! Clean. Sure as hell wasn't working with them, was he?

A minute later two more cars pulled into the station. Sonny ran back and forth, filling a Datsun with unleaded, an old Buick with regular, collecting money from another driver, racing to the office for change.

The phone rang.

"Standard. Can you hold on?"

"Is Sonny Baer there?"

Someone honked for service.

"That's me. Hang on."

"This is Donna. Where the hell have you been?"

Another car rolled in. Bing-bing. He wanted to rip the bell off the wall. A driver waved a credit card in the air at him. "Always," Donna said. "*Always* leave a number where I can reach you." A station wagon full of Cub Scouts descended on the place like an invasion of guerrilla terrorists. Bright yellow scarfs darted here and there, headless ghosts. A chubby Scout with braces banged on the office door. "*We lost a quarter in the machine.*" Another whined for the key to the bathroom. A man shouted across the station for his change.

"Lemme call you back."

"You got the job."

His heart skipped a beat.

"You'll start Monday. The producer's on a tight budget but you know how that goes. As it stands you'll work ten days for no less than four thousand. We're going back and forth with him now, so keep your fingers crossed. I may be able to get us more. He really, really liked you, Sonny. What did you *do?*"

Gas streamed down the side of the Buick. The lady inside jumped out, screaming toward the office. *"I'm not paying for that."* Another car drove in. The bell rang. Three Cub Scouts were shaking and rocking the Coca-Cola machine.

"Hello . . . Sonny?"

He couldn't speak.

"Are you there?"

Mr. Hill burst into the office, jowls vibrating. A Brahma bull, breathing fire. *"Are you out of your mind?"* He threw his ice cream cone in the waste can and pointed to the pumps. *"Get to work."*

Sonny cocked his head, smiling. "Know what you can do with your job?"

Tania strolled into Don the Beachcomber, holding her head high, clutching Dan's arm. The host led them through the darkness to a table overlooking a small waterfall behind glass that fell silently into a pond of pink and white lillies and goldfish. Green and yellow floodlights shone below the surface, indistinct, the colors wavering in the ripples of the water. They ordered sweet drinks served in hollow pineapples and sipped them through thin red straws. "Hold still," he said, reaching across the table. He gently wiped a speck of foam from her upper lip with his finger.

Tania drew her hand lightly across her mouth. "Is it gone?" Her other hand fluttered up to check her hair. He nodded, grinning, his cheeks red from liquor like a robust Santa Claus.

"What do you think about marrying me?"

"You're drunk," she said, laughing.

"If we left tonight we could be in Vegas by morning."

"Are you jokin'?"

"I'm not joking."

She made a goofy face. "I work Monday."

"Only if you wanted."

"You are jokin'."

"I'm not."

"Then you must be drunk." She poured his drink into hers. "No more."

An hour later they were on their way to Las Vegas. Plastic party cups, a bottle of vodka, and Collins mix lay on the floorboard of the car. Tania giggled like a schoolgirl up to something naughty as they barreled across the dark highway. Goddamn it, she thought, it was her life and she could damn well do what she pleased. She was tired of being lonely, tired of going to bed alone, waking up alone, always alone. Lonnie would live with them in a house where a family belonged. The other boys were plenty old enough to move out on their own. Dan knew her situation, and obviously it hadn't kept him from proposing. They'd discuss the details later. Tonight was their night and nothing was going to spoil it. She couldn't let the boys control her life.

Tossing her shoes in the backseat, she rubbed a stocking foot along the inside of Dan's calf while she made drinks, spilling mixer in her lap, not caring. The radio played easy rock. Solid road purred beneath them over the drone of the engine. Mountains surrounded them, only the crest visible, a smooth, rolling outline, black and vast like an ocean bay at night. Resting her head on his shoulder, she licked his ear, in and out, as if she were sucking an oyster. Goosebumps rose up and down his arms and he shivered. Tania rubbed them away, then reached down to his pants. Unzipped them. Smiled. They swerved over the line occasionally, hitting the turtleback reflectors, the tires going thump-thump-thump as she teased him hard.

He flipped off the kitchen light and they stumbled out of the apartment. "All you gotta do is deliver, collect, split," Alex said. "I take care of the rest." Lonnie slid down the handrail, cigarette in mouth, feigning indifference. His brother wanted an answer bad and he felt a power over him. "And you always get coke for yourself. No cost. That's one of the fringe benefits." They hopped into the Riviera and drove down the alley. "Know what we need? We need a tattoo." He punched Lonnie in the shoulder. "Get it right there. Real professional like."

"They fade when you get old."

"Not professional."

"Yeah." Lonnie nodded. "Professional, too."

"Know what? You think too fuckin' much." Alex was switching stations on the radio when a car pulled out from behind the loading dock on the other side of the alley. *"Look at that asshole."* He honked the horn. Headlights shone in their eyes. It sounded like a cherry bomb only tinnier and more sudden. The front window shattered. A gust of wind swept through the cab. Glass ticked against the dash and the walls of the car like a flurry of party ice. The Riviera zigzagged through a picket fence, its front end rising off the ground, crushing row upon row of rose bushes, spinning in a half-circle before it stopped dead in the middle of the yard. Lonnie doubled over under the glove compartment, cradling his head. The radio was static. A burning cigarette smoldered on the floorboard. Alex fumbled for the door handle and fell out onto the soft, damp lawn. Dazed. A light inside the house flashed on. Suddenly he heard the screech of tires, the roar of an engine accelerating.

"Bastards," he screamed, stumbling to his feet, running. He threw his jacket open and pulled out the .38 just as the Chevy was turning out of the alley. Extending his arms, bracing his legs, he squeezed the trigger. Click. Nothing. Click. Click. Click. No fucking bullets. The roar of the engine faded. Alex groaned, dashing to the end of the alley. Bits of glass tinkled from his hair to the ground like confetti. Far away, past two intersections already, were the red tail lights of the Chevy. *"Bastards."* Iron gates barred the windows and doors of the shops along the deserted street. He ran to the end of the block and stumbled off the curb and fell. The red tail lights disappeared into the darkness.

"Bastards." His voice sounded guttural, strained, like the bay of a bloodhound. A car with one headlight passed silently on the street. Moaning, Alex picked himself up and limped back down the sidewalk to the alley.

A woman in curlers stood staring from the window of her apartment. Other window shades were drawn, rooms lit, doors open. People in bathrobes and slippers watched safely from stair landings and balconies. A kid pressed his head through the metal bars of the handrailing while his mother screamed at him to get inside.

Alex glared at the kids as he crossed the yard to the Riviera, his vision blurred with tears. The driver's door was open, the dome light burned dimly, the engine still idled. Lonnie was slumped over in the front seat with his head in his hands. His eyes were shut in a tight wince. Blood colored the cracks between his fingers and he was panting as if he couldn't get enough air. "I'm here, man. I'm here." Alex eased himself into the front seat. "You're gonna be okay." He took his brother's wrist in two fingers and lifted.

At first Lonnie resisted but then he moaned and let his hand relax. A small patch of skin and hair, like a ragged piece of cloth, flapped open and dangled from his temple. A bit of skull showed white. The hair around his ear was soaked black and the ear itself was mangled, a bloody little knob. Alex grimaced as he let go of the wrist and pitched backward. Lonnie immediately covered the wound. "There's gonna be cops. Can you hear me? There's gonna be cops and they're gonna ask questions." He reached to turn off the engine and noticed that his fingers were bloody. Gasping, he wiped them on the seat. "Don't say nothin', nothin' to nobody." He gulped, feeling sick to his stomach. "Understand? Nothin'."

Lonnie rocked back and forth, groaning. "Call an ambulance."

"Did you hear me?"

His lips trembled, his chest jerked.

"Don't say nothin'."

Moaned. "Call an ambulance."

"We don't wanna get busted."

He tried to scream it but it came out weak, choked and hoarse. *"Call a fuckin' ambulance."* Blood rolled down his forearm and dripped off his elbow onto his pants leg. Alex gulped, holding his breath to keep from gagging. "It *hurts,*" he moaned, rocking further toward his knees. "It *hurts.*" A second later, when Alex made no move to leave, he opened his eyes and tried to sit up and reach for the door handle. Blood stained the dash where he had first cradled his head. The carpet on the floorboard was damp, black.

"Hold on, A. I'm going." Alex breathed in and out through his mouth, deep and fast, hyperventilating. "Hang on." As he backed out of the car he grabbed his brother's shoulder and pulled, forcing him to stretch out along the seat. "You're gonna be okay." Lonnie tossed, kicking at the door, groaning, cradling his head tighter. "Stay still, god-damn it."

Then he felt the seat rise, the dome light went off, and he was alone again. The side of his face burned and he curled up, chest to knees, his forehead beaded with sweat. Blood trickled from behind his neck down the front of his T-shirt.

The wail of a siren sounded in the distance. Sharp pains like hot needles tingled in his groin. His Levis clung to his thighs, binding him as he bucked his hips. He felt feverish, then cold—feverish—cold—shivering then sweating. A loud ringing vibrated in his head. The stench of blood and sweat mixed with the smoke from the smoldering cigarette. He thought he heard a voice. Footsteps. "Alex?" he moaned. Silence. The side of his face had gone numb. "Alex?" Grasping the top of the seat, he struggled to pull himself up. The siren grew louder. Another joined it. He collapsed beside the steering wheel. His eyes kept wanting to roll back into his head but he was afraid if he let them that he'd lose consciousness.

He heard a voice again, lots of voices, and knew a crowd had gathered in the alley. Sirens wound down, power cut. Car doors opened and closed. He traced a finger along the ridge of his ear, wincing, tasting the salt of blood on his tongue. Swallowed dryly. There was no lobe. He bit his lower lip. The skin bubbled beneath his hand as if it were afloat. He felt again. Wet. Gritted his teeth against the pain. There was no lobe. Suddenly the sky was bright with spotlights. The rush of men, coins and keys jingling in pockets, the rustle of jackets and stiff leather holsters, surrounded the Riviera. *"Who shot you?"* Flashlights darted through the cab, blinding him from all angles. *"Who shot you? Who shot you?"* Lonnie turned the side of his face up for them to see, letting his eyes drift back into his head.

15

The clock on the wall in the emergency waiting room showed ten-thirty P.M. The lieutenant motioned him through a pair of swinging doors into a quiet hallway.

"It was a Chevy?"

"Yeah."

"What year?"

"Old. Sixty-seven, sixty-eight."

"Make?"

"Impala."

"Are you sure?"

"Yeah. It was the kind . . ." Alex stopped himself from saying *spics*. "The kind a lotta guys make lowriders outta." He was sure the cop knew. There were thousands all over L.A. "Want me to try my mom again?" The cop nodded. Alex walked to the phone booth down the hall, slipped a coin into the slot, dialed. His eyebrows were furrowed in concern as he listened to it ring on the other end. Could've been Pete, he thought. Could've been the punk he fought last March who vowed to kill him. Could've had to do with the Riviera, could've been a lot of assholes he knew. Had known. The only thing he felt sure of was that they were aiming for him, not Lonnie. On the tenth ring he hung up and shook his head. "Nobody home," he said, stepping out of the booth.

A fluorescent light flickered overhead. The flowers in the dark display window of the gift shop were wilted. Now and then a nurse carrying a stainless steel tray glided past in soft-soled shoes. An old man sat slumped in a wheelchair in a baggy white paper gown at the end of the corridor. Alex shrugged. "I don't know where she is." The cop removed his glasses and methodically cleaned the lenses with the slack of his shirt.

"*Was* it a lowrider?"

He nodded.

"What color?"

"Blue." No. "Gray, it was primer gray."

"Did you notice anything else? A dented fender, maybe? A broken tail light? Did it have special rims?"

"I didn't get a good look."

"How many were in the vehicle?"

"Three or four."

"But you're not sure?"

"Hadda be at least three."

"Would you recognize them if you saw them again?"

"It was dark." He snapped his fingers. "It happened like that."

The cop blinked, replaced his glasses, and glanced up from his notebook. Alex pinched the bridge of his nose, shielding bloodshot eyes. He knew his pupils were twice normal size, that he looked high, but so far the cop hadn't said anything about it to him. Considering all he'd drunk and snorted in the past few days, he hadn't once slurred his words or stumbled walking. And he was clean. The .38 and his coke, his razors and straws, he hid in the apartment when he went to phone an ambulance.

"Was the shot fired from inside the Impala?"

"Yeah."

"Was the vehicle in motion?"

"Yeah."

"From which side of the vehicle was the shot fired?"

"The backseat, I think."

"Were you able to see that person's face?"

"Sorta. It happen real fast like I said. They just kinda whipped in front." His nostrils flared, he made a fist. Those dirty motherfuckers. "They just done it. Like they didn't even know him, like they didn't never even seen him before."

He waited a moment for Alex to calm down. "The person in the backseat," he said. "Could you identify his ethnic group?"

"Yeah, he was an ethnic all right."

The cop sighed.

A woman's voice squawked over the PA system:

DR. LOW LINE THREE . . .
DR. LOW LINE THREE.

"Was he black?"

"Uh uh."

"Hispanic?"

"You mean Mexican?"

The cop nodded.

Alex's face lit up. Now the sonofabitch was getting warm. "These hadda be cholos," he said. They were the only ones who pulled that potshot shit. Them and niggers.

"Why's that, son?" the cop asked, removing his glasses again, staring squarely at Alex. "Why Mexicans?"

" 'Cause I saw 'em, that's why."

He wrote in his notebook, face expressionless. "Do you have any idea who it may have been or who may have set your brother up? An old enemy? Someone who has a grudge against your brother or yourself? For any reason? Has anyone in your family been in a fight recently, or had an argument with someone you think might do something like this? Is there any reason for anyone to want to hurt your brother?"

Alex shifted nervously, glancing down the hall. His palms were sweating. He shook his head sadly but wisely, as if he'd already given those questions a great deal of thought. "My family's decent people. Not everybody likes us, that's for sure, but nobody, nobody in my family hangs with scum. I mean the scum like you know I mean." It had to be someone he knew, he thought, some customer maybe, someone who knew how much cash and coke he carried on him. Whatever the case, he didn't plan to tell the cop any more than necessary. The worst thing that could happen would be to have a parade of patrol cars cruising the neighborhood, making a beat of it, sticking their noses into everyone's business. He intended to take care of matters himself. Later. His own way.

"Why don't you try your mother again?" the cop said, slapping his notebook shut. Alex fished a coin from his pocket as he stepped into the phone booth, leaving the door open, showing he had nothing to hide.

A tow truck hauled the Riviera from the yard. All Sonny saw was the rear end disappearing around the corner as he turned into the alley. It could've been anyone's car. The picket fence lay flat across the garden, a track of broken slates and wire. Old Man Wheat puttered about the dark yard with a shovel while the last two remaining cops stepped into their patrol car. He thought of stopping to ask what had happened but figured it would be gossip by tomorrow. Some drunk must have run into it. After parking the 'Vette, he rushed upstairs with a bag of liquor under his arm, set it on the kitchen table, and hurried to the bedroom to look for Lonnie. His smile faded to a frown. The room was empty. He checked on Alex. The bed was made. Mom's room was empty too. "Wouldn't you know it?" he mumbled, popping the cork on a bottle of Dom Perignon. It hit

the ceiling. He shook his head. "Wouldn't you goddamn
know it?"

The phone rang.

"Sonny?"

"Where is everyone?"

"Mom around?"

"No one's around. Is Lonnie with you?"

He ground his teeth. "No, but I know where he is."
Christ, he thought, biting his lower lip, this was going to
be hard.

"Don't go away." Alex heard footsteps in the background followed by the loud clang of cans. "Hear that?"
Sonny said. "Foster's. Hear this?" The clink of bottles.
"Dom Perignon. It finally happened for me, man. It finally
fuckin' happened. I declare a truce, a cease-fire for the
night. Get Lonnie and come home."

Holding the receiver against his chest, Alex waved the
cop over. "It's my older brother," he said, stepping out of
the booth. "Could you do it for me?" A pale light shone
through the doorway down the hall and fell across the
linoleum floor as Alex leaned against the wall, waiting.
Two nurses strolled by, talking in low voices. The air was
stuffy. The PA system crackled. He caught the glint of
chrome spokes in the flicker of the fluorescent light. The
withered old man was rocking the wheelchair, trying to
make it move.

A half hour passed. The PA system squawked again:

NURSE DAVEY SEE DR. LOW . . .
NURSE DAVEY, SEE DR. LOW.

He squeezed between a Puerto Rican woman and a teenager at the counter in the emergency room, ignoring the
dirty looks they gave him. The cop had left twenty minutes
earlier. A receptionist sat behind his desk at a typewriter,

phone receiver clamped between cheek and shoulder, asking questions and typing the answers as they came. "How's my brother?" Alex said, leaning over the counter. The receptionist kept typing. An unshaven man coughed convulsively on the lobby couch, his chest shaking, rattling like a rusty can of loose bolts. Occasionally he wiped phlegm from a pink hole in his throat with a soiled handkerchief and then glanced shyly around the waiting room as if to apologize. "How's my brother?" Alex said again, only louder. The receptionist continued to peck at the typewriter. He sighed, aggravated. He imagined capturing the hoods, driving them to a deserted spot in Griffith Park late at night, making them kneel, then blasting two of them in the back of the head. The third punk, the bastard who actually shot Lonnie, would sob and plead for mercy as Alex stuck the barrel of the .38 into the fucker's mouth. But, just as he was about to pull the trigger, he'd throw the gun to the ground. For one pitiful second the sonofabitch would think he'd had a change of heart. Then, from behind his back, would come an axe. Down. Again and again and again.

A hard tap on the shoulder. He jumped, spinning around. Sonny stood glaring at him, his pants greasy from work, his breath smelling of tobacco and wine.

"How's Lonnie?"

Clasping Sonny's arm, he smiled sadly, testing him. "I been workin' on it." Sonny glanced down at his arm as if he'd been spit on. A small muscle in his jaw quivered. Alex removed his hand and nervously patted his pockets for cigarettes although he knew he didn't have any. "This guy's an asshole," he said, nodding at the receptionist. "He won't fuckin' answer me." Sonny grabbed his brother's meaty bicep and yanked him backward. His head jerked involuntarily, not from the force of the pull, but from its suddenness. *Never jump, never blink*, he thought. *Control, A. Control is what it's about* . . . "Go ahead." Alex jerked his head again, pretending to flick stray hair from his eyes as he backed quickly away from the counter. "You're better

with words, you always been better with words." His voice
cracked in midsentence. "Fuckin' A, you know how to deal
with these kinda people." He coughed to clear his throat
then dropped to baritone. "I'm on your side. Don't forget
that." *Control is what it's about;* his lips silently formed the
words. Sonny's hands lay flat on the Formica counter top,
his back to Alex, torso shaping upward to shoulders more
like an H than a tapered V. He and Lonnie were built the
same, Alex thought. Barrel-chested, thin and narrow from
behind, but thick and strong in profile.

"Does Mom know?" Alex asked. Either Sonny hadn't
heard or he was ignoring him. "Does Mom know?" Definitely ignoring him. He was about to tap his brother on the
shoulder when the receptionist hung up the phone and
pulled the paper from the typewriter. The Puerto Rican
woman and Sonny lunged forward, butting the teenager
from the counter.

"I need to know how Lonnie Baer is," Sonny said. Stern.
"He's my brother. I want to see him if I can."

"What's his name?"

"Lonnie Baer."

The receptionist slipped the paper back into the typewriter.

"Did you hear me?"

"I heard you," he growled. "How do you spell the last
name?"

"B-a-e-r."

The receptionist made a phone call.

Two men scuffled through the electric doors, holding a
young girl up between them, her stocking feet dragging the
floor. They set her down on the couch and her head rolled
limply to her chest while her skirt rode up her plump thighs
to the dark line of pantyhose. Soon she was whisked down
the hall in a stretcher. A few minutes later a nurse entered
the waiting room and the brothers descended on her.

Dividing eye contact equally between them, she said that
Lonnie was in satisfactory condition. Fourteen buckshot

had been removed from the right side of his face. His ear was badly damaged but, fortunately, it wouldn't affect his hearing. He was lucky. Another inch and he might've lost an eye. Other than that, there was nothing more she could tell them. Lonnie's doctor had left for the night. She suggested they do the same. Tomorrow was another day. It's late, your brother has lost a good deal of blood, he needs sleep. The nurse lightly touched Sonny's arm with a cool, dry hand. Go home, she said.

As she walked off, Alex eyed her legs and the swing of her ass. "C'mon." He nodded toward the electric doors. "I'm fuckin' beat." The muscle in Sonny's jaw twitched again. Cocking his head, Alex grinned, trying to appear relaxed. "I'll tell you everything on the way home."

"He was with you?"

Alex rolled his eyes toward the people on the couch and whispered. "This ain't the place to talk."

"He was with you?"

"I was drivin'." He started for the doors then stopped. "I'm tired, you're tired. Let's go. I need a ride or I wouldn't fuckin' bug you."

"Where'd it happen?"

"In the alley."

"In Old Man Wheat's yard?"

"I don't know." He shrugged, motioning him toward the doors again. "C'mon." Sonny didn't move. "Why you starin' at me like that? I didn't do nothing'." His eyes were wild, wide. He stepped toward him, Alex stepped back. "Don't look at me like that. It wasn't my fault, A. I love him like you love him. Just as goddamn much as you." Sonny clenched his fists, his nostrils flared. Alex raised open palms. "Don't make me hit you. I don't wanna hit you. Please don't make me hit you." His voice trembled as he rocked his head from side to side. "You're drunk, man. You don't know what you're doing."

The first one came high and fast, a blur, grazing his temple. Alex stumbled backward into the wall.

"Fight!" the Puerto Rican woman screamed. *"Fight!"* Sonny sunk his fist deep into hard stomach. A great whoof of air burst from Alex's mouth. The people on the couch scrambled to their feet and huddled in the corner of the waiting room.

Barring his face with forearms, Alex doubled over, catching a flurry on top of the skull, his head swinging left to right with each blow. The coughing man broke from the crowd and grabbed Sonny by the shirt collar. *"Break it up, you."* Sonny spun around, batting the man in the knee, sending him sprawling to the floor.

Sonny landed a clean left. Silver specks swirled in front of Alex's eyes. *Now he's gone and done it.* Groaning, he shifted his block, leaving an opening on the other side. Sonny slammed his eye. *Now he's REALLY gone and done it.* Dropping his guard, Alex popped Sonny hard in the nose. Blood sprayed across the front of his shirt. The Puerto Rican woman gasped. Alex grabbed him around the waist and hurtled him into the wall. Sonny's head hit with a thunk, he slumped to the floor, cupping his nose.

"You had enough?" Alex said, panting. Sweating. Fists cocked. Placing one hand on the floor, Sonny leaned forward to get his balance. "Don't get up." Alex raised his leg to kick him in the mouth but then changed his mind. That was cold, dirty, he couldn't kick his own brother when he was down. "No more. We're even, A." Blood the color of chocolate stains absorbed into Sonny's blue work shirt. He fell at an angle as he rose to his feet, like a sprinter off the block, all his weight behind him, fist on jaw, solid like a home run. A perfect connection, a firm crack. His body followed the whip of his head. He spat. A tooth skittered across the linoleum floor. Sonny charged. Alex wrapped him in a headlock and pounded his face with his free hand as they stumbled through the waiting room, bouncing against the walls, bumping into a table, knocking over the lamp. Suddenly Alex yelped, grasping his side. *"He bit me! The dirty fucker bit me!"* he screamed to the crowd, shocked.

A sharp kick between the legs lifted him off the floor. Clutching himself, Alex groaned and doubled over. Another blow to the base of his skull dropped him.

"Get up," the Puerto Rican woman hollered. *"Get up."* Sonny was banging Alex's head on the hard linoleum when four male nurses pushed through the crowd. A strong forearm crossed his throat. Sonny gasped. More hands clamped shoulders while another pulled at his leg.

For a full five seconds after they had hauled him off, his arms kept pumping up and down like jackhammers, waving two fistfuls of brown hair.

An ambulance rolled quietly up the driveway and stopped in the red zone outside the emergency ward. No victim in the wagon. Across the street stood a lighted billboard picturing a tall glass of milk, white like a nurse's uniform. A few cars were scattered about the lot, probably owned by janitors and nurses and the others who worked swing shift. Sonny dug for his keys, grimacing, his bloody knuckles rubbing the inside of his pocket. Unlocking the door, he reached under the seat where he had stashed a bottle of champagne, eased the cork free, and took a long drink. The cab filled with the heady odor of wine. He looked up at the massive hospital building, imagining Lonnie asleep in one of the darkened rooms, tubes from suspended bottles running into his arms as if he were some kind of human machine. He felt lonely and scared for his brother.

Switching on the dome light, he leaned close to the rearview mirror. A purple half-moon ran beneath one eye; a large bump on the bridge of his nose jutted left. He couldn't tell if it was only swollen and bruised or if it was broken. He moaned. They couldn't film him like this. Shit. Sonny switched off the light and stretched out, covering himself up to his chin with his jacket. His body ached in places he had never ached before. Balancing the bottle on his chest, he rested his head against the door panel, bent his knees.

First thing tomorrow morning he'd check on Lonnie.
There was no sense going home for a few hours and then
having to come back. As he lay there, cramped, drinking
champagne, he pictured himself on film with a broken
nose. It wasn't such a bad image. A broken nose might add
character, offset the all-American prettiness. Handsome
but bold like DeNiro or Pacino. Kind of tough. Other parts
would probably come easier. People in the right places
would see him and be impressed. His performance would
stand out, shine. Who knows? In a couple of years he might
be working fairly steady, doing features, making thirty or
forty thousand a year. The chance was there. This was a
good start, anyway, no lousy one-liner, no commercial, but
a *leading* role. And wasn't he the best? You're goddamn
right. He frowned sternly, had another drink, then set the
bottle on the floorboard.

Soon he fell asleep, snuggled under his jacket, smiling
like a fool. They were paying him four thousand dollars.
Maybe more.

He winced everytime the bus hit a bump. And everytime
he winced or blinked his left eye throbbed. The driver ran
over so damn many potholes Alex wanted to scream. Although there was only one other passenger on board, he
kept his face turned toward the window and shielded his
profile with a hand. His lower lip was twisted and bloated,
the gum underneath so sensitive that he could barely touch
it with his tongue without bringing tears to his eyes. The
back of his head was lumpy with knots. One eye had swollen shut, puffy as a blister ready to burst, glossy and
smooth. The eyelid was dark purple laced with fine thin
lines of green. A single drop of blood stained the side of his
shirt where Sonny had bitten him.

An empty lipstick container rolled off the seat as he rose
for his exit. The aisle was littered with transfers, and the
grooves of the safety mat were level with grime. Flattened
balls of gum dotted the floor here and there, hard and black,

a permanent part of the mat. "El Loco Wolf x-con-x Gold Lady" was scrawled across the back doors in fancy cholo style lettering.

The stench of urine hit him and, with his good eye, he glanced down to a damp spot on the bottom stair where some punk or bum had had the gall to piss. Suddenly the doors flapped open. He'd barely stepped to the curb when the bus roared off as if the driver was terrified of the neighborhood. Alex nervously scanned the dark streets for hoods who might be scouting a victim but there was no one in sight. Far away he heard the freeway roaring softly like the ocean. Occasionally the headlights of a car came from behind and made shadows of his body on the sidewalk before it passed and disappeared.

He wondered where anyone would be going this time of night. Home, like him? From where? Coming off a night shift? What kind of life could a man have working those hours? Soon the distant roar of the freeway gave way to the hum of the dynamo at the end of the alley. A lamp in an apartment carport burned behind a wire cage so heavily meshed to protect against being broken that little light could escape. Alex passed the remains of the fence and stopped for a moment. Although he hadn't actually thought about whose yard they had ended up in, he didn't see how he ever could've figured different. In his mind, picket fence had always been synonymous with Old Man Wheat's garden. He could still hear it crackling under the Riviera like a string of dry, rickety tinder. There were marks in the ground as if someone had tried to drag the fence off the garden but hadn't had the strength. The manicured lawn was torn with tire tracks, almost neatly, as if pared with a knife. Long strips of grass, dark moist earth clinging to the roots, had been piled to one side of the yard. And the rosebushes that were crushed beneath the fence had been placed in individual clay pots and lined up along the porch like a bunch of wounded soldiers. One still had a complete flower. The others looked pathetic. Pitiful.

"Poor sonofabitch," he mumbled. Old Man Wheat was the only one in the neighborhood who took pride in his place. He almost felt sorry for him, felt an urge to apologize, offer to help rebuild the fence and plant another garden. Then he realized they were just stupid roses and it didn't fuckin' matter. The old man was crazy. Soft, Alex was getting too damn soft.

As he turned down the narrow path leading to the apartments, his foot bumped something and he jumped backward, startled. Stormin' Norman sat in a heap, half his ass on the concrete path, the other half in a strip of dirt.

Stormin' Norman stared at the side of the garage three feet in front of him, his back to the cyclone fence that separated the yards. There was a rim of gold around his mouth and a brown paper bag in his lap. Beside him lay a dirty canvas sack full of maps to stars' homes. He raised his head in stages, by fractions, until finally he was staring up at the giant before him. He swayed from side to side like someone was gently and lovingly guiding him through a slow dance, eyes droopy, glazed with a milky white film.

Norman giggled.

"What happen to your face?"

A storm. His head roared.

"Ya look pretty."

He pulled a can of spray paint from the canvas sack and shot a short blast into the paper bag. "Want some?" Over the roar, Alex heard a voice in his head telling the kid to get out of his way. Norman held the bag out to him. "It's gooood, A," he drawled. Dreamily. "It's gooood." Alex kicked him in the hip, hitting bone. Norman only frowned and looked at him with dopey, disappointed eyes. "Why ya always wanna hurt me? I don't wanna hurt you. I wanna be friends, A. Let's be friends." He leaned over to put his face into the bag and then seemed to remember his manners and offered it to Alex again.

The kid was a mouse, Alex thought. A whimpering, sniveling mouse. No, a diseased sewer rat. His old man had given him a rotten, uneven crewcut that made the shape of his skull appear much too large for the skinny little body. All lips and head on a pencil neck. Visions of Norman as a wasted old bum wandering around downtown, begging, passed through Alex's mind so clearly that he felt no prediction could've been more true or accurate.

Again he heard the voice telling the kid to move, but again he said nothing. "Suit yourself," Norman muttered. "Gold's real good." When he cupped the bag around mouth and nose, Alex kicked between the hands and split his lip. Sent him spinning. The bag flew into the air while the can of spray paint rolled down the path.

Norman popped to his feet and clung to the cyclone fence like Spider-Man. But Alex grabbed the back of his shirt before he could scramble to the top and yanked him down. Body hit concrete with the whack of bone. For a long second he lay stunned, his shirt ripped open, a trace of blood on his chin. His small round belly was cluttered with sloppy daggers and Nazi crosses, a cobra on one breast and a pirate skull and crossbones on the other. Alex kicked again and again, the roaring growing louder—in the back, the legs, the head—rotating between left and right boot, Norman moaning and whimpering, rolling farther along the concrete with each blow. At the foot of the apartment stairs he paused to stare down at the trembling, wasted figure. Sewer rat. He stepped on his hand. Norman shrieked. Then, kicking him clean off the path, Alex left him curled in the dirt and hurried upstairs to his room.

As he spread his suitcase open across the bed, a fuzzy outline appeared around the edges of his vision, radiating. Alex blinked and shook his head, trying to clear his vision. The walls wobbled and breathed like huge lungs. He ran his tongue along the empty space in his mouth where the tooth was missing. Fucking Sonny. Someday he'd get even. He packed what he could, his best shirts and slacks, folding them carefully but quickly. His mind was made up. There were no choices. No excuses. Taking the .38 from between the bed mattresses, he wrapped it in a pair of jeans and placed it in the suitcase. Tomorrow he'd buy bullets. Go all the way or not at all. He rushed to the closet for his coke/meth. Using the tip of his pocket knife, he dipped it into the plastic bag, into one of the tiny envelopes, and raised a large mound of powder to his nostril and sniffed. Once, twice, three times. In a minute the stinging subsided and his vision cleared. Snapping the suitcase shut, he glanced around the room and sighed. He'd have to leave his stereo behind, at least for now. All his records, too. Alex shuddered at the thought.

As he headed for the front door, he wondered if he should leave Mom a note to let her know what he was doing. But what the hell for? She didn't give a shit about him. Suddenly an idea hit him. He set the suitcase down, hurried to Sonny's room, and flipped on the light. Underwear flew from the dresser over his shoulder. A pair of boxers snagged the bedpost and hung there. A T-shirt landed on the windowsill. But he couldn't find anything worth taking except a pair of gold cufflinks that Mom had given Sonny for high school graduation. He'd always liked them and he'd be damned if he wasn't going to have them. They *owed* him. Stuffing the velvet jewelry case in his pocket, he reached behind a bookshelf that ran clear to the ceiling. Stepped to one side. Gave it a good quick yank. The shelf paused at an unbelievable angle before it crashed across Sonny's bed with the flutter and tear of binding and pages. The floor shook. Books scattered everywhere. His lip cracked where a scab had begun to form as he grinned. Somebody was in for one hell of a nice surprise.

A sense of freedom and power, of satisfaction and determination swelled inside him on the way downstairs. It was a beautiful night, a beautiful morning, he thought. The sky was clear for once, and the air was cool on his face. He knew he was doing the right thing. A man his age needed a place of his own, a place to bring a lady for the night, a place where he could have a party now and then if he

wanted, a place he could do what he wanted when he
wanted. Privacy. Alex threw his head back, sniffling. A
surge of warmth ran the length of his spine. Coke and meth
made your mind clear, vision sharp, body strong. He
couldn't see himself without it. Sleep no longer dictated his
life, and to be free of sleep was to be free of a curse, to be
alive. His thoughts came as revelations, geniuslike, pro-
found and accurate, too great for words. Only the sweet
voice of Smokey Robinson could ever approach his reverie.

Something stung him square between the shoulder
blades and he dropped the suitcase. Then again, in the
thigh. He spun around, seeing no one. Something swished
by his ear and bounced off the garage. A rock. One hit him
in the chest. Another whistled past his head, wind raising
hair. He looked up. They were coming from everywhere.
A fucking meteor storm. Norman stood on top of the apartment roof, arms flying, spray paint and bag beside him.
Alex grabbed the suitcase and zigzagged down the path like
he was dodging gunfire.

16

Her eyes glowed red like a cat's in the strong flash. A bouquet of white roses rested in the crook of her arm. Her other hand held tight to Dan's elbow. He smiled sheepishly in his suit and tie. Over their heads an archway, entwined with plastic daisies, read LAS VEGAS, NEVADA. Lonnie stared at the cheap Polaroid for a few seconds. His hands shook. A police lieutenant and a homicide inspector had left the room ten minutes earlier.

He tossed the photo onto a pile of magazines on the bedstand and lay back on his pillow. The top left side of his skull was wrapped in white gauze. Yellow pus stained the small area surrounding the wound. He brought his hand to his chest. His heart beat fast. The police had questioned him for over an hour and he had done his best, without being rude, not to give them a single straight answer.

On the other side of the room were two more beds. One was vacant and the other had its curtains, which hung from a rod attached to the ceiling, completely drawn. A black-and-white TV was suspended from a metal bar over the doorway. The boy behind the curtains couldn't control his bowels and the room often smelled of shit and the antiseptic the nurse's aides used. For the first two days Lonnie slept long hours, tossing, in and out of dreams, doped and never fully conscious. He might wake to darkness, not remembering where he was, frightened, or he might wake to a room of sunshine and suddenly feel anxious. Then as if he'd broken a fever, as if his body had stored all the energy it could, he became restless. Couldn't sleep. On the morning of the fifth day he was taken off liquids and given oatmeal. Soon he graduated to eggs, tasteless eggs that chewed like rubber. Then toast, an orange or an apple. Fruit cocktail.

The strange warm smells of sickness and antiseptic seemed stronger at night. Long after the TV had been turned off, he lay awake listening to the sounds of the nurses moving about in the hall outside his room. Sometimes he caught the murmur of a passing conversation. Sometimes he heard the slosh of a janitor's mop. The heaters along the wall crackled on and off, metal buckling while the room grew suffocatingly warm. He'd drop his feet over the side of the bed and steady himself. Blood rushed to his head, pulsing against his temples. In a white paper gown, Lonnie weaved across the room, past the boy behind the curtained bed, to the lavatory. The floor was tiled and cold on his bare feet. The air was cool and he could feel the weight of it in his lungs, heavy and moist. He liked to linger there, a hand on the washbasin for support, staring through the cracks of a small louvered window overlooking the parking lot below. Street lights shone across the city in the distance. Once just before dawn he saw a thousand city lights go out one after the other until the streets lay in partial darkness. Sometimes he stayed here for a good hour. Sometimes, after only a few minutes, the boy behind the curtains whimpered like a puppy as he fumbled along the bed railing for the call button. Lonnie crept back to bed, his wound throbbing with each step. He wasn't supposed to be on his feet yet. Soon a small lamp shone behind the curtains, a nurse slipped into the room, the bed creaked. A soft, embarrassed voice of apology followed the crinkle of paper brushing skin.

"How's the forty-three-year-old midget doing today?" A newspaper rolled into a tube poked from the back pocket of Sonny's jeans.

Lonnie smiled, sat up, stuffed one of several pillows behind him, and patted the mattress. "Have a seat."

Pulling the newspaper from his pocket, Sonny sat at the foot of the bed. "I can't stay long," he said. "I have to take a load over before it gets too dark."

"You about settled?"

"Everything's still in boxes. I stayed there last night for the first time."

"Spooked?"

He shrugged. "Me?"

"How is it?"

"It's got new wall-to-wall carpets and fresh paint but it's nothing fancy. Just a studio, somewhere to sleep. At least the rent's almost affordable."

Lonnie nodded, trying to keep his smile. "Sounds good," he mumbled. "I'm glad you found a place." Two old women in hats wobbled down the hall and stopped, looked about the room, then muttered something to each other and ambled on. The brothers exchanged curious looks. A phone buzzed in another room. "Hear from Alex?" he asked.

Sonny shook his head. "He came back for his records when I was on the set. I don't know where the hell he's staying, though. Mom said he told her you could have his stereo. Hey . . ." Sonny reached inside his coat pocket. "You got a letter." Water had gotten on the envelope and the ink had run, smearing the return address. "Open it."

Lonnie pressed a button on the bed railing and the top half of the mattress rose humming. He slid his finger under the seal then suddenly changed his mind and flipped the letter on the bedstand. "I'll read it later." A long silence passed. The boy behind the curtains coughed.

"Whatta you say about helping me decorate when you get out of here?" Sonny said, slapping his brother's thigh beneath the sheet. "You can spend the weekend. We'll buy some beer and hang pictures and talk. Have a good time."

"Yeah," Lonnie said, trying to sound enthused. "Have a good time." On his wrist was a plastic yellow name band, the ends crimped together with aluminum. He lowered his head and played absently with the bracelet, turning it round and round on his wrist. "When they gonna let me outta here?"

"When you're okay."

"I'm okay now."

"What's the doctor say?"

"He says they gotta watch for infection. *Infection.* Shit. Ain't no infection. They just wanna keep me forever so they make money." He hit the mattress with the meaty side of his fist. "I'm fuckin' sick of laying here."

Sonny placed a hand on his shoulder. "Take it easy," he said, letting the tube of newspaper unravel in Lonnie's lap. *Variety.* "Look at page twelve." In the bottom right hand corner was a small black-and-white shot of Sonny leaning against a chain link fence, an eyebrow cocked, cigarette dangling from his lips. Lonnie glanced from the picture to his brother a couple of times as if he wasn't sure they were the same people.

"Pretentious, huh? My agent paid for it. Why, I don't know. I always thought that picture was obnoxious." He scooted closer to him so he could look at it again. "There was a small piece about the movie in the *Reporter* last week, too."

"Yeah?"

"Yeah."

"You get your name in it?"

"Twice."

"Great."

"Uh huh."

He rattled the newspaper. "Mine?"

"That's why I brought it."

"Thanks."

"Don't give me this *thanks* bullshit. We're brothers, remember?" He pitched backward, looking him up and down in fake amazement until Lonnie smiled. "Anyway, you know Mom. I have a whole stack in the car. She wanted twenty copies."

Letting his gaze fall to his lap, Lonnie tugged on the bracelet again. "They gettin' along?" he mumbled.

Sonny nodded. "It seems like it. Mom gave her notice at Denny's already." He spread his arms wide. "Dan has a big house in Encino. They took out a loan to put in a pool with a Jacuzzi this summer. I can just see you lying around the water, drinking beer, wearing sunglasses, getting a tan. Ahhh. Talk about luxury."

Lonnie didn't know what to say. He wasn't sure if he'd heard right. Frowning, he looked his brother in the eye.

Sonny's smile faded. "C'mon, man," he said, patting Lonnie's thigh beneath the sheet again. "People have to do shit they don't want to sometimes and this is just one of those times." Lonnie jerked his leg away. "It won't be that bad. I talked with Dan and he seems like a decent man. He won't pull any father bullshit on you. Do you hear me? Things'll get better but you have to hang on. You have to keep getting back up no matter how hard you go down." Sonny paused for a second, started to place his hand on his brother's knee, then withdrew it and laughed. "Hey, ever hear of *Teenbeat?* Wipe that grin off your face." Lonnie wasn't grinning. "This lady came on the set the other day and interviewed a few of the cast. Whatta you think?" He winked. "Your brother, the teen idol." But Lonnie was staring across the room, no longer listening. Taking a pen from the bedstand, Sonny wrote on the back of *Variety.* "Here's my address and phone number. Call me." He stood up. "Mom said to tell you she's going to come by with Dan later tonight. Don't give them a hard time, okay?"

"Sure."

"See you later."

"All right."

He paused in the doorway. "Need anything special?"

"No."

"See you, then."

"Bye."

When Sonny had left Lonnie crossed his fingers, shaking them . . . *like this, ese* . . . *like this, huh?* He watched a nurse wheel another boy into the room, slip her hands under his armpits, and help him from the wheelchair into the vacant bed. Lonnie wondered, as he reached for the letter on the bedstand, what was wrong with the new kid. Didn't look sick or injured.

The writing was impressed deep into the paper by a firm hand uncomfortable holding a pen.

> Dear Lonnie,
>   Sorry to hear about the trouble you've been having. It should work itself out in time. I guess you didn't hear I sold my garage. I called your mom when the sale was final but she must have forgot to tell you. I'm a real estate agent now for Century 21. This July I plan to apply for my broker's license, move to Sunnyvale, and open my own office. You also probably don't know I'm engaged. Her name is Dianne. I'm sure you'll like her. We're taking a trip to Arizona in June to look for property. When do you get out of school? The best time to visit would be late August or early September. Say hello to Alex and Sonny for me. I'm glad to hear the police recovered his car. Give your mom a hug.
>
>   Your uncle,
>   Ernie

The nurse was leaving the room when he waved her over.

"How are you feeling?"

"Not too good."

"What's the problem?"

"My stomach's upset."

"Can I get you a glass of Bromo Seltzer?"

"I just wanna rest," he said. "If anybody comes to visit, could you tell 'em I'm sleeping?"

A half-hour later Lonnie dozed off. When he woke, the room was dark and he was shivering. The sheets were damp with sweat. His heart pounded. The same dream, the same scene. He was clutching his head in one hand, raking the nails of his other along the wall behind him, groping for the door handle of the Riviera.

The notice was tacked to the bulletin board inside Pearl's:

FOR SALE

Classic '67 Riviera. Hydraulics. Cherry paint job. Chain steering wheel. Rebuilt AT. Needs new windshield. Sacrifice $1400 FIRM. 555-1320 after 9 P.M.

Alex tore it down. He'd just sold the Riviera to a sixteen-year-old Samoan from Montebello. The clock on the wall read ten-fifteen P.M. He had picked up his car two days ago from a garage downtown. Because the plates didn't match the registration, he had a hell of a time explaining what had happened. A tracer was run. The ID on the engine block checked out under his name and, since the car had never been reported stolen, all the police could do was scold him for not coming to them. Minus fifty dollars in storage fees, Alex was now thirteen hundred and fifty bucks richer. When the garage attendant handed him the bill, the first thing he thought was, *Why should I pay? The fuckin' pigs impounded it.* But if getting the Riviera back signaled an end to the investigation, the end of cops and questions, then it was well worth fifty dollars. No complaints. Later that same day he filled a bucket with cold water and detergent and scrubbed the inside of the cab. The dashboard above the glove compartment was encrusted with blood the shape of Lonnie's forehead. The carpet on the floorboard was stained the color of rust. Buckshot had torn the top of the backseat. The stuffing was shredded, bulging. The windshield on the passenger's side was shattered. Twice, while washing the front seat and door panels, he gagged and nearly vomited. Cursed the attendant. For fifty bucks the prick should've at least cleaned the car. The bucket of water was pink when he finished.

He crumpled the notice, turned to see if anyone was watching, and swaggered from the bar to an alcove behind the storage room. As he climbed the narrow staircase he shook the rickety banister. Some of the spokes were loose, others were kicked out. The hallway was dark and stank of cat piss. At the top Alex stopped, glanced down the staircase to make sure no one had followed him, and slipped his key into the dead-bolt lock. He shoved the door shut, chain-latched it, double-checked it, then pulled off his leather jacket and collapsed on the tattered fold-out sofa. The sound of traffic mixed with the bass thump on the jukebox below. His only window overlooked Hollywood Boulevard. Bolted to the side of the building, next to an old iron fire escape, was a large neon sign flashing PEARL'S—PEARL'S —PEARL'S every night until two in the morning. He had to nail a heavy cotton blanket over the window to keep it from driving him crazy.

The place had been fumigated for cockroaches last week and still reeked of poison. The walls were bare, the ceiling stained a dingy orange from years of tobacco smoke. A sixty-watt bulb burned dimly overhead. On an empty cable spool in front of the sofa was a round plate of smoked glass powdered white with the residue of cocaine and methamphetamine. Two plastic baggies, slit down the middle, lay spread open on the glass. Alex sat up, took the thirteen hundred fifty plus twenty-five hundred from his wallet, and tossed it on the table. A black shoulder holster crossed the side of his breast, under an arm, around his shoulder blade. The .38 was strapped and loaded. Dum-dums. They made a pinhole in a man's chest but came out the back with a chunk of flesh big as a fist. Crater makers. The kind cops used.

A scab had formed on his lower lip where Sonny had whacked him. Half of it had fallen off last night when he bumped his mouth drinking from a bottle of whiskey. His left eye was still bloodshot although the swelling had gone down enough for him to see out of it. Alex gritted his teeth. Should've kicked Sonny's ass. Never should've let him up when he was down. He thought of Lonnie, wondering if he should visit him tonight. Surprise the kid. He'd spoken with Mom; she said Lonnie looked better, but he hadn't seen him since the shooting. Been too damn busy. Lonnie understood that. Tough little bastard. Built like a rock. He'd be okay. What was he thinking about, anyway? He didn't even have a car now. It was late, visiting hours were over. Alex leaned toward the cable spool and, with the razor, scraped enough powder from the inside of the bags to draw himself four long, thick lines. In a minute he was high again, cheeks hot, rushing.

A nail holding the blanket over the window suddenly popped out of the wall. The room blinked purple—green —purple . . . He spread the wad of bills across the smoked glass, wagging his head, counting silently. Three thousand eight hundred and fifty bucks. He grinned, smacked his lips. Three thousand eight hundred and fifty fuckin' bucks.

Sonny parked in stall twenty-three of an apartment complex off Cahuenga Boulevard. The 'Vette squatted under the weight of boxes of books and clothes. He yawned. Sighed. He'd been up since four A.M. studying his character, studying the scene the director had planned to shoot today, and he was exhausted. But at eight sharp this morning, when he'd arrived at the studio, he had been told that the schedule had been changed. His day was spent sitting around the set on call, watching the other actors act.

On the way upstairs he noticed the manager had misspelled his name on the mailbox—Bear, not Baer—and reminded himself to correct it tomorrow. Another detail. Moving was always a long hard job full of minor complications. He decided to leave the rest of his stuff in the car until morning. No one would steal a bunch of old paperbacks. A manila envelope was tacked beneath the peephole, and Sonny, balancing a box of books on his knee, pulled it free as he unlocked and booted the door open.

Setting the box on the floor, he switched on the light, yawned again, then opened the envelope. A paperclip held a note attached to a glossy folder with an aerial shot of Ventura Boulevard on the cover:

Was in the neighborhood. Dropped by about nine P.M. Sorry I missed you. Thought you'd like to see this.

Donna

He opened the folder:

UNIVERSAL PICTURES
100 Universal City Plaza
Universal City, CA 91608
Monica Dye, Publicity Dept.

Subject: Sonny Baer

A very interesting-looking young fellow of twenty-one with a dedicated attitude which makes him seem more mature. Medium build, rather olive complexion, great smile. I caught him in *Looking Glass, Amen* at Martin's Theatre and was impressed (Sternberg thinks he's a young Robert DeNiro). Saw an answer print of *Long Days—Go Get 'Em Tiger* in which he played a dope-

addicted high school boy. Was impressed with his sen-
sitivity and authority. It's incredible in view of his
almost total lack of formal training and age. Watch out
for this young man!

Monica Dye

He slowly reread the letter, then let it fall from his hand,
fluttering to the carpet. Monica Dye was responsible for
grooming nine-tenths of Universal's major actors.

Two days later the bandages were removed. A heap of
white gauze fell into the waste can. The top clinked shut.
The air felt cool on Lonnie's temple where his hair had
been shaved. A stocky nurse stood nearby, sipping coffee,
watching the doctor. On the wall was a blood pressure
barometer and, over a padded table covered with stiff white
tissue that crinkled when he moved, hung a dome light on
a chrome ball joint. Cold metal. The snip of scissors. A tug.
Two tugs. He winced, feeling string slide through his skin,
catching, being tugged harder and then slipping free.
Twenty-two stitches in all. His ear would need cosmetic
surgery. The doctor told him to come back in a week and
he'd refer him to a good plastic surgeon.

The nurse taped a square gauze bandage over the gnarled
ear, leaving his temple exposed to heal, and then walked
him back to his room. Mom sat in the chair beside his bed,
a Broadway bag in her lap. Her cheeks were pink with
rouge and her eyelids were painted a soft shade of blue. She
was watching a morning game show on the TV over the
doorway. The obnoxious cackle of an emcee, the shriek of
a contestant, filled the room. The stack of magazines and
the wedding picture were missing from the bedstand. The
sheets and the blanket had already been stripped and the
mattress was bare. In another bed the face of a boy was
hidden behind a crossword puzzle magazine. Mom blinked
as she stood up. Lonnie caught her glance at the wound. A

tendon in her neck quivered and he knew, by the sudden
stillness of her chest, that she had lost her breath for a
moment. He bowed his head, feeling ugly and ashamed. As
she handed him the bag her lips slowly broke from what
could've been a wince into a nervous smile. "I got you some
new things," she said, looking him up and down in his
gown. A small laugh. "You can't go home like that." He
smiled for her, raising his head slightly. Tania wore high
heels with black hose, a black dress with white lacing along
the neckline; a new dress, an expensive dress. A present
from Dan, he thought. "Why don't you go change," she
said. Lonnie nodded and, without looking at her, headed to
the lavatory.

He set the Broadway bag on the floor, turned his head
sideways and peered into the mirror over the washbasin. A
jagged gash the shape of a sickle ran from the top of his ear
across his temple, almost to the base of his skull. The ugli-
ness of it startled him. He looked away, repulsed. His knees
grew weak. He opened and closed his eyes once, swallowed, then forced himself to look again. The stitches had
left a long centipedelike trail along his temple. The holes
where the needle had gone in and out were hard crusty dots
the size and color of tiny blackberry seeds. A fine pink gap
ran where the skin had been slit. He leaned closer to the
mirror, narrowing his eyes. His scalp was shaved naked
two inches on both sides of the gash. It would never grow
back, he was sure. His breathing became jerky and shallow.
Pinching a strip of tape between his fingers, he began peeling the bandage from his ear, wincing, when he heard
Mom's voice just outside the curtain door.

"You all right in there?"

"Uh huh."

"Need any help?"

He quickly smoothed the tape back in place. "No,
thanks."

"The pants fit okay?"

"I'll be out in a second."

Lonnie opened the Broadway bag. Brown corduroy slacks, a blue polo shirt with a small alligator embroidered on the pocket, tube socks. A pair of soft suede Hush Puppies. Red jockey shorts. Untying the gown from behind his back, he let it drop to the tile floor in a heap about his ankles. He dressed swiftly, mechanically. There was no point arguing. The corduroy slacks felt loose around the waist but the length was perfect. The shirt clung tight to his chest. When he bent over to put on the new shoes his wound began throbbing and he grabbed the washbasin for support.

Mom greeted him with a smile, a vinyl night bag in hand, her purse slung over one shoulder. Her eyes went from his shoes, the pants, up to his face. This time, though, her smile didn't falter. "You look fantastic," she said, handing him the vinyl bag containing his toiletries, the magazines, the picture. Just then a nurse entered the room with a wheelchair. Lonnie frowned. "It's policy, baby," Mom said. There was no point arguing. He sat in the chair, set the bag in his lap, and let the nurse push him. As he was wheeled down the hall to the elevator, he spotted the nurse's aide who had taken care of him, who had made his bed and brought him pitchers of water, who had given him sponge baths. She was making someone else's bed now, smoothing a sheet across the mattress with her palms. He wanted to wave good-bye to her as he passed the room but instead he bowed his head.

They rode the elevator to the first floor in silence. The nurse stopped the wheelchair just outside the main entrance. "You're on your own now," she said. Lonnie thanked her then rose to his feet. He crossed the parking lot with Mom, one step behind her. The night bag bounced against his thigh and he switched it from one hand to the other. "Want me to carry that?" she asked. He shook his head. The sky was overcast, hot, hazy with a ceiling of smog. The strong glare of the sun hurt his eyes, making him squint. He felt himself sweating under his arms, thought of taking off his shirt. He became conscious of the new shoes and how light they felt and how the soles gave to the rise and fall of his steps. He was used to fence climbers with laces that wrapped firm around the foot and soles that didn't give so easily.

Digging through her purse, Mom found her keys and unlocked the passenger side of a huge Chrysler. Dan's car. Power steering, automatic transmission, V8. A relic of the past. "The clutch went out on the Toyota again," she said as she walked around to the other side of the car. "I hadda take it in." Cellophane candy wrappers overflowed from the ashtray. The cab smelled like he imagined Dan's house to smell, like the man himself, like his family—the scent of strangers. He missed the familiar tobacco odor of the Toyota.

A bus pulled out in front of them. Mom flipped on the blinker, sat forward, and glanced into the rearview mirror. Another car was approaching in the next lane. She sat back, sighing. The Chrysler handled like a boat, shocks absorbing every bump in the road. Lonnie watched the streets pass with a cold stillness, shops and stores, building after building, light poles and shaggy telephone poles. Two Mexicans in coveralls, goggles atop their heads, stood outside an auto body shop. He heard the faint whine of an electric sander, glimpsed the red spark of grit on metal in the darkness of the garage, caught a whiff of paint. Then he smelled a bakery somewhere. Then a Mexican food stand. The bus veered to the curb and Mom stepped on the accelerator as she swayed into the other lane to pass. A few seconds later they stopped for a red light. She leaned over to squeeze his knee but couldn't reach him. "Sit closer, baby. I don't bite."

He didn't move.

The blinker was still flashing.

He saw her as he saw the streets, indifferent and detached, fading back like a passing image seen through glass. On the freeway he looked out over the city and it appeared almost artificial to him, one-dimensional like the setting of a low-budget movie. The tops of the skyscrapers were hidden by a layer of smog. Soot and exhaust covered the ivy bordering the freeway. Up ahead, on the side of an over-pass, was a green road sign with white reflector letters:

WESTERN AVE ½ .

He felt the vibrations of the motor on the bottom of his feet, through the floorboard, accelerating gradually but steadily. The speedometer needle rolled from fifty to fifty-five, wobbled a moment, then leveled at sixty. When they shot under the overpass, past the exit they had taken a thousand times before, his body tensed and he glanced down the ramp. A Harley turned right onto Western. He drew a hand slowly across his forehead to the back of his neck and squeezed. Tania stared straight ahead. Then it was behind them. Soon they passed the Hollywood Bowl and were climbing a grade, then going down, breaking air pockets, making a shooing noise as they zipped by a long string of cars waiting to exit at the Universal Tours off-ramp. He remembered taking the tour with Sonny and Alex when they first moved to L.A. and how, like the others on the tram, they had looked hard to spot a star.

Alex swore he saw Raquel Welch.

No one else did.

Now Sonny was working there.

Two lanes merged. They crossed over the deep concrete pit of the L.A. River, murky and swift, running through a narrow channel. The freeway rose high over another free-way. "A letter came for us," Mom said, switching lanes. "The hearing's on the twenty-first. Dan's gonna take off work." Lonnie saw the San Gabriel Mountains far in the distance, barren, granite blackened by fire. Thousands and thousands of houses on neatly sectioned plots of land spread across the flat, dry valley. Great sheet metal boxes of air conditioners dotted rooftops. Here and there were light blue pools of different shapes and sizes. Cool, cool water. His throat swelled. So damn many people, so damn many homes. The valley was a massive complex without a center, divided by redwood fences and a tangled maze of asphalt, sprawling for miles in every direction.

The sun broke through the overcast. It grew hotter and hotter as they rode deeper into the valley. Tania took the Havenhurst exit in Encino, followed it for a few blocks past a shopping mall, then turned up a residential street. Hung a left, a right. Another right. Every house, though painted and landscaped differently, had a composition shingle roof and the same size front yard.

They passed a small clean park with picnic benches, a slide and swing set, a jungle gym. Some people played volleyball. A young woman arched backward to serve the ball and her blouse came untucked. Lonnie caught a flash of firm, white belly, taut and smooth, just before the Chrysler dipped to one side and rolled into the oil-spotted driveway of a ranch-style house. An orange basketball hoop hung over the garage.

Shutting off the motor, Tania closed her eyes and rested her head on the steering wheel. Lonnie sat motionless, staring through the heat waves rising off the hood of the car, listening to the radiator hiss. His upper lip was moist with sweat, his wound ached. A long, silent moment passed. Tania slowly raised her head, opened her eyes, then ran her tongue over dry, chapped lips. "Honey, don't ruin it for Momma." The sun beat hot through the windshield. He heard the laughter of the people in the park. "Give me a chance. Dan's a good man. He wants to help us." She slipped out from behind the steering wheel, placed her arm around his shoulders, and squeezed him to her. His body stiffened. A V like wings darkened his shirt between his breasts. The air in the cab was thick, heavy, hot. He concentrated on his breathing.

"Nobody's gonna bother you. You're gonna have your own room and everything." A drop of sweat rolled from between his eyes and stopped in the curve of one nostril. "We're gonna put in a pool this summer," she said, leaning back to look at him, smiling weakly. "That sound nice, honey? You like to swim?" He saw a wood plaque over the front porch, through the heat waves rising off the car, wavering like liquid in the glare of the sun. THE DE MARTINI'S. A cherry tree grew in the middle of the yard while rosebushes bordered a concrete walkway embedded with gold and silver glitter. She tightened her arm around him and tugged, pressing the side of her breast against his arm, soft and warm. He felt her breath hot on the back of his neck. "It's gonna be good." She stroked his hair. He smelled her perfume, her sweat. "Please don't ruin it for me." Suddenly he broke away, grasping for the door handle. "Don't push your luck, baby. I've run out of patience."

A model airplane dangled over the bed from a string tacked to the ceiling. Bicentennial curtains patterned with bald eagles and Mayflowers and Paul Reveres covered a window facing the front yard. Lonnie watched the airplane slowly turn as he lay on the quilt of a strange bed, fully clothed, fingers laced behind his head. Mom had showed him to his new room earlier that afternoon and he hadn't come out since. His PAL baseball trophy rested on the dust cover of Alex's stereo on top of an Early American–style dresser. His clothes hung neatly in the open closet. All of Sonny's books, all of his belongings, were missing. The bedding, the quilt, smelled of a different brand of laundry detergent. Another hour passed. The sun went down and now he lay in darkness. Popcorn popping in the kitchen blended with the noise of the TV in the living room.

A knock came on the door. Lonnie quickly tugged the quilt over him, rolled to his stomach, and closed his eyes. He heard the knob turn. A bar of light from the hallway fell across the side of his face. A dozen seconds passed. Finally the door closed. "He's still asleep," Dan said.

Exhaling, he rolled to his back again. He needed to get out of here, out of this house, take a walk, but he was afraid to cross through the living room. They'd all stare at him.

Mom would ask him to sit down and watch TV with every-body. Or else no one would say anything and pretend they didn't even see him. Their thoughts, though; their eyes. He knew what they would think. He'd stayed in the room too long to come out now without embarrassment.

Later that night, when it had been quiet long enough for everyone to have fallen asleep, he threw the quilt off him, stuffed Sonny's *Variety* in his pocket, and felt his way along a dark, carpeted hallway. A glass bowl of burned popcorn kernels rested on the coffee table. The moon shone through the sliding glass door in the dining room. Round chunks of redwood steps led to a garden fenced off with antique wagon wheels. He froze and listened for footsteps or the creak of a bed.

He thought of Mom asleep with Dan but felt neither resentment nor concern. He heard crickets in the back-yard. He smelled liver and onions from the dinner he'd missed. As he closed the door to the den, he turned the knob so it wouldn't make noise catching, then moved silently toward the outline of a rolltop desk. His hand slid along the stem of a metal lamp to the button switch. Pressed it. He froze and listened again. Only crickets, the tick of a clock. Lying flat on the desk, underneath a sheet of clear plastic, was an appointment calendar. An oversize clothespin held a pile of bills. A file cabinet stood against the wall beneath an oil painting of the Golden Gate Bridge.

The clock on the desk read five to twelve. Lonnie pulled the *Variety* from his back pocket and looked at the calendar. Today was the nineteenth. In a few minutes it would be the twentieth.

Nibbling his lower lip, he reached for the phone. Dial tone.

A woman's voice. "Hello?"

"Sonny there?"

"Hang on."

He heard loud music and laughter in the background, the noise of a crowd. Several minutes passed. He jerked the receiver from his ear, wincing. Someone had dropped the phone. A pain burned in the pit of his stomach. The line was dead.

Lonnie woke to the roar of an engine. Sitting up, he looked through a crack in the curtains. Mom was backing out of the driveway with Dan. A bit of shaving cream clung to Dan's chin and his hair was neatly parted on the side. When they were down the block Lonnie rolled out of bed and put on his black pocket T, a pair of Big Ben's, his PR fence climbers. His stomach growled but the thought of food nauseated him.

A knock on the door.

He pulled on his night watchman's cap as he kicked the pants and jockey shorts, Hush Puppies, and polo shirt under the bed.

"Come in."

Dan's boy, Tim, poked his head into the room. His glasses rested halfway down his nose. The thick lenses made his eyes look dull. "Phone call," he said.

Lonnie hurried to the den.

"Hey."

"Alex."

"What's happenin'?"

"Where you been?"

"Busy, my man, busy," he said. "Got a new ride to support."

"Whatcha get?"

"You sittin' down?"

"Yeah."

"A Transam."

Lonnie whistled. "Making money, huh?"

"Making fuckin' good money, A."

"You seen Sonny?"

"Sonny who?"

"C'mon."

"Fuck Sonny."

Lonnie glanced over his shoulder. Tim and his little sister stood listening in the doorway. She was chewing a piece of toast. He glared at them until they got the hint and disappeared. "I gotta get outta here," he said, almost whispering. "Can you pick me up?"

"When?"

"Now."

"I got business now."

"After, then."

"It's a long drive, A."

"So I'll take the bus. Where you at?"

"Right over Pearl's. Apartment B."

"See you in a while."

"If I ain't around go down and have a beer on me. Tell Eddie, he's the cook. Tell him you're my little brother. He'll fix you up."

He found Dan's kids staring at him from the breakfast table when he strode out of the den. The little girl had a milk moustache. Tim rose from his chair, smiling awkwardly as Lonnie headed for the front door. "Your mom told me to tell you . . ." He paused to swallow a mouthful of cereal. "Your mom told me to tell you not to go anywhere."

"Ain't you supposed to be in school?"

"Our bus comes at eight."

"What time's it now?"

Tim checked his wristwatch. "Quarter to."

They'd be long gone before Mom got back.

"Tell her I went to get some smokes."

Twenty minutes later he stood at the bus stop on Ventura Boulevard, smoking like a fiend. A pile of butts lay in the gutter near his feet. The bandaged ear made a strange bulge in his cap. Drivers stared at him as they passed. Bowing his head, he flicked another cigarette butt into the street. Mom could drive by any second and spot him and he wished the bus would hurry the hell up. If things had gone right, he thought, if he'd worked hard he might've graduated to the eleventh grade next month. But he'd fallen so far behind that it was futile to even think about it.

It was a long twenty-mile ride from the suburbs of Encino and he had to transfer once, walk across the street, then wait for another bus. He got off on La Brea near Grauman's Chinese Theatre and stretched his neck. A group of tourists compared their handprints and footprints with those of the stars, old stars and dead stars, embedded in the concrete slabs around the box office.

Lonnie kept his head down as he walked, hands jammed in pockets, shuffling his feet like an old man might. He hadn't slept much last night and he felt tired, weak, his legs rubbery. A sign on an office building on the corner of Hollywood and Highland flashed 83°—10:43—83°—10:44. The air was muggy and hot like it was yesterday. Although his scalp itched with sweat, he didn't remove the cap.

Up the street a cop ticketed a car with out-of-state plates. A bum rummaged through an industrial garbage bin in an alley behind the Bank of America. Some Japanese businessmen passed, gibbering in their native language, 35mm cameras strung around necks. Lonnie stopped in front of the Hollywood Wax Museum, thought of going in, then changed his mind and walked on.

A few blocks from Pearl's he heard a honk and turned around. Alex sat behind the wheel of a silver Transam, grinning, cruising with the windows down and the tape deck blasting rock. He pulled to the curb.

"Hey, *ese.*"

"Nice car."

Alex leaned back. "Yeah," he drawled. Casual. "It'll do for now."

As if you've driven better, Lonnie thought, stepping into the Transam and shutting the door. There was gaudy rainbow tape on the dash. The car was a couple of years old but it was well taken care of inside and out. They rolled down the street, Alex grinding second gear while Lonnie gritted his teeth. His brother's shirt was unbuttoned to the navel.

A gold chain dangled from his neck.

"I'm sorry I couldn't visit, A," he said, staring at the bulge in Lonnie's cap. "But you know how it is. Business." He spit out the window. "Picked up a ounce this morning. Cost me two thousand, right? I turned around, put six grams on it, and sold it for twenty-four. Over a thousand profit in fifty minutes. Not too shabby, huh?" Alex laughed.

"The punk weighed it out and give me this look like hey-you-know? I told him his fuckin' scale was off, take it or leave it. He ain't got no connections 'cept me. No more gram shit, either. I'm moving up to quarter-pounds next week." He fumbled through a paper bag under the seat and handed Lonnie a warm beer which he clamped between his thighs but didn't open. "Cops talk to you?" No answer.

Suddenly Lonnie wished he was somewhere else. He'd thought he wanted to see Alex but realized now he'd made a mistake. His brother irritated him.

"Whatcha wanna do?" Alex said. They made a right onto Sunset Boulevard. "I was thinkin' maybe we go to Santa Monica. Drink a few beers, do a little coke, check out the ladies. Like old times, A."

Yeah, Lonnie thought, old times. He shrugged like he didn't care what they did although really he would've preferred Alex stop the car to let him off.

"You get my stereo? I told Mom I wanted you to have it. Everybody needs a fuckin' stereo. I got me a Marantz turntable and some big-ass speakers. It cost eleven hundred cash but they threw this in for free. Listen." Alex turned the tape deck up full blast.

Lonnie winced, tolerating it for a few seconds before turning it down. "Sounds good," he mumbled.

They swerved through Beverly Hills, past the mansions and their magnificent front yards, down a winding road past UCLA, through Westwood. Every once in a while his brother floored it and then, as if he forgot he was driving, he slowed to a crawl and forced drivers behind him to pass. "So what'd you tell the cops?"

Lonnie rolled his eyes, ignoring him. Alex was only interested in himself.

"I have friends, A. Word's out. Those cocksuckers are gonna pay. Wait and see. We'll have a party after."

Lonnie wondered, while he looked through the case of tapes on the floorboard, why his brother was such a jerk. He'd never known anyone more full of shit. Every time Alex opened his mouth he somehow managed to make an ass of himself. The frightening thing was that he actually *believed* his own bullshit.

Sunset fed into Highway 1. They drove south along the coast to Santa Monica and parked in a crowded lot. The ocean lay a hundred yards ahead. Alex opened the glove compartment, took out a mirror, a glass vial from his boot, a hundred-dollar bill from his wallet. After he'd drawn four long lines on the mirror, he rolled the bill into a tube and handed it to his brother. Lonnie wrinkled his nose and shook his head. He didn't feel like getting high today. Alex looked at him in amazement. "Never seen you turn down coke before," he said, shrugging, setting the mirror on his lap. In one fast sweep, he sniffed up all the lines and then shoved the hundred-dollar tube in Lonnie's shirt pocket. "Keep it. Just remember it was me give it to you, not Sonny." They hopped out of the Transam. The breeze off the ocean was cool and felt good on Lonnie's face. As they crossed the parking lot, Alex put his arm around him. "You been thinking about what I said?" he asked. "The offer still stands. It's easy money, A. All you gotta do is deliver."

They straddled the four-foot-high retaining wall near the bathrooms. Asphalt on one side, beach on the other. Here and there clusters of people lay on towels and blankets, sunning themselves. Lonnie balanced his unopened beer on the wall and stared at the ocean. It was as calm as a lake. In the distance he could see the remains of the Santa Monica pier where he and Sonny used to play the slot cars.

Now much of the boardwalk was gone, ravaged in a storm, sucked into the ocean. Lonnie looked away. Broken glass sparkled in the sand beneath his feet. Nearby three tanned surfer girls rested belly-down on a blanket, skin slick with oil, bathing suit tops unlatched across the back. "My hearing's tomorrow," he mumbled, as if to himself. A few seconds passed. "Did you hear me?"

Alex was on his hands and knees, frantically scratching at the sand.

"I said my hearing's tomorrow."

"Shuddup and help," he hollered. "I dropped my fuckin' coke."

Lonnie wagged his head in disgust as he jumped off the retaining wall. His brother hadn't changed. Never would. He picked up a handful of sand and watched it trickle through his fingers.

17

By six o'clock that evening Lonnie was back on Hollywood and Highland, waiting for the bus to Encino. The Transam had just disappeared around the corner. He stepped off the curb and looked over the tops of the cars down the street. His bus was approaching, swaying side to side, packed with people just off from work. Squeezing a hand into his pocket, he withdrew a couple of quarters and dimes. As he stepped back to the sidewalk, he glanced up at the sun, lifted the brow of his cap, and wiped sweat from his forehead. Eighty-seven degrees. His head reeled. The people sitting on the bench were gray and blurry and the atmosphere had a kind of dreaminess about it as if he were looking through a silk stocking. He spun around, darting across the street. A driver laid on his horn. When the bus squealed to a stop, Lonnie was inside the phone booth at a Union station, dialing Sonny's number, watching the big orange 76 ball go round in the sky.

One ring.

Five rings.

Nine rings.

He replaced the receiver on the hook and looked at the address scribbled on the page he had torn from *Variety*.

Cahuenga Boulevard. Less than a mile away. He wondered if he should call Mom first. Naw. He shook his head, then nodded. Yeah, he really should. But he was already a block from the gas station by then and he didn't want to turn around.

Lonnie hurried down the street, past the Hollywood Wax Museum again where a mime stood doing his act for a crowd of tourists. A Bengali in a turban, a red dot painted in the middle of his forehead, sat nearby in the ticket booth. A sign on the glass door read AIR CONDITIONED in frosty letters dripping with icicles.

He found himself walking faster and faster, eyes concentrated straight ahead, moving in and out through the people. Salsa music flowed from the doorway of a Mexican import shop. His foot caught an empty paper bag and he kicked it free. Five teenagers wearing matching brown jackets and Big Ben's, two carrying oversize radios tuned to the same station, strutted toward him. He took his hands out of his pockets in preparation. You never knew. A moment later they passed without a word. Lonnie turned down Cahuenga, walked by a twenty-four-hour newsstand with long racks of magazines on the sidewalk, crossed Sunset.

Birds of paradise and dwarf palm trees grew outside the main entrance to a huge apartment complex. Two floodlights were aimed at the raised street numbers mounted on the white stucco face of the building. Three-twenty-seven. This was the place. Shuffling up the front steps, he pushed open the glass door and entered the lobby. The row of mailboxes must have been a hundred long. He followed the hallway leading into a courtyard with a pool and stopped. Apartments surrounded him on all sides. The back of his neck grew tense as he climbed a staircase and walked along an open corridor, silently counting the numbers on the doors until he came to apartment twenty-three.

Adjusting his cap, tucking in his shirt, Lonnie raised his fist and knocked lightly on the door. Nothing. He forced a smile, then knocked again. Nothing. He peeked through a space in the drapes but it was too dark inside to see anything. Sighing, he fitted his legs between the banister spokes and sat with his feet dangling over the courtyard below. A woman in a bikini was reading a paperback on the lounge chair beside the pool. The water was still, light blue. He spotted a penny on the bottom near the drain. An hour passed. The sun went down. The woman slipped into her robe, some sandals that slapped the soles of her feet as she walked, and disappeared into a ground-floor apartment.

Lonnie glanced around the courtyard and, seeing no one, stood up and went to Sonny's window again. It was shut tight. He tried the doorknob. Locked. But it was a spring lock, a five-pin tumbler with a twist button on the other side—a cheap, standard apartment door lock. He took an old celluloid library card from his wallet, placed his shoulder against the door, and shimmied the card back and forth until it was firmly wedged between the door and the frame. Jiggling the knob, forcing the card deeper, he felt the bolt slip into its sleeve and ease the pressure from his shoulder. Then he looked left to right down the hall and crept inside.

He found the range light over the stove. Switched it on. The kitchen table was cluttered with empty beer cans and bottles, potato chip bags, glasses. In a bowl of dip, the hardened remains clinging to its sides, was a mound of cigarette butts. He opened the refrigerator. A jar of mayonnaise, four eggs, a gallon bottle of wine two-thirds empty. Three grocery bags full of discarded paper cups and more beer cans were propped against the bottom cupboards on the floor. Boxes of books and clothes were strewn around the single bed in the other room. On the wall was an old poster of *The Raven* with Jack Nicholson. A small stone Buddha rested on top of a shaky bookcase built from shipping cartons and concrete blocks.

Suddenly he heard laughter in the hallway outside and froze. The thought of being in the wrong apartment sent a wave of fear up his spine.

The door opened.

He stiffened.

Sonny entered with his arm around a woman and a bottle of sherry in his other hand. Before he could flip on the light, she pulled his head to hers and kissed him. A few seconds later she gasped in his ear, pushed him away, and pitched backward. "What's the matter?" Sonny said, frowning. "Did I hurt you?" She pointed with her chin, looking beyond him. He turned around. *"Where the hell did you come from?"*

Lonnie stood behind the kitchen table rubbing the back of his neck, blinking and stammering, searching for words. The woman crossed her arms over her chest and gave him a long, mean look. "S'cuse me," he mumbled, starting for the door. He'd seen that face somewhere before. Michelle. The one who flirted with his brother at the cast party.

"I'm sorry I hollered," Sonny said, stepping in front of him. "You just startled me is all." He closed his eyes for a moment, exhaled, then nodded toward the door. "Let's go outside."

Michelle tossed her hair back. "Hurry up, okay?"

"Give me a few minutes."

"Leave the sherry, then."

He glanced at the bottle in his hand as if he'd forgotten about it. Michelle sat on the edge of the bed, crossed her legs, lit a cigarette. Two streams of smoke shot from her nostrils with an angry force. Lonnie waited beside the door while his brother rushed to the kitchen and returned with a glass of sherry. "I can't stay late, you know?" she said. "Don't take all night."

Bitch, Lonnie thought. Vicious bitch. Don't cater to her.

The sky was dark now as they walked down the hall. Rolling his eyes, Sonny wiped his brow with the back of his hand. "I'm not going to ask how you got in," he said, feeling his shirt pocket for cigarettes. "I already have a good idea." They stopped near the end of the hallway. Lonnie rested his foot on the bottom rail of the banister, his elbows on the top rail, and leaned over the side.

"You have a party?" Steam rose off the surface of the pool. A powerful light shone through the water beneath the diving board.

"Just a few friends," Sonny said. "It was nothing important or I would've called you." He opened a fresh pack of Camels and offered him one. "Smoke?"

Lonnie reached for his own pack, struck a match, lit his brother's cigarette and then his own. He watched the match burn until the flame grazed his fingertips before dropping it over the side. "How's your actin' job coming?" he said, staring across the courtyard below. Moths fluttered around the light down the hall on the ground floor.

"Good." They lowered their heads as they smoked for a while, not speaking. "What's on your mind?"

"I don't know."

"I get worried when you're quiet."

Lonnie smiled weakly.

"Tell me what's the matter."

He started to speak, then stopped.

"You don't like living with Dan?"

"That's part of it."

"What's the other part?"

"We don't see each other anymore. *That's* the other part, man. I wanna do something together. It's like you're way far away, Sonny. We don't talk no more or nothin'. Everything's all fucked up and like . . ."

Michelle leaned out of the apartment door and shouted down the hall. "Telephone."

"Tell them I'll call back."

"It's your director."

He sighed as he started for the apartment. "This shouldn't take long."

"Sonny?"

"Yeah?"

"Ah," Lonnie said, wrinkling his nose. "Forget it."

Five minutes later Sonny stepped into the hallway and his face turned pale. He cursed and dashed downstairs to the sidewalk and scanned the streets. No one in sight. Sonofabitch. He ran back upstairs and found Michelle lying on the bed.

"You get rid of him yet?"

"Shuddup."

Her mouth dropped open. "You asshole, you."

"Get outta here."

She flicked her cigarette at him but missed. Sonny grabbed her shoes off the floor beside the bed and hurtled them out the open door, over the banister, into the pool.

"Get outta here."

A white neon tube outlined the picture of a sleek greyhound in midstride. Lonnie paused beneath the sign for a moment, watching the cars pass on the street behind him in the reflection of the glass door. The night was warm, muggy. He thought of Sonny, of Alex and Mom, but his breathing remained calm and steady. Pushing the door open, he stepped into the glare of the fluorescent lights and headed for the ticket counter. A young sailor was banging his pelvis into the coinbox of a pinball machine at one end of the station. Nearby sat a woman with a Pekingese dog in her lap, stroking its head, cooing in its ear. Lonnie looked up and saw himself, shabby and worn, in the television monitor suspended from a corner of the ceiling. The pinball machine buzzed and chimed.

The smell of exhaust carried through an open door near the ticket counter. A bus idled in the narrow driveway. People, suitcases and bags on the floor beside them, waited in line to board. Lonnie rested his forearms along the counter and pointed with his chin.

"Where's that bus going'?"

"Houston."

"How much is it?"

"Eighty-five dollars," the clerk said. "A hundred and seventy round trip."

Reaching into his pocket, he pulled out the hundred-dollar bill and handed it over. "One way, please." Through an open door he watched a porter and the driver stow luggage into the deep metal side compartments of the bus.

"It'll be leaving in five minutes."

"Fine."

"Any luggage?"

"No."

The clerk gave him his change.

Four Vietnamese waited at the end of the line to board. A skinny woman clung to her baby wrapped in a wool blanket while the small bony men, eyes jerking nervously, stared at the silver bus ahead. Outside the station two cops lifted an old woman to her feet and led her, stumbling between them, into the back of a black-and-white van. A single light glowed in the window of an office building across the street.

He hurried to the pay phone down the hall next to the men's room.

"How you doin'?"

"Lonnie?"

"Who else gonna call you?"

"Don't be joking around."

"Sorry."

"Why'd you take off like that?"

"It was time to go."

"You scared the fuck out of me."

"I didn't mean to."

"There's something I wanna tell you."

"There's something I wanna tell you, too."

The loudspeaker sounded in the background: *Five-oh-three to Houston is now boarding . . . Five-oh-three to Houston is now boarding.*

"What was that?" Sonny said.

"Ah, nothin'."

"Where are you at?"

"I just called to say good-bye."

"Oh, shit, Lonnie."

The line of people moved forward. He swallowed hard.
"I gotta go now."

"No, you don't."

"Ain't no choices, man."

"Your hearing's tomorrow."

"They're gonna lock my ass up."

"You don't know that for sure."

"Why take a chance?"

"Because you could get probation."

His voice cracked. "Then what?"

"Hey."

"Yeah?"

"You listening to me?"

"I'm listening."

"You listening good?"

"Yeah."

"I want you to live with me."

"What?"

"I said I want you to live with me. You and me. Here."

He pulled the receiver away from his ear for a moment.
The doors to the bus shut with the solid thump of a tight
seal. Hands rose here and there in the windows, grasping
for small but powerful reading lamps overhead. He heard
the faint cry of the Vietnamese baby over the sudden roar
of the engine. The bus dipped down the driveway as it
turned onto Vine Street. Lonnie imagined himself sitting
inside, watching the road pass beneath him with increasing
speed until the broken white line appeared solid.

"Hey, Sonny," he said. "Can you gimme a ride home?"